WHERE *the* ROCKS
say YOUR NAME

WHERE *the* ROCKS
say YOUR NAME

❧

BRENDA HASIUK

thistledown press

Library and Archives Canada Cataloguing in Publication

Hasiuk, Brenda, 1968-
Where the rocks say your name / Brenda Hasiuk.

ISBN 1-897235-11-9

I. Title.

PS8615.A776W43 2006   jC813'.6   C2006-903735-3

Cover and book design by Jackie Forrie
Typeset by Thistledown Press
Printed and bound in Canada by Marquis Book Printing Inc.

Thistledown Press Ltd.
633 Main Street
Saskatoon, Saskatchewan, S7H 0J8
www.thistledownpress.com

Thistledown Press gratefully acknowledges the financial assistance of the Canada
Council for the Arts, the Saskatchewan Arts Board, and the Government of
Canada through the Book Publishing Industry Development Program for its
publishing program.

Canadian Patrimoine
Heritage canadien

Canada Council Conseil des Arts
for the Arts du Canada

In memory of Robert Arnthor Sigurdson
1967-2000

For Duncan — who feels like home,
and for Roberta — who remembers.

Fish hibernate for the winter down in the depths of the river; squirrels go off to find their stores of nuts in the fir-groves; birds fly away to warmer lands. And what of him? Why couldn't he spread his wings and fly away? After all, he was twenty years old. As though to excite and inspire him, a bright shooting star traced its path through the night sky above his head. Then the star burst, and in its greenish light he saw his own house, low to the ground, painfully familiar, its roof coated in frost.

— From *Two Winters and Three Summers*, Fyodor Abramov, 1968

The metabolic rate of history is too fast for us to observe it. It's as if, attending to the day-long life cycle of a single mayfly, we lose sight of the species and its fate. At the same time, the metabolic rate of geology is too slow for us to perceive it, so that, from birth to death, it seems to us who are caught in the beat of our own individual beating hearts that everything happening on this planet is what happens to us, personally, privately, secretly.

— From *Continental Drift* , Russell Banks, 1985

IMAGINE A LATE EVENING IN EARLY JULY. Three of them were on their way home after a long summer day of wetting themselves in the lake, then drying themselves on a rock, over and over, only interrupting the cycle now and then to drink warm beer and spit sunflower seeds at each other. It had been one of those miraculous afternoons of pointless harmony between a small group of people, the kind that most of us probably only get to experience once or twice in our long lives.

But to understand this one in particular, you need to know that in this place the winter lasts a good eight months, when the days are almost inhumanly short and frigid, and in summer, the sun stretches long and hot — so hot that the smallest spark can set miles of dense forest ablaze within minutes. Each year, the people who live there wait for this heat, for the sweet kiss of burning sun on their face, like those in the tropics wait for the rains.

On that blazing afternoon, the heat itself seemed to burn away all that had happened before and all that was to come. It wasn't until the light began to lose its intensity, bouncing soft and gold off the water's surface, that the spell began to fade.

If you'd been sitting precariously above the highway as night fell — legs dangling from the craggy rock which had been blasted away decades earlier to make way for the bulldozers and asphalt — and looked straight up, you would've seen a very pale slice of moon, a smudge of white crayon in the darkening sky that bore no resemblance to a real place where human beings have actually walked. Straight ahead of you, the sun would've been disappearing quite quickly behind a dark wall of spruce trees. And down below, you would've seen a white pickup truck winding its way north in the dusk, driving just over the speed limit and jerking strangely now and then on its way home.

Rina was in the front seat with her bare feet propped up against the dashboard. She was leaning forward and trying to paint her toenails *cranberry crush*, and Toby, who was driving, rested one hand on the soft curve at the bottom of her neck. Ally sat in the cramped back cab, watching Toby's thumb slowly move over Rina's vertebrae like he was strumming a ballad on a guitar.

For the last ten minutes, Rina had been teasing Toby about the one thing he held strong opinions about. The windows were open and she spoke loudly over the rush of wind. "But why can't you do something, Toby, that maybe the people, they actually like to watch?"

Toby was nineteen, exactly thirteen months older than Ally, who'd told him this made them the same age since girls mature faster. They'd both lived in this place of hot and cold their whole lives, on land so rocky that sewage pipes had to be enclosed in wooden boxes above ground. They took for granted the towering presence of the smelter's smokestack, endlessly spewing its industry over the houses and the shops and the new hotel down by the highway, and the dense forest all around. They didn't blink at bear traps in driveways.

But Rina had grown up far away, across an ocean and most of a continent, where there'd been buildings and roads almost a thousand years before this rocky land was even on a map. This meant there were times when she had something funny to say on the tip of her tongue and had to let it float away, just like that, because it was in the wrong language. It meant that though she was the youngest of her friends, wouldn't turn eighteen for another two months, you would never have guessed it. For Rina had seen things that don't belong in someone's childhood, or anywhere else.

Still, on this night, none of that seemed to matter. She was acting more drunk than she was and felt the kind of giddiness that pretty girls do when their olive skin has turned fawn-coloured in the sun and they feel free to enjoy the effect they're having. When she turned to Toby, she could actually hear his longing in the way he breathed. "Or, you know, " she went on teasing, "a sport that maybe any of the people has even heard of."

Rina held the nail polish brush in mid-air and braced herself. She knew exactly what was coming. This time, when Toby jerked the steering wheel quickly, left then right, she didn't get *cranberry crush* all over her toes again. Instead, she painted a bright red line across his forearm.

A half-ton truck flashed past and Toby had to steady the wheel with both hands. A more skittish person might've been shaken, but for him there was only the usual lazy contentment. With the rush of speed and wind lingering in his ears, the nail polish strangely cold against his skin, all he could do was shake his head and smile. He wasn't consciously aware of loving the wildflowers in the ditch, quickly disappearing into the blue dusk, or the presence of Ally behind and Rina beside him, or the smell of the descending dew, sweet and familiar, rushing in to mix with their sweat. He simply sensed them all at once and knew it was good.

Toby couldn't even be bothered to think of a good comeback. It was as if all his life he'd instinctively known that the best way to ruin things was to think too much.

Rina ran her fingers over the red line on his forearm like she was admiring a scar.

"Tell her, Ally," he said. "Tell her that the best sports are a blend of endurance and skill."

Ally undid her seatbelt and leaned in between them. With the windows rolled down, their voices had been drifting out past the gravel shoulder before they could reach her, floating over the wildflower ditch until they were lost in the growing darkness of the bush.

Rina dipped the brush in the bottle and aimed towards Ally's nose.

"Everybody thinks you're weird," Ally said. "The *bi*-athlon sounds like something *bi*-sexuals do."

Toby threw up his hands as though he'd finally given up and wanted to end it all.

"You should be a hockey player," Rina said, still fingering his scar, "or what do they call it, when they go down the snow on the one ski."

"Snowboarder," Ally said. "They say nobody gets the women like a snowboarder."

Before Toby could defend himself there was a small black shape in the headlights. He swerved into the opposite lane and Rina was thrown against his shoulder. Tiny yellow eyes flashed still for a moment, bright and terrified, then disappeared into the murky dusk as quickly as they'd come.

As he eased back into the right lane, Rina stayed where she'd landed, gripping the nail polish bottle in one hand and resting the other on his chest. Ally did up her seatbelt again.

"Lucky bugger," Toby said. He could still feel the adrenalin pulsing through to his fingertips. Rina's damp hair smelled like apples and it was almost more than he could stand. "You remember that time, Al?" he asked, "on the school bus with the ducks?"

Ally leaned forward as far as she could. "What ducks?"

"Don't you remember?" Toby asked. "There was this family of ducks just walking along in a line across the highway, and we could see them up front but the driver could only swerve a bit and try to miss some."

Ally rested her head back and let him lead her through the familiar routine. He was always remembering things from when they were small. "And?"

"The last three in line got squished."

"You remember how many got squished?" she asked.

"Yeah," Toby said. "The last three or four of them got the pancake treatment."

Ally shook her head and smiled to herself in the dark. "You remember how many?"

"Yeah," he said. "Don't you remember?"

Rina pulled away from him and hugged her long legs against her chest. "Toby, you talk about stupid things. Even the biathlon is more fun than dead ducks."

Toby kept both hands on the wheel, calmer now, and feeling like an idiot. The scar of nail polish had dried itchy and tight against his skin.

Ally settled into the darkness and closed her eyes. In her mind, she followed the yellow eyes past the gravel shoulder, over the wildflower ditch and deep into the woods. Though it was totally black now, she could see herself lying there, curled up in a clearing of damp moss, having a snooze. Toby was nestled in behind her, his knees tucked inside hers. They were covered with a beach towel, but her imagination didn't seem to care whose it was, his or hers.

"But do you remember that, Al?" Toby shouted above the wind.

"No," she replied. "Not really."

So we start with only three. That evening, when a small fox was spared, only three of them were there. Adam, the failed warrior, had not yet come back. But he would, soon, because this is a story of eight weeks in the lives of four people, not quite fully grown, and the people who loved them.

Just one summer is all you get. Twice, the moon grew full, then thin again. Animals tended their young and began their mad scurry to fatten themselves for the hard months to come as if for the very first time.

Two calendar pages fell near the beginning of the twenty-first century.

Fires burned. Hearts broke. And then there was only one in a small, northern town in the middle of a large, northern country that most of the world still regards as a rather wild landscape populated by peaceful and polite, if rather boring people.

EARTH FIRE WATER AIR

1

SOMETIMES THE WORLD can seem like nothing but a series of opposites, as if the unseen conflict between gravity and space sets the tone for all of life on earth. Everything seems to exist as hot or cold, cruel or kind, alive or dead.

In the northern mining town of Franklin, the seasons have always been the most obvious extremes. Depending on the time of year, the world even sounds different. When you're camped out in dense summer bush, where the darkness is nearly thick enough to touch, every distant crack and rustle seems a foot away and the wind in the towering poplars bears down on you like the rush of a waterfall. On Franklin's main shopping strip, where they dropped Ally off that night, the streets were nearly deserted but filled with noise.

When she sat down on the curb just after ten, there was only a smattering of people and cars moving to and from a fast food place and the beer vendor at the hotel. Yet the sounds of the night grew and expanded in the open sky. Every car seemed to need a new muffler and people's laughter lingered long after they'd disappeared out of sight.

In winter, all this would be buried under a thick coating of insulation. Movement would be reduced to the hushed crunch of cars easing over packed snow, all laughter immediately lost inside scarves. In the leafless bush, where the night would never get much darker than a muted grey, even the roar of a snowmobile could sound oddly faded and lonely.

One time, just before he left, Ally's father Harry had taken her ice fishing even though he hated it.

"Listen," he'd said, in the middle of the frozen lake. "Listen."

Five-year-old Ally had pulled the toque from her ears and done what she was told. After trudging through the drifts, all she could hear was the mad beating of her own heart.

"Nothing," Harry had said. "Eerie, unbelievable nothing."

It could be said then, that the people of this place experienced their share of the world's extremes through their climate, while the people of Rina's birthplace, a temperate land where civilizations had moved back and forth and risen and fallen for centuries on end, looked to their history.

Now, sitting on the curb, Ally reached into her straw bag that was starting to tear along the seam, and fingered some chocolate-covered raisins that had melted into a giant clump. She was hungry, and knew that Toby and Rina would be having sex soon, maybe in Toby's parents' basement or in the back seat where she'd just peeled away her bare thighs from the vinyl, and that her mother Ruth would be at the kitchen table fanning herself with a magazine even though the air conditioning was on full-blast.

It wasn't like Ally to sit there all by herself, fishing around in the slimy chocolate mess and sucking her fingers one by one. Like so many northerners, she was most at ease in the company of others, and as an only child of a distracted mother and absent father, she craved company even more than most. She smoked because she liked to trade cigarettes back and forth and to come to the rescue with a light. She'd let a defenceman from the school hockey team kiss her twelve-year-old breasts and reach into her panties because she was drunk and because he asked.

Ally had a quick, straightforward laugh and saw the world as a practical matter. When her old best friend's family had picked up and moved south to the city, she'd simply gone up and introduced herself to Rina, who after four months in town was still regarded as the new doctor's leggy, but sullen daughter. To Ally, it was simple: she needed a new best friend from the limited supply available in a small high school in a small town, and Rina needed someone to tell her what was what.

Of the three of them, Ally was most in her element as they'd lazed there by the lake, pack-like, a trio of healthy wolf cubs sunning themselves on a rock and swatting at each other playfully.

"Our Ally," Rina had said, rolling over onto her stomach and poking at Ally's shoulder. "Our Ally is turning pink, Toby." So he'd poured warm beer down Ally's back and then Rina and Toby had grabbed her at either end and carried her into the water.

Then they'd all floated there for a long time, their toes and fingers bumping into each other now and then by accident.

Six months before, on a bitter February night, Rina and Ally had sat together in the stands of the local hockey arena, happy to get out of the house and out of the cold.

"I saw the professionals play one time in the city," Rina said. "All of us poor little refugees, they give us the free tickets at the school and then we go and we sit so high up the men look like little ants."

"They call that the nose-bleed section," Ally had said, though she'd never been herself, not even after her father Harry moved south to the city.

"But this is what I don't understand, okay?" Rina went on. "Even here, so close, you can't even see what they look like under all the helmets and the pads. Where I come from, they wear the football shorts, so you can see what they look like. With this, how do you even know what shape they are?"

Ally squinted her eyes while slowly exhaling cigarette smoke, just like her mother Ruth always did. In a place where neighbours had no choice but to work in close quarters to carve out a life, the fast, rough, passing game of ice hockey suited them well. Young men who excelled on skates got hero-like status, a paycheque from the mine and plenty of time to practice.

"What do you want, you want them out there with no padding?" Ally asked. "They would be breaking things all over the place if they were just out there in shorts. Plus their testicles would get all small and shrivelled in the cold."

Rina laughed and shoved Ally away. From the very beginning, she'd liked the way there was something innocent about Ally even when she said something crude. "You are a pig," she said, still laughing.

"I'm just saying," Ally said, and flicked her finished cigarette at a trashcan down below.

Toby was walking passed on his way from the snack stand. The smoking butt bounced off his left ear and he stumbled, spilling steaming hot chocolate down his jeans. He glared up into the bleachers.

Ally pulled a piece of licorice from her pocket and took a bite, then pointed it at her friend. "You'll have to excuse her," she called down to Toby. "She's not from here. Where she comes from, they can't throw and they watch soccer because you can see their asses."

Rina leaned forward, elbows on her thighs. Toby was trying hard to ignore his scalded knees and his face contained a masculine gravity it normally lacked. "Don't listen to her," she said.

He recognized Ally from a grade or two below him at school, and from her mother's store. Rina, the doctor's daughter, he'd only seen once or twice on the street. From where he stood, if you followed her tight jeans all the way to her crotch, it made a perfect V.

"Nobody ever scores in soccer," he said.

Rina made a small snorting sound that he would come to know well. Then she leaned forward further because she didn't want him to walk away. "So I guess you like the hockey, or the snowmobiling. Everyone here does the snowmobiling."

"He likes to ski," Ally said. "Even in the summer."

A player came flying into the boards with a *thwump* and Toby instinctively stepped forward, spilling more hot chocolate. Two miners he worked with waved him away with mock frustration.

"Maybe you should watch the game," one of them said, expecting Toby to good-naturedly flip him the finger like he always did.

"You see that crazy son of a bitch the other day," the miners on his shift would say, loud enough for him to hear in the lunchroom, "skiing on fucking wheels. I almost ran him over." And it would always be the same — Toby would smile and flip them the finger.

But this time, he'd felt the doctor's daughter's dark, snorting eyes still on him. "I train for the biathlon," he said to Rina. "You know, skiing and shooting."

Ally threw a piece of licorice down to him and Toby caught it with one hand, not spilling a thing. Her face was nothing but friendly and round and pink from the mild chill that kept the ice from melting.

"I know," she said.

One week later, Ally was showing Rina how to hold a cue so it wouldn't wobble, when Toby and some friends came into the pool hall, puffing from the cold. When they weren't at the arena, young and old gathered in places like this — smoke-filled rooms with three televisions all playing a different channel, where you could enjoy idle conversation and the warm release of a few strong drinks.

Toby pulled a wool sweater over his head, revealing a swatch of curly hair around his belly button.

"I guess soccer players aren't the only ones with nice bodies," Ally called out. Toby's friend Josh came over and grabbed the cue from her. He scanned the table for a shot. "Don't waste your time with him. He's got a small dick."

Toby picked up another cue and poked it hard at Josh's chest. "Don't be an asshole."

Josh stepped back in surprise. "What's your problem?"

Toby shoved his hands in his jeans' pockets and straightened his elbows, a habit his sisters called his penguin imitation. He shrugged and pretended to look for some chalk. He didn't have an answer. All he knew was that the doctor's daughter had been watching him.

Ally leaned across the table to rack the balls, bending over further than she needed to, and waited for Josh's hand on her bottom. "Come on boys, no fighting," she said. "Let's play."

That night would be the true beginning of the way Toby and Ally would laugh together until her drink drizzled from her nose, the way Rina would be lulled by their giddiness, waiting for the moment when Toby would finally look at her and shake his head in sheepish glee.

After a few games of pool and a couple of drinks, he'd playfully poked Ally in the shoulder, but looked at Rina. "It's true. Don't you remember, Al? This asshole climbed onto the roof of the elementary school and then couldn't get down. He climbs up on a snowbank and then the plow comes and moves it, but they don't see him. He yells and yells for maybe three hours and then finally somebody hears. The whole frigging volunteer fire department showed up."

Before they left, as Josh had slipped Ally's parka over her shoulders and casually cupped her breasts, Ally had turned to Toby. "Are you just going to make googly eyes or are you going to ask her out?

Then she'd grabbed his hand and written Rina's number on his palm.

But that was months ago. Now, though her tailbone was getting sore from sitting on the curb, Ally stayed where she was. Somewhere a stereo was playing so loud she could feel the beat in her stomach, pounding as if to remind her how empty it was. To her, this was the sound of a summer party, the kind where young men let out alcohol-fueled yelps in the night and young women lose their virginity on blankets in the bush.

A blue van eased past on the other side of the street and the driver shouted at her above the music.

"What?" Ally automatically yelled back.

But they drove on out of sight, leaving her alone while the relentless beat lingered in the air. She felt like shivering in the heat.

Once, when she was eleven, Ally had asked her mother Ruth: "Why did Dad cheat on you?"

It was just after Ruth had risked everything they had to open up the first bulk-food franchise in town. They were enjoying the novelty of having air conditioning in their new apartment above the store and Ally was watching her mother's fingers fly over the adding machine, the paper streaming onto the floor in a curly mass. She'd watched with the same childish awe as when Ruth cleaned out a chicken or told off a bank teller.

"Because he's a cheater," Ruth said.

"But it was only once, right," Ally said.

Ruth's furious fingers didn't pause from their work. "Once is enough."

Then for a moment, though she hadn't seen her father in over two years, though she had chosen her mother hands-down, Ally suddenly wondered if this were true. Was once enough? Was it that simple? What if her mother was wrong? Chewing at her nails even worse than usual, she'd felt something close to terror.

"Stop that," Ruth said. "It's disgusting."

After that, her mother had gone and made them peanut butter and banana sandwiches and things had returned to normal. The awful doubt had faded away, just like that. Until this moment on the curb.

The whole way home in the back seat, she'd imagined herself reaching out and running her fingers through Toby's hair, which had been sticking up adorably after swimming all day, like a little kid who's just woken up. She was still imagining it even now, as she sat there cleaning the melted chocolate from beneath her well-chewed nails. And just like before, when she was eleven, she felt it — that fleeting sense of complete and utter separateness. It was as if she'd betrayed something by her very thoughts and could never take it back no matter how alone she felt.

For several minutes, Ally remained on the curb, all by herself, not wanting to go inside. And nothing in her upbringing could account for this.

All the new development in town was near the highway that led south, towards the tiny airport, the pristine cottage-ringed lakes, and the distant city. On the way home earlier that night, Ally and her friends had first passed the new hotel with its cinder-block walls painted in the latest colours and its restaurant that served mid-priced entrées instead of suppers, then the new residential development of attached garages and freshly landscaped lawns where Toby and Rina lived. After that they'd headed over the bridge and up, up, up.

Two large, weedy lakes split Franklin in two, with everything new to the south and everything else rising from a series of granite ridges, where tiny bungalows with rocky yards seemed to teeter over the water, each ridge higher than the last until you got to the giant industrial shapes of the mine stretched across the horizon, hovering over the tops of squatty downtown buildings. Visitors often found themselves speechless at their first sight of it — the towering metal structures used to extract and smelt and refine even more metal seemed to emerge from the wild forest like skyscrapers in the desert.

Still, Ally would've noticed this no more than she would've noticed the back of her own hand. She took for granted all that you might find in an industrial town only recently established in the twentieth century — the three banks and two law offices, the Co-op grocery and gas station, the hastily built churches, the smokestack that managed to dwarf even the huge windowless box of the hockey arena, the white manhole-sized satellite dishes that perched near the roof of every dwelling and establishment, bringing faraway channels and a daily connection to the wider world. The only suggestion of anything from a more distant past was the imaginatively named *Souvenirs and More*, a former shoe store across from Ruth's that now sold overpriced, traditional handicrafts and tacky trinkets to the few tourists the town saw. This too Ally took for granted, paying no attention to the steady stream of suckers shopping across the way, city men with too much money who came in small planes to spend their weekend fishing the quiet lakes and hunting game in the last great wilderness.

There were many things Ally barely noticed. When she finally went up to the apartment that night, she didn't even consider their home a mess. It was just the way it had always been.

Ally's mother was very organized about some things, but let others slide. Down in the store, the narrow wood-planked aisles were always swept and the bulk bins of dry goods kept full. The plastic bags and twist-ties were kept well-stocked and never more than an arm's-reach away. The stockroom was well-ordered, with frequent sellers like cinnamon and popping corn in the front shelves and black licorice bits and curry powder near the back.

But up in the apartment, it was another story. Gritty boot racks were left by the door even in summer. A plastic Co-op bag propped up against the cupboard below the sink tended to sag with garbage, often spilling over before being taken out. The front window was new but its frame left unfinished. An old storm window facing the lane was taped over with plastic to keep out the cold.

Once, when Ally's father, Harry, was still around, he'd gone behind his wife's back and bought a new fold-out couch, dark chocolate brown with sleek, modern lines.

"The old one was perfectly good," Ruth had said.

He'd only laughed at her, carefully stripping away the plastic wrapping and running his hands over the velvety fabric.

"Feel that," he'd said. "Just feel that."

Worn now in places, faded to just plain brown, his couch remained parked a few feet in front of the TV, exactly where he'd left it.

When Ally came inside, Ruth was still at the kitchen table, surrounded by paperwork. Her hair was pulled back in a ponytail, revealing a broad shiny forehead with little lines that had just become permanent in the last year. She was holding a cool glass to her cheek and watching a game show where people compete to answer the most trivia questions.

"Hey," she said, not taking her eyes off the television. "I made some iced tea there."

Ruth was exactly the kind of person these shows were aimed at. She would marvel at how the contestants managed to know so many little things and take courage from its central message — those who keep their nerve shall be rewarded.

Ally threw her bag by the door and tripped over a runner that was missing its laces. She kicked it across the floor on her way to the pantry.

"This guy just won $500,000," Ruth said. "They're going to buy a motor home and travel around with their dog."

Ally shoved a whole oatmeal cookie into her mouth. A bald man was waving stupidly at the camera while a woman wandered back and forth with a little black poodle squirming in her arms.

Ruth waited for Ally to respond. *Am I the only goddamn one talking here?* she wanted to ask. But minutes earlier, she'd made a pact with herself not to raise her voice when Ally got home.

She turned to her daughter and laughed. Ally looked like a raccoon in reverse — round white eyes where her sunglasses would've been inside a beet-red face.

"What?" Ally asked, her mouth still full.

Ruth got up and grabbed the bag of cookies, sorry that she'd laughed out loud. She poked Ally's shoulder and said the first motherly thing that came into her head. "You burned yourself. They say skin cancer is the most common kind, you know."

Ally pushed Ruth's hand away and rubbed the white little mark that was left. Not long after she'd met Rina, Ally had told her "they say because we're so dry up here the cold is easier to take. Like in places where it's more damp, they say it can be the same temperature and ten times worse." Rina had snorted. "Who is 'they'?"

Ally could hear her snorting even now. "You smoke," she said to Ruth.

"Don't get smart," Ruth said. She went back to the kitchen table and shuffled papers around until she found the remote control. "You know what I mean."

She switched to the channel where viewers could buy what was on the screen simply by calling a number. Though Ruth never did this, she liked the idea that she could, anytime.

"I've seen this blender before," she said. "They say this thing will make whipped cream out of skim milk. It has a special beater that attaches."

Ally went to the fridge and drank iced tea straight from the plastic container. The couple on TV had reminded her of Toby carrying around his old cocker spaniel just before it died. The dog had been old and sick and had to wear a diaper or it would pee all over the house. Rina had kept bugging him to put her to sleep. "It is undignified," she'd said. "Would you like to smell so bad?"

But when the morning with the veterinarian finally came, Rina had a math exam and it was Ally who'd met him at the animal clinic.

"What are you doing here, anyway?" he'd asked, after the dog was dead.

"I skipped history," she said.

He'd nodded approvingly. "Do you remember when I brought her to school for show-and-tell and she shit on the floor beside the fish tank?"

"I heard about that," she said.

He hadn't cried. He'd just stroked the ends of the dog's ears until she stopped breathing and then for a little while after that. It had been one of those strangely mild days in March that turns the road to gritty slush that will inevitably freeze again into deep, ugly ruts. They weren't even wearing gloves. Ally remembered because she'd watched his hands, bare and trembling on the steering wheel, as he took her back to school. He'd come from work and there was still some black under his fingernails.

Ruth shuffled around again for her cigarettes and plunked herself down on the couch. "Last night," she said, "they were selling a cross-country ski machine that all the professionals use. You should tell your Toby. They said it's just like the real thing."

For years, Ally had told Ruth what was on her mind, had gone to her with hurt feelings even when it didn't help at all. When she was seven and a boy at school said she needed a diet on her legs, Ruth had let her lick the icing bowl and said, "I got a lot worse when I was your age." Still, Ally always went back. Two years before, when she'd had sex with a hockey player while Ruth was down in the store, and then he acted like it never happened, she'd climbed crying into her mother's bed. Yawning, Ruth had wiped Ally's nose with a tissue she kept rolled into the sleeve of her nightgown. "Are you on the pill, at least?" she'd asked.

Ally had always gone back. But not tonight. Instead, she drained the last of the iced tea and imagined herself crouched in the snow, shivering under an umbrella of spruce trees and holding the cocker spaniel, who was also shivering. Then Toby came by, gliding over the powdery surface without a sound. When he saw her, he stopped so fast he nearly fell over. *What are you doing here?* he asked.

She ran away and I found her, Ally said.

Then the dog was gone, and Toby grabbed Ally by the hand and pulled her up. *You must be freezing.*

Then he pulled her mitt off and held her cold fingers against his lips.

I have to tell you something, she said.

He raised his eyebrows and his breath was so hot that her fingers ached.

"Do you think I'm made of electricity?" Ruth asked. "Close the fridge."

Ally opened the crisper drawer and closed it with a *bang*. "I'm still getting something. And there *are* no professionals." She slammed the fridge. "And he's not my Toby."

"You know who I mean," Ruth said. She lit a cigarette and inhaled deeply. "The one following that Rina around like a puppy." She squinted her eyes as she exhaled. "So Adam's coming to stay for a bit."

Ally stopped chewing her cookie. "Adam who?"

"Vincent's Adam," Ruth said. "He called from the city. He'll be on the overnight bus."

Ally went and stood in front of the television. "You don't even talk to Uncle Vincent."

Ally hadn't seen her uncle and cousins since the brown couch was brand new. She had no idea what her cousin Adam even looked like. All he conjured up was a whirl of blue-black hair, a tumble of grass-stained knees, and a vague tension. "If he's been into the bottle too much we're turning around and coming home," her father Harry would say on their way to visit Uncle Vincent years before. "I know he's your brother, Ruth, and I know he's got his reasons, but I'm not sitting around there while scratches his balls."

Ruth would slowly nod and get out the snacks.

"Just an hour or so," she'd say. "Then we'll go."

The gravel road to seemed to go on forever, the pine trees getting thicker and darker until they opened into a clearing of long, low buildings. Most of the houses looked exactly the same except that some had been left without siding so that you could still see the plywood and framing. As soon as they pulled in, dogs would come running from all around.

"You little buggers," Harry would say. "They've got enough rifles out here. Why do they let them run wild like this? It's a menace," and Ruth would nod some more.

At the house, Harry would say: "Remember, I've got an eye on you guys," and the adults would go off into the kitchen.

Then Adam and his brothers would show off for five-year-old Ally — wrestling in the living room until the television screen was nearly bashed in, catching a groundhog in the field by setting a tiny noose around its burrow. They would take turns jumping off the roof into a pile of dry grass, or see who could carry Ally the longest, even the one who was younger than her.

Eventually, Harry would come and stand there with his hands on his hips. "Let's go, Alison. We're going."

On the way home, she would feel almost dizzy with exhaustion. The tension in the front seat would be silent now and the snacks gone. She would close her eyes, and with the boys' exhilarating shrieks of laughter and the sweet smell of their dirty hair still with her in the backseat, she would fall into a twitch-filled sleep.

Later, Vincent and his family followed Harry south to the city. They lived just across the river, but might as well have been worlds away.

Ally swallowed the last of the oatmeal cookie. It felt dry and thick in her throat. "Where's he going to sleep?"

Ruth tried to concentrate on the features of the hand blender. They said you could whip up omelets of perfect consistency. "Right here."

"In our living room?" Ally asked. "Don't you think you could've checked with me?"

Ruth patted around a pile of old magazines, looking for an ashtray, but had to settle for a dirty plate. When Adam had called from the city bus depot, sounding distracted and probably stoned, she'd known he was in some kind of trouble.

"Just for a while, eh, Auntie Ruthie," he'd said. "How long's it been, eh?"

It had been a very long time since anyone had called her Ruthie. He'd taken her confused silence to be consent, and then it was too late.

"We'll give him three days and then he's out," she said.

Ally picked up the remote and muted the TV. Somewhere outside, she heard the speakers throbbing again. "What?"

Ruth stubbed out her cigarette. For so long, Ally had been such an easy child, eager to please and ready to give her mother the benefit of the doubt. But not lately. "I said some of us were here working while some of us were lying around all day doing goddamn knows what like they goddamned owned the place."

Most animals instinctively leave their parents by the time they reach sexual maturity, but humans have evolved to linger. After her period had begun and even after she'd begun to let hockey players into her room, Ally had continued to live with her mother. Everyone, including Ally, expected she would stay and help Ruth in the store when she was done school, and this meant they were bound to argue. But for Ally and Ruth these days, there was more to it than that. Other things lurked beneath their bickering, things that had been brewing for years, that could never be undone no matter how far you moved, or how old you got.

That night, it had taken Ruth all of three minutes to raise her voice and break her pact. And Ally stood her ground in front of the television screen, remembering Toby's words to her at the vet — *what are you doing here, anyway?* — wishing that when Ruth had touched her sunburned shoulder she'd slapped her mother's sweaty, fleshy arm as hard as she could.

While Ally glared at Ruth, across town in his parents' basement, Toby watched Rina doze on the musty carpet, feeling both so horny and so protective that it left him lightheaded.

Oblivious to his gaze, Rina dreamt of a place where a crowd of people in black wound their way down a lush, green mountain and onto the muddy road, like a giant snake. Far to the south, Adam wandered through the snack shop at the bus depot, filling his pockets with things that he not only didn't need, but didn't want. And somewhere hidden alongside the highway where Toby had driven Ally and Rina home that night, where the bus carrying Adam would wind him north into their lives the next morning, the fox that had been spared lay curled beneath a batch of fern, sleeping the lonely and fitful sleep of a small predator.

2

IT WAS NEARLY MIDNIGHT before Adam's bus left the outskirts of Winnipeg. For several hours and several stops it travelled northwest over vast prairie lowlands, until boreal forest began to close in on either side. Over ten thousand years ago, there was a dramatic geographic shakeup — hills had risen, valleys had been carved, massive fresh water lakes had dried up — so as hour nine approached, the forest walls suddenly turned to towering Precambrian rock cuts, as if some spiteful witch had stopped by one day and turned all the jagged jack pines into stone.

As the bus wound its way through the rocky pass, Adam kept his jacket draped over his head, completely oblivious to it all as either geological phenomenon or fairy tale. It wasn't that he took the landscape for granted, as Ally did. In the inner city neighbourhood where he'd grown up, congested winter streets coughed up car exhaust thick as fog, and summer evenings reeked of garbage left in a dumpster too long. By the time he was ten, he'd become a master of ignoring his environment.

Adam kept his eyes closed beneath the jacket, but the early morning sunshine seemed to taunt him, not heating the air-conditioned bus, not glaring through the tinted windows, just there, bearing down on him. It had been almost four hours since his last cigarette and his left leg began to fidget. For as long as he could remember, his oldest brother had called this twitching his "junkie withdrawal symptoms."

Out of habit, Adam pulled out a stolen marker and tugged the lid off between his teeth. He'd just begun tracing the curved outlines of a graffiti-style letter "A" on his palm when he felt a jab against his leg.

"You shouldn't do that."

It was the old woman beside him. Early in the trip, with nothing but the ink-black prairie going by, she'd kept him awake, first by eating something that smelled like mouldy cheese, then by snoring. With the rancid smell still lingering, he'd eventually closed his eyes and drifted in and out, his own breathing falling in rhythm with her snorting and hissing. But in his mind, over and over, he'd taken the rolled-up jacket from under his head and held it against the old woman's face until there was nothing but the soft *whir* of wheels on the highway.

The stink and the snoring had infuriated him, and the fact that it infuriated him made it all the more infuriating. For months now, he'd tried to feel nothing, had craved numbness like a starving man craves bread. Sleep was one of the only things he looked forward to these days.

It had been the very opposite when he was small. His father Vincent always said that little Adam would do anything to stay up, including wandering out after midnight to find a rusty nail to step on so they'd have to rush him to emergency. When he and his brothers would laze on the couch in their underwear watching music videos, Adam was always the last holdout, padding around in his sock feet, flipping through channels, afraid of the darkness behind his own eyelids. His mother, Lucille, usually let him be, called him her little nighthawk, except on those days when the principal called asking if she knew her child was dozing off in class.

"Get out of my face," she'd say to Adam later. "You got school tomorrow. Go lie down, for Christ's sake."

Now, there was something in the old woman's voice that reminded him of when he was in school. He'd been famous for being able to talk himself out of anything — vandalizing school property, hot-wiring cars — with a particular kind of female teacher, usually quite young and from neighbourhoods very different from his own. Later, after a growth spurt and the loss of his right eyetooth, these same kind of women tended to avoid him on the street.

"It's not good for you," the old woman went on. "You'll get ink poisoning."

Adam bent forward until his draped jacket fell to the floor. He spit the pen lid out and shoved his fist in the woman's face. F-U-C-K was tattooed on his knuckles in green capital letters. "I did it myself," he said. "And I'm still here."

She pushed his fist away as if swatting at a fly. "What a stupid thing to do."

It wasn't the reaction he'd expected. For the first time, he noticed how small she was, about half his size, and how old. She was like the sick, old people he'd seen on television, wandering the hallways in hospital gowns and looking lost. There was dried spittle in the corner of her mouth.

She began peeling a banana with shaking fingers and Adam wondered if she might be crazy.

"You from around here?" she asked.

The sun, higher in the sky now, bore down on him, exposing countless flecks of dust in the air. He closed his eyes and shook his head, leaning back as if going to sleep. In his mind, Adam grabbed the banana and shoved it up her nose until she began to gag for air, her mouth open wide like a baby bird's.

For his first six years of life, Adam believed the world was berry bushes and snowmobiles and stray dogs, and then one day it became concrete and bus fumes and stray cats. Though his family didn't have to cross political borders like Rina's, he too had to leave everything he knew and start again.

When his family first arrived at the main floor of a rental property that was to be their new home in the city, Adam walked over to his mother Lucille and began punching her tailbone. It was a rainy September day, unusually humid for that time of year, and when Vincent saw his six-year-old son throwing a temper tantrum against his wife's ass, he let go of the mattress he was shoving through the door and doubled over with laughter.

When feeling nervous or under stress, Vincent's first instinct was to laugh. All his life, people with authority had told him "wipe that grin off your face."

Lucille, who was unloading glasses onto a kitchen counter covered with cigarette burns, turned and looked at her husband. Even then, trouble — like dealing with men — gave her a smooth pallor of resignation. It would keep her looking younger than her years. "Are you just going to let him pound me like that?"

Vincent squeezed his way in between the mattress and the doorway. Still laughing, he grabbed Adam's wrists, hard. "Cut it out."

Adam kept struggling, even though it made it hurt even more. With four older brothers, he wasn't intimidated by a little pain. All he could think of was how far it would be to run all the way home, away from this strange place where traffic passing over slick streets seemed to shake the house with noise.

"It stinks here," he said.

His younger brother, Leonard, was sitting on the floor stroking a soggy cat that had wandered in through the open door. "Yeah. It stinks."

Vincent suddenly let go of Adam, and Adam stumbled backwards, almost stepping on the cat.

"I don't have time for this shit," Vincent said, small drops of water dripping down his forehead. His hair was still long then and he was always brushing it from his eyes. "You can plug your nose, can't you?"

The boys looked at him as if they were actually thinking it over. Maybe they would just walk around holding their noses for the rest of their lives.

Vincent started to laugh again. Adam began marching around the room with his fingers up his nose and Leonard followed. All three of them were laughing.

Lucille banged a glass down on the counter. "That mattress is getting wet."

Vincent lunged at her, close enough to practically spit in her face. "You think I don't see the fucking mattress?"

Adam was already used to his father's polar changes. Baby Leonard had been the same, screaming one minute and giggling the next. "You think I'm fucking blind?" Vincent shouted.

Lucille kept taking out glasses and arranging them on the counter.

Adam felt dizzy from holding his nose and thought he might cry. He could feel Leonard watching him, his mouth buried in the squirming cat's mottled fur, looking for a cue for what to do next.

As Vincent yelled out curses at his older sons who'd deserted him in this dump, the little bastards wandering off to the convenience store to gawk at the dirty magazines, Adam understood right then that no matter how fast he ran, or for how long, the distance they had come was too great for a small boy.

There was nowhere to go.

He put Leonard in a headlock and dragged him across the floor. The frightened cat jumped screeching from his arms.

"Stop repeating everything I say," he said, pulling his brother by the neck down the steps of the back landing, until Leonard bit him hard on the forearm and he had to let go.

The old woman on the bus jabbed Adam's leg again. "You have family up here?"

He leaned forward and pretended to search for the pen lid on the gritty floor. With his head between his knees and blood rushing to his face, he felt trapped. It was like the old woman, with her stinky cheese and banana peels, was there to drive him as crazy as she was.

"Did you hear me?" she asked.

Adam straightened up but kept his eyes on the floor. He didn't want to encourage her. "My auntie."

"Every year, my niece asks me to come," the old woman said. "But she can't cook and there's no decent place to eat out. When I was young I worked in an office and I used to go out for lunch every day of the week."

Adam began filling in the letter on his palm. The marker he'd just lifted from the crappy store at the bus depot was already starting to dry out.

"But family's important," she said. "Your aunt work in the mine? Seems everybody works in that awful mine."

For Adam, this was the last straw. He had no idea what Ruth did, or what she must've thought when he called from the bus depot, out of the blue. He had no idea what he was doing, or where he was going.

He chucked the useless marker to the floor and leaned back again so fast he saw stars, little flashes of silver dancing in the yellow brightness. In his mind, he pulled out a pocket knife from his jacket, and holding it just inside his shirt sleeve, leaned over as if to pick the banana peel up from the old women's lap. With a swift upward stroke, before she could take another breath, he stabbed her once, twice, three times. When the blood came, spreading against her white blouse the way flowers open on television, sped up for effect, he lifted the paper bag at her feet and placed it in her lap. He reached over and closed her eyelids with a brush of his hand, like he'd seen them do in movies, and dropped the knife, slippery and bloody, into the bag. Then he slowly and calmly followed the other passengers down the aisle as they got off, and disappeared into the town.

"I didn't work in a mine," the old woman said. "I worked in an office."

She looked down at her hands like she was inspecting something of great, antique value. "I could type sixty-five words a minute."

Adam hadn't been to Franklin for close to fifteen years, not since he was six and his family had still lived at the end of a gravel road. Shortly before they left for the city, Vincent had brought him along to the local taxidermist after an argument with Lucille. It was an argument that they would repeat again and again over the years.

"Why don't we just eat it?" she'd asked. "I thought we were supposed to use every part of the hunt, not go decorating the house."

Vincent waved dismissively at Adam, who was at his father's feet, pouring his juice onto the plywood floor to see which way the stream would go. "He won't even touch fucking fish," Vincent said. "None of them will. This is a once-in-a-lifetime. You got to splurge when it's once-in-a-lifetime. You just have to shit on everything I do. That's the biggest fish this place has ever seen."

"I'm not going anywhere," Lucille said

Vincent picked up Adam under the armpits like he was still a toddler and held him awkwardly in the air. "I'll take my boy with me, then."

Lucille grabbed hold of her son's ankle. "He's had his juice," she said. "We were going to lie down."

It was times like this that Vincent would often say it was no wonder she was so fat, because all she did was lie around. But he also loved this about her. He never felt so safe as when he was resting in the gentle folds of her stomach.

"Let go," he said. "I'm taking the boy," and she'd turned away without a word.

Once in town, Adam insisted on carrying the newspaper-wrapped fish that was almost as big as him. He made it as far as the shop doorway, then stopped dead. There was an elk head up on the front counter, its hair still matted with blood where the neck had been severed, its giant antlers branching out awkwardly over the cash register.

"They're not going to hurt you," his father said. He took the fish from Adam and dragged him in by the elbow. A small beaver sat perched on a wooden shelf by the door. Vincent picked it up and imitated its large, funny-looking teeth. "See? All dead. Touch it. He's soft."

Adam poked cautiously at the glossy fur, then jumped away. It felt so real, and he was suddenly aware of dozens of dead animals all around the shop, all staring down blankly with their glass eyes. He didn't care what his father said. They looked neither dead nor alive, like they could see him and not see him. It was like they'd fallen under some evil spell.

Afterwards, when Vincent told Lucille how Adam had waited outside on the curb for almost half an hour without a peep, she laughed harder than she had in months.

The bus eased into town, its wheezing brakes announcing its arrival. Several people stood waiting in the shed-like depot, including the old woman's niece and a miner who'd come to reconcile with his estranged wife. Adam pushed through the small crowd and zeroed in on a pair of unattended sunglasses. A moment earlier, the distracted miner had left them behind on a bench. With just one glimpse, Adam felt his adrenaline begin to flow and without even slowing his pace, he swept the glasses up and kept on going out the door.

When he was about to lift something, the rest of the world dissolved into slow motion. He would feel the rush and know only he was fast enough to get what he wanted. But lately, once he'd gotten away with it and the world sped up again, his stomach would tense with fear, as if he were on an amusement ride that only went faster and faster and faster. He'd want to escape inside somewhere, into a small room, where he could close the door and turn out the lights.

Once outside, with the cheap sunglasses pinching behind his ears, Adam felt the familiar fear rising again in his gut. From where he stood just south of the bridge, most of the town lay hidden atop a series of staggered ridges. Even the towering smokestack was hidden; the only evidence of its existence was a grey smudge of smoke hanging in the cloudless sky.

The dramatic changes in elevation made it hard for Adam to get his bearings. In Winnipeg, the only real hill was a grown-over garbage dump, and for a moment, he wondered if this was all there was — a squatty, pale-yellow hotel just behind the bus depot; a pizza place with picnic tables in the parking lot; a gas station with a sign that said: "ice cream and bait in cooler;" a newly-paved intersection like you might see in the city suburbs, except that it had giant lakes flanking either side. The only thing that seemed familiar were the splashes of graffiti high against the rock faces, and even that looked alien against the rocky, nature show wilderness.

Adam lit a cigarette and inhaled greedily, waiting for his left knee to steady itself. It's easy, Ruth had said. Walk straight up the hill towards the smokestack, then turn left at the gas station, then turn again and walk until you see the store. But Adam's knee showed no sign of letting up.

By the time he was twenty-one, he'd broken into over forty different suburban homes, yet he had never been alone in a strange place. One or more of his brothers had always been around as they grew up on top of each other in a string of cramped rental houses, and then later, as they shared cramped apartments where they would pass out alongside various friends and acquaintances in whatever room was handy. There'd been a steady stream of girls if he wanted, wandering to and from the bathroom in the middle of the night with glazed eyes and scrawny, bird-like legs sticking out beneath their T-shirts. Even during a break-in, he always had a partner, someone to sample the liquor cabinet with, someone to carry out the merchandise as he scanned the deserted midday street from an upper-floor window.

All his life Adam had been surrounded. Until one March night it had all exploded in a surge of revenge and betrayal that would make newspaper headlines and come to haunt him in rays of sunlight.

He checked his pack of cigarettes. There were only three smokes left and he couldn't decide if Ruth had said right, then right again, or left, then left. With nothing else to do but panic, he found himself clinging to the one thing he recognized.

The graffiti covering the cliffs was unimpressive, mostly amateur stuff, but the sheer height of it was unbelievable. Some of them — *DJ and Teddy Forever, Murphy Sucks* — looked like whoever did them must've had wings. Did they use a rope? he wondered. How long had it been since he'd been up on a rooftop with his own black garbage bag full of spray cans?

As if he'd been thinking out loud, Adam noticed a guy in uniform approaching with a familiar, concerned expression. Just from the way they guy moved, the keys on his belt jingling, he could tell he was one of those security dicks who got paid shit and made up for it by acting like a big shot.

"Can I help you here?" Mr. Big Shot asked.

It wasn't really a question. Adam shrugged and tossed his butt at the guy's feet, then turned purposefully to the left. He walked up towards the bridge as if he'd planned on it all along, not even pausing to light up another cigarette.

After such a long, cramped journey, the climb did him good. As his muscles strained up the sloping streets, there was almost no one else around except a few kids madly pumping their bikes up, up, up. Inevitably, they all got off and walked them in defeat. It was going to be a warm day, but for now, a light breeze from the west held the heat off and filled the air with something strangely sweet-smelling.

Breathing hard as he climbed, Adam began to remember snippets of his cousin Ally: a fat face with curly blonde hair that was almost white, hiding between her mother's legs. He remembered his Auntie Ruth was the opposite, her long black hair blowing across the rhubarb pie she always brought when she visited. He even remembered Harry, the white guy Ruth had married. Harry had a patchy blond beard and walked through the yard like he had a stick up his ass.

After turning left at the gas station, Adam found his way easily and according to instruction through the anonymous streets. His heart pumping, he actually began to feel some of the cockiness of his school days, back when the lady teachers would drape their arms protectively around his shoulders; back when he always had a plan. By the time he got to Ally and Ruth's he even knew what the smell was.

It was trees. After so many years away, Adam found himself enjoying the sweet smell of aspen sap before the morning dew dries up.

From behind the cash desk, Ally watched him pace back and forth on the sidewalk for a while before she said anything to Ruth. It had been months since she'd felt that anticipation in her gut, the flutter of meeting someone for the first time. She wanted to keep her long-lost cousin to herself for just a minute.

Ally had expected some kind of family resemblance, but all she could make out was that Adam and her mother were the same — dark, like Rina with a tan. He was a bit shorter than Toby but a lot wider, his big shoulders hunched and round, like the young miners who got in fights outside the arena, or felt her up when she'd been drinking, after they'd pleaded and teased and pulled.

"Is that him, or what?" she finally asked.

Ruth was struggling with a heavy bag of cinnamon, trying to empty it into a bin. Each time she heaved the bag up, too much poured out, leaving her surrounded her by a brown cloud. She rested the bag awkwardly on her hip and sighed. "Are you going to help me here?"

Before Ally could reply, the bell above the door sounded.

"Auntie," Adam said, pointing down at Ruth. Then he pivoted towards the cash register. "And little Ally."

Ruth rested the half-empty bag on the edge of the bin and wiped the sweat above her lip, smudging cinnamon like a mustache. She'd been annoyed with herself all morning. While sweeping in the back, she hadn't noticed a lineup of customers for a full two minutes and then she'd given out the wrong change to her hairdresser — all in the first half-hour of opening. *Three days,* she'd told herself, *three days tops and he's out.*

The boy reminded her of Lucille, big-boned with round cow-like eyes. His clothes, hanging loose over his bulky frame, looked like they hadn't been washed in weeks and he wasn't carrying a thing — no luggage, no bag, no knapsack.

"Where's your stuff?" she asked.

Adam's knee started up, bouncing like it had a life of its own. The boy might look like his mother, Ruth thought, but his mannerisms were all Vincent. Just one twitch of the leg and it was like her little brother was right there in her store, bearing down on her with his quick, nervous energy.

"Yeah, they're sending it," Adam said. "I was in the can and I almost missed the bus. They'd already packed everything underneath, so my bag got left there. They didn't see it. They're sending it on the next bus, eh."

The bell tinkled and a woman came in towing three small children. Ruth smiled over at her, holding up a finger to signal she'd be there in a moment.

"We'll get that later, then," Ruth said to him. "Go upstairs, have a shower, have a nap. You must be tired."

Adam nodded, running his fingers through his hair and delivering a sheepish, very Vincent-like grin. "Yeah, that's great," he said. "The girl I talked to at the depot said they'd actually left three people's stuff. Must've been a new driver, maybe."

The woman with the kids pretended to finger a display of fancy nuts. She was a good customer with a big mouth.

Ruth took Adam's elbow. "I'll take him up," she said to Ally. "Give the little ones there a sucker."

Adam let Ruth lead him away, smiling so wide Ally could make out the gap where an eyetooth should've been. "We'll catch up later, Cuz," he said.

Ally had always found this hard to resist. The only problem was trying to figure out when guys like this were joking, and when they weren't.

"Later, Cuz," she said.

When Ruth questioned his lack of baggage, Adam's old carefree cockiness had nearly disappeared as quickly as it had come. He'd had hours to anticipate this question, and yet he hadn't. How long had it been, he wondered, since he'd been so off his game?

But in the end, it was his cousin's eager expression that had saved him. Buoyed by Ally's sunburned and expectant face, old habits had kicked in. He'd remembered that the key was in the details, and afterwards, when he'd had a hot shower, and filled his stomach with toast and jam, and then drawn the blinds, he stretched himself out on the worn fold-out sofa bed, practically light-headed with satisfaction. Little things, like it being blueberry jam, his favourite kind, or the endlessly *whirring* air conditioning that allowed him to cover up with an afghan even in midsummer, were like unexpected gifts.

As he drifted off in the gloriously cool, dim silence, he remembered how his journey on the awful bus had ended. After they'd eased to a stop and he was already standing in the aisle, the old woman had poked him one last time.

"Lye soap and water."

He'd stared down at her, so small and shrivelled.

"It'll take that pen ink right off," she said.

Holding out his fist, he waved his tattooed knuckles at her again. The scent of space and freedom waiting just twelve feet away and down two small steps had made him generous.

"Yeah, I'll try it with this, too, eh," he said.

The old woman had laughed, a girlish giggle, delighted that she'd gotten him to speak a complete sentence.

3

⌒ FOR A WEEK, Adam stayed in pretty much
the same horizontal position on Ruth's couch, with the blinds
drawn and the remote control close at hand. Wrapped up like
this in the cocoon-like apartment, he felt freer than he had in
a long time.

He ventured out only once, on the morning of day two,
telling Ruth he was off to the bus depot to get his stuff, then
lifting a knapsack and a few T-shirts from the sporting goods
shop and a toothbrush from the Co-op. When he returned, she
spent some time throwing open cupboards and showing him
where things were in the kitchen.

"Now you can help yourself," she told him, "because I sure
as hell won't be serving you."

He figured his best bet was to lie low and stay out of her
way.

During the days he dozed, smoking cigarettes from a carton
he'd found above the fridge, absently flipping channels until
his eyes closed again. By dinnertime, he would often be fast
asleep and would stay that way while Ally and Ruth puttered

around the apartment carrying out their nightly routines. He slept for long, air-conditioned stretches, sometimes twelve hours at a time. On day three, he briefly wondered how long it had been he'd slept like this without any booze or other chemical help, but then he pushed the thought away. *Don't question*, he told himself. *Don't fucking question it.*

It wasn't until day four, during a period of half-sleep in the afternoon, when there was nothing but the distant little bell issuing customers in an out of Ruth's shop below, that bits and pieces of his early childhood began to return. They came as flashes, more like sensations than memory.

There was hot tea in a plastic cup and the heavy breathing of bundled figures huddled around a fishing hole in the ice. The steam drifted up into his frozen nostrils, tingling yet soothing, and then his brothers laughed as he danced around open-mouthed, trying to cool his scalded tongue. Or there was the old man sitting on a step, always on the step, always looking the same, smelling of scorched wood and cigarettes, whittling a stick and humming something in the back of his throat.

On the morning of day five, he found himself fighting the urge to tell Ally what was happening to him. He'd been vaguely aware of her tiptoeing around him all week, staring from a distance like he was an animal at the zoo. But that morning, he opened his eyes to see her standing over him, eating her cereal.

Don't fucking wreck it, he told himself. *Make nice and send little Ally on her way.*

"He says he's got a cold," Ally told Ruth, "but he never coughs."

"Ask me if I care," Ruth said. "Next week, he's gone."

For years, Ally had accepted Ruth's estrangement from Adam's father Vincent as a fact of life, like her parents' divorce or mosquitoes in summer. Ruth had explained things in typical Ruth fashion: "You can only get burned so many times before you wise up. I wised up."

But with Adam there in the flesh, in the middle of the apartment, impossible to ignore, Ally couldn't help studying the way he dozed on his back, knees pulled up, feet sticking out from the afghan. Even when talking to Rina on the phone, she still couldn't bring herself to look away.

"He just lies there," she whispered on day six. "That's it."

"I can barely hear you?" Rina replied. "How can you stand it so crowded in there?

"He barely even moves," Ally said, louder, but still whispering.

That night, a regular Friday at the pool hall, Toby and Rina took turns playfully lecturing her.

"I think Ruth's finally lost it," Toby said. "Your cousin sounds like a prick."

Rina gently poked her pool cue at Ally's shoulder, whispering loudly: "Our Ally is too trusting."

Ally set down her third beer of the night. "I like pricks."

Toby laughed and Rina raised her eyebrows, waiting for him to explain the joke. "Very funny," was all he said.

On day seven, Adam began remembering gophers. Snoozing on the couch late in the afternoon, he felt the long grass tickling against his legs, then heard the brushing sound of his little brother Leonard leading them through a field. Leonard passed him something, a tiny little body, a newborn with eyes still closed, squirming sickeningly in his hand. He tossed it back to his brother, and suddenly they were playing catch, back and forth until the squirming body was rubbery and still. Then Ally's father Harry was there, dragging them both by the arm with a look of horror.

When he opened his eyes, Ally was there for real in the doorway. Her sunburn had faded to the same dull pink as the baby rodent. She had the same thin lips and red ears as Harry.

Adam sat up and pointed at her like when he'd first appeared in the store. "You used to chase us around," he said, "and your dad, he didn't like it. I think he thought we were going to eat you."

Ally kicked her sandals across the floor. She'd come up to go the bathroom before helping Ruth close the shop. "You remember my dad?"

"Kind of," he said. He grabbed Ruth's cigarettes from the coffee table and offered her one.

Ally relaxed against the armrest, watching him expertly light first one, then the other. It seemed this giant stranger that Ruth had let in really was her cousin, someone who could actually remember things about people that she didn't.

"He's in the city now, by the university," she said. "He does computer stuff."

Adam nodded as if he were impressed. "There's a lot of money in that, eh."

Ally shrugged. The last thing she wanted to talk about was Harry. "Do you live with Uncle Vincent?"

Adam flicked the ashes of his cigarette into his palm and shook his head. "You don't want to go where I fucking live."

Ally squinted her eyes as she inhaled and watched him pull the afghan up under his chin like it was the middle of winter. She wondered if he really might be sick.

"So why don't you live with your rich daddy?" he asked.

"He's not rich," Ally said. "And he's an asshole."

Adam leaned back in surprise. With his cousin perched there on the armrest, squinting at him as if she were confused, or maybe offended, he'd begun to regret opening his big mouth. But he'd underestimated her.

He smiled wide enough to reveal his missing tooth. Ally handed him a dirty plate to dump the ashes from his palm and blew a long tunnel of smoke at the ceiling, looking very pleased with herself.

Before leaving work that night, Toby lingered awhile near the fluorescent-lit lunchroom listening to the steady hum of the drink machine, wondering if Rina would be there or if he'd have to wait until later, when they were supposed to pick up Ally for a game of pool.

One of the other miners eventually looked up from his card game. "What? You like this fucking place so much you don't want to go home?"

Toby flipped him the finger.

"Come here and do that, you little dink," the miner said.

Toby walked away with an exaggerated strut. This was his playfully crude world and he knew his way around it with his eyes closed. "Some of us are out of here. I hear it's really fucking nice out."

"Little dink!" the miner yelled.

All his life, Toby had never been easily upset or excited. It's why he was so easy to kid and so well-suited to biathlon's pattern of ski and shoot. He could race five kilometres, pushing himself until his muscles started to burn even in the bitter cold, then fall to the snow and slow his breathing to measured, even puffs of steam as he aimed at a small tin can that shone silver amidst the barren trees.

But not tonight. As he stepped out into the light after his shift, he held his breath with a kind of hesitant anticipation. The sky was still flaming orange in the west and it took his eyes a moment to adjust. Gradually, he made out her silhouette, one hand on her hip, making a perfect triangle. She was standing in the heat with her legs slightly apart so her bare thighs wouldn't stick together, as if at military attention in her cut-off jeans.

He kept walking towards her, not stopping until their noses were maybe two inches apart. He knew she loved it when he could reach out and touch her, but didn't.

"I'm sort of smelly," he said.

This was an ongoing joke between them. He'd never really gotten used to her seeing him before he'd had a chance to jump in the shower, but she always insisted he just hurry out to meet her.

Rina leaned forward, arms at her sides, legs still slightly apart and darted her tongue softly between his lips. They were the same height and she buried her face in Toby's sweaty hair though she knew it would make him pull away in surprise.

All day she'd waited for the setting sun hot against her back and his breath coming soft and quick while the late day shift drifted home all around them. After their third date, she'd decided that having Toby in her house was more trouble than it was worth. Each time he'd come to pick her up, she'd come downstairs to find him trapped in the front landing by one or both of her parents, and looking ready to bolt. So she'd begun slipping out after supper to wait for him outside the mine. Throughout the bitter cold of February and March and early April, she'd hung around the chain-link fence, patiently waiting for Toby and the other miners to emerge like ants leaving their hill.

Tonight, she was in the mood for teasing. "You ski down the street to do exercise," she said on the way to the truck, "but you won't walk even three minutes on a beautiful night. My dad, he lived for forty years before he learned to drive a car. Now my mother thinks he looks like a farmer in that big red truck."

Toby never knew what to say when she went on like this. If Ally had been there, she would've jumped in: "You stay on your feet in the store all day and see if *you* feel like trudging around when you're off work."

But he'd never thought about why everyone in a five-kilometre-square town drove from place to place, slush or snow, rain or shine, or why they bought trucks or SUVs that might be worth more than their houses. He'd never tried to explain to himself or anyone else why getting behind the wheel might become a habit — was it the cold, the steeply climbing streets, the dozens of hours it took travelling around narrow curves to get to the fishing hole, the snowmobile trails, the far-off city?

"I like my truck," he said. "What's wrong with that?"

Before going to get Ally, they stopped off at Toby's place so he could shower.

When the three of them were sick of the pool hall, the arena, even the lake, they always ended up at Toby's. With a rusted swing set in the backyard and a basement his father Lyle had outfitted with a bar sink and built-in television cabinet, it was a natural gathering place. When Toby's three older sisters had still lived at home, there'd been a steady flow of young people coming in and out, and now Lyle missed the noise and banter.

"You don't have to get your own place yet," he'd told Toby. "You got lots of time to worry about bills."

For her part, his mother Sharon had never even been able to bring herself to remove the child-safety plugs from the electrical sockets. When Toby's twenty-year-old sister had delivered a surprise grandchild that April, at least their house was prepared.

The mining town had been good to Toby's parents. Their families had worked in a cannery for generations on the East Coast, until the fish began to disappear and the unemployment lines got longer and longer. Relatives still on the Coast would sometimes ask how they could stand the endless, mid-continental deep-freeze, and for twenty years, Lyle had replied: "I'm too busy spending my money to notice."

Now, when Rina and Toby passed through the living room, his father muted the television. "You still with that bum, Rina?" Lyle called. "I tell you, you're too good for him."

Toby's mother rolled her eyes. "Ignore him."

It was a standing joke, and there was something about the easy affection in Toby's family that always gave Rina pause. Part of her always wanted to plunk down in the chair where the footrest magically popped out from the bottom and just rest. She wanted to stay there surrounded by framed photos of the family looking charmingly, uncharacteristically stiff and watch the weather channel with Sharon and Lyle.

But Toby kept going, shaking his head at his father with mock disgust, and Rina let him pull her away, down the stairs and into the rec room that always smelled of cool, damp concrete and lemon air freshener. "You should talk to your parents," she said. "They're too nice to you."

"You don't have to live with them," Toby said, but he didn't really mean it. He knew he was the envy of all his friends when it came to his parents, who'd been leniently doting with their teenage children. They'd made it clear that what Toby did in his basement bedroom was his business.

"Better you do it under our roof," Lyle had said more than once. "At least that way we know you're not dead in a ditch somewhere."

By the time Toby was in the shower, the water streaming hot and glorious down his back, he suddenly felt a sense of well-being so powerful his whole body tingled. All he needed in the world was right there — the sound of his parents gently bickering above him and Rina lying silently in the next room on his unmade bed, her knees drawn up and cut-offs gaping to reveal the edges of her white cotton underwear.

When he was done, he wrapped a towel around his waist and softly padded across the carpeted floor where he used to play ping-pong and hair salon with his sisters. He stood dripping over Rina as she snoozed, letting little beads of water land on her shoulder and neck and cheek. He was so turned on that it almost frightened him. It was as if he had to have her now and if he couldn't, if someone interrupted them or she didn't want to, he wasn't sure what he might do.

When Rina opened her eyes, she had to cover her mouth so he wouldn't see her amusement. With his wet hair slicked back from his face, he looked like he was ten years old.

By the time Toby and Rina arrived to pick her up, just past nine, Ally almost felt like her old self again. She was ready and waiting to perform introductions.

"This is Adam," she said. He still lay beneath the afghan and she swept her arm over him like a game show assistant presenting a prize. "He lives on our couch."

Then she pointed to her friends in the doorway. "Toby's a lifer here, like me," she said to Adam, "but Rina's just here because her dad couldn't get a job anywhere else."

Rina stuck her hand in the back pocket of Toby's jeans and felt him, predictably, catch his breath. "My father left the city by his own choice," she said.

Ally parked herself on the armrest at her cousin's feet. "I was just kidding," she said. "You know, ha-ha."

Rina had forgotten that Ruth's nephew would be here. All week, Ally had gone on about this mysterious Adam in her living room and Rina had found herself vaguely irritated. Now, with just one look at him, she felt more than annoyed. She knew young men like Adam all too well from the time she'd spent living in a cramped Winnipeg apartment after emigrating, when Slavenka worked for a house-cleaning service and cried in her ugly uniform while Merik frowned over his medical books. She'd passed plenty of Adams on her way to school, posturing on street corners like self-made soldiers in their ridiculous colours and caps. They'd rarely showed any interest in her — a gawky, tightlipped little immigrant with books clutched to her chest and somber eyes on the ground, yet their mere presence had left her complaining of stomach aches when she got home.

Ally tapped Adam's knee beneath the afghan. "Rina lived in the West End. Anywhere by you?"

Adam sat up just far enough to get a better look at them. "I've lived all over," he said.

Rina moved in closer to Toby, practically stepping on Toby's feet.

Adam grinned. "So where you kids off to?"

Toby didn't like his tone. Though Rina's hips were pressing pleasantly against his, he tried to catch Ally's eye, give her the signal it was time to go. But she wouldn't look away from her cousin. When she was trying too hard, Toby knew Ally could have a big mouth. "Play pool," he said.

Adam lit a match and let it burn until it snuffed out between his fingers. "Is that your game?"

Toby paused, not sure what he meant.

"He does the biathlon," Ally said.

Toby wanted to shove a sock in her mouth. Adam's smirk got wider.

"Cross-country skiing and target shooting," Toby said.

Ally went to the kitchen counter and slipped Ruth's lighter into her pocket, then settled herself back against the armrest "Pool is better," she said. "It's sticks and balls and little openings. What's not to like? You should come, Adam."

"If we don't get moving there won't be any tables left," Toby said.

Rina pulled away from him and went to the couch, slipping her arm through Ally's. Early on, Ally had been embarrassed by Rina's offers to walk arm-in-arm in public, but after a while, she'd come to like it as much as Toby did.

"All the time, girls walk together like this back home," Rina had explained. "What's the big deal?"

One of Toby's favourite things was to follow just behind them when they did this, his arms draped casually over both girls.

Now, as Ally let herself be led to the door, Ruth appeared at the top of the stairs. She was huffing from carrying up a small sack of flour. Toby turned and smiled at her, waiting for her to tell him to help her with this goddamn thing or get out of the way.

Instead, she just stood there huffing, looking at them like they weren't familiar faces but just a barricade in her way. For the first time, Toby noticed that Ruth's salt-and-pepper hair, gathered in a ponytail high on her head, seemed suited for someone much younger. Someone without any wrinkles around their mouth.

Adam settled back into the couch. He'd decided the guy was hardly worth noticing, the kind of ordinary, friendly faced athlete he and his friends might harass at two in the morning outside a downtown nightclub. But the girl was something else. She was nothing like the needy teenagers who'd crawl in and out of his bed, nothing like the earnest teachers he'd known at school.

This one looked at him like he was part of the furniture.

The key, he told himself, *the key was to stay right here with his long-lost auntie who talked tough but still made no move to kick him out.*

Here, in his cocoon, nothing could touch him. Not even the kind of girl who looked at you like you weren't even there.

"Pool's not my game, eh," he said. "You kids have fun."

That night, as Ally had hovered over her new houseguest, Rina had felt a surge of protectiveness. She understood that when people don't leave the house it's for a reason. But when she'd ushered Ally out the door, she wasn't merely rescuing her friend. And though she believed she kept meeting Toby after his shift to avoid an uncomfortable scene with her parents, there was more to it than that.

Every evening, she waited for him as the miners emerged into the sunlight, most of them taking her in with envious eyes and muttering the odd crude comment amongst themselves, until she could distinguish Toby from the rest, could see him walking out of the dirt and the danger, his face so sweaty and tired and yet so clear and faithful she felt comforted in a way she never had before and never really would again.

4

JUST OVER A WEEK after Adam's arrival, long-held patterns began to shift. For nearly a month, a high-pressure system of uninterrupted sunlight had remained stubbornly fixed over the town, turning Rina fawn-coloured and Ally baby-gopher pink, and giving people something to talk about.

"Isn't this heat something?" customers had said while scooping their flour, or raisins, or individually wrapped toffees.

"It's something all right," Ruth would reply, as she had so many Julys before.

But one Sunday evening, the sky grew thick and overcast. By Monday lunch, customers actually stopped what they were doing to make predictions.

"With this heat we could be in for something," they said, or, "you can feel it in the air out there."

For the next few days, the clouds remained heavy and threatening, yet produced nothing, leaving the ground hard and the trees parched. The only rain that came fell in dreams.

On Wednesday morning, Ally went through the mindless routine of opening the store — breaking rolls of pennies into the cash drawer, checking the bins for misplaced scoops — and the dull grey light made it seem too dark to be out of bed. After such a long stretch of brilliantly early sunrises it was as if her body had forgotten that for most of the year the store would be still covered in darkness until she flicked on the lights by the stairs. She couldn't stop yawning, and couldn't stop wondering if Adam was awake yet, holding a cigarette between his thumb and index finger like he always did, letting the match snuff out against his skin like he had the other night.

When Ruth came down, Ally watched her pass by without a word. She watched her get out the ladder and sweep away the beginnings of a cobweb, then just stand there on the fourth step with the broom in mid-air, staring into space as if she was some kind of statue holding a sword. All week, Ruth had been acting strange, hiding down in the store doing god-knows-what until after ten, letting the day's paperwork pile up on the kitchen table.

Ally inspected the back of her mother's legs and decided Ruth's shorts were too short. Her thighs were the skinniest part of her, but ripples of fat were beginning to gather around the upper edges.

"It's been almost two weeks," Ally said. "You haven't kicked him out."

Ruth started a little, as if she'd forgotten her daughter was there, opening the store like always. She climbed down, legs jiggling with each step. "You think I haven't noticed that?"

Ally ignored Ruth's tone. She needed to talk about her cousin, like an itch that needed scratching. "Do you at least know what he's doing here?"

Ruth struggled to push the ladder closed without putting down the broom. This, at least, was typically her — always overestimating what she could physically accomplish. "Why don't you ask him?" she said.

Ally tried to take the broom, but her mother wouldn't let go.

"What's with you?" Ally asked.

Ruth looked past her as if she wasn't even there.

Ally turned and saw Adam at the foot of the stairs. He'd padded down silently in his white sweat socks and now stood wrapped in the afghan, the skin on his legs indented with its flowery knitted pattern. His hair was flat and matted on one side and his left cheek seemed slightly squished in. It looked like he'd just been punched in his sleep.

"I can't find the toilet paper," he said.

Ruth shoved the broom at Ally. There was a time shortly after Harry left when Ally would bawl like a baby over trivial scrapes and Ruth had fantasized about hitting her. She'd imagined the soft skin burning against her palm and it had filled her with such horror that she'd learned to block it out, just as she'd learned to block out her brother Vincent. Piece by piece, choice by choice, Ruth had learned to turn her back on failure. Just moments before, up on the ladder, she'd wished she could just sweep Ally away.

Yet seeing Adam so unexpectedly there — his sweat socks pushed down around his ankles, his limbs jerking busily even when standing still, his broad face still puffy with sleep — a forgotten tenderness had risen up in her. It wasn't until the shop bell sounded that Ruth could make herself turn away from him.

"I got stuff to do here," she said to Ally. "You show him."

Up in the apartment, Ally opened Ruth's bedroom closet and reached into a cardboard box as deep as her arm. She handed Adam a roll of toilet paper.

"We buy in bulk," she explained, following him to the bathroom "It's really stupid. There's only two of us and there's like a hundred and fifty rolls per box. We usually keep a stock under the sink but I guess we ran out."

She stopped just inside the doorway and Adam twisted around in his sock feet. He shed the afghan to the floor and stood glaring at her in his grey boxer shorts. His belly button was a perfect little "o" and even with his arms crossed, she could tell his chest was almost completely hairless. Three of his T-shirts had obviously been rinsed out in the sink and hung to dry over the towel rack.

"We have a washing machine," she said. "And a dryer."

Adam hugged his arms closer against his chest. "If you don't fucking leave, I'm going to shit on the floor."

Ally couldn't tell if he was serious or not. She settled against the door frame, not sure when her next chance to see him awake might be. "I'll go if you tell me why you're here. You going to work in the mine or what?"

Adam grimaced. He'd been searching for toilet paper for over twenty minutes.

What do you do with someone so clueless and relentless? he wondered. She just stood and stared all the time, shoulders rounded and unchallenging, thin lips curved up into full cheeks, invisible blonde eyelashes blinking slow and gentle.

"You think I want to get killed in that fucking mine?" he asked. "Some fucker snitched on me."

Ally backed out and gently closed the door, looking like a little kid who's just found out there's no Santa Claus.

Adam gazed absently in the mirror. It was covered in tiny specks of toothpaste and dust. He sank down onto the toilet.

Early that morning, as the sickly light of dawn had begun to appear behind the blinds, he'd found himself somewhere deep in a forest, digging. It had been raining hard in his dream, not a storm, but a good, steady downpour, and the trees overhead seemed to provide little shelter. He'd been on his hands and knees in only his boxers, trying to dig a hole with his bare hands. But the more he'd dug, the faster the edges of the hole had collapsed. In his dream, he'd dug for hours but was left with only a shallow, water-filled trench.

As the soggy earth had continued to seep through his hands, he knew everything depended on this hole. Pausing, he could suddenly see Ally and her friends a few feet away, huddled together just as they'd been the other night, their faces blurred in the rain. At their feet, there'd been a small body covered in a jacket.

It was the old woman from the bus.

Fucking help me! he'd shouted to them. *I can't get it deep enough!*

But they hadn't heard him or understood what he was saying and all he'd been able to do was keep digging. All he'd been able to do was splash uselessly at the mucky water, with no idea whether he'd killed the old woman or not.

Now, even after Ally had left him in peace, even after he'd left the whole bathroom reeking of his dump, there was no relief. All week, he'd known it was only a matter of time before he would fail. It was almost five months since he'd watched his brother bleeding in a doorway, almost five months since his mind had begun to turn on him. Yet he'd never managed to stay numb for more than a few days.

She was probably down there telling her mommy right now, he thought.

He flushed the toilet and felt his brief calmness swirling away like shit down a drain.

"So I think the police are after him," Ally said.

It was Sunday and she and Rina had come to watch Toby target practice in his backyard. Rina sat cross-legged on the grass with her long church-going skirt pulled tight against her knees. Toby stood perfectly still in the gravel driveway, cradling his air rifle in position. He'd constructed a biathlon-style target range against his parents' garage, tailored out of tinfoil plates and clothespins. He said the girls' talking helped test his concentration.

"Who?" Toby asked, his jaw barely moving.

Ally climbed onto the picnic table like she always did. "Adam. Who do you think?"

Rina kicked off her sandals and rolled onto her stomach. She'd just spent over an hour in a church full of worshippers, watching Slavenka practically chew on her fingers as she prayed while Merik played model citizen, helping pass out the sacrament to his patients. For some reason, the forced singing and shuffling feet of the fresh-scrubbed miners and their families usually left her in a bad mood. It wasn't until she got to Toby's that she would start to relax, watching the graceful way he aimed, precise and beautiful as a cat stalking its prey, waiting for the ridiculous *thwak* of pellet against tin foil.

"It could be anything," Rina said. "The gangs, they're into all kinds of things. Pimping, joy riding, dealing."

Ally nodded as if all of these things had already occurred to her then been dismissed. "I think he was going to tell me but then he had to take a shit."

Rina rested her cheek in the cool grass and went on with her list. "Arson, assault, B and E."

Ally raised her eyebrows at the last one.

"Break and enter," Rina said, lifting her head before the grass could leave ugly red imprints on her cheek.

As he reloaded, Toby glanced up as if surprised to hear Rina use slang with such authority. When she kicked her bare feet playfully in the air, he left the box of pellets in the gravel and grabbed onto her ankles.

"Maybe he's just yanking your chain," he said to Ally, pretending to bite Rina's toes. He held on tenderly, swaying back and forth with each kick.

"No, you're not listening," Ally said. "He's freaked out about something. He's started wandering around all day even though he's supposed to be hiding."

Toby went back to his gun and Rina rolled onto her back. She wondered what it would take to make Ally stop talking.

"New girl," Ally had shouted at her that first day, following Rina down the stairs of the school and onto the sidewalk. "Hey what's-your-name. Do you speak English?"

Rina had kept going. "What do you think?"

"I don't know," Ally said, almost caught up. Trying to match her stride with Rina's, she'd stumbled along, half-running, half-walking. "I never heard you say anything. Where I come from, we talk to people. That's how we make friends. We say, 'Hi, my name is Ally; who are you?'"

As Ally stumbled along beside her, round and persistent and breathing hard, Rina had begun to feel an odd mixture of amusement and exasperation and protectiveness. She'd slowed down. "So I'm talking."

Now, it was hard for Rina to keep the irritation from her voice. "So he's told you this secret. He'll maybe be gone by the time you get home. These guys, they move around all the time. No fixed address. N-F-A."

Ally leaned forward, her face red instead of pink. "I'll bet he'll still be here after you've buggered off."

Rina got up, not bothering to brush the grass from her long church-going skirt, not even glancing at Ally as she made her way to the back door. She was afraid that if she stayed another second she might begin to scream uncontrollably.

What do you two know, she would scream at them, *you in this ignorant, godforsaken place? Nothing, you know of fucking nothing.*

She went inside to Sharon's deserted kitchen, sat at the wooden table where Toby and his sisters had engraved their names long ago. With her hands carefully folded together like an obedient student's, Rina listened to the steady hum of the magnet-covered fridge and the gentle *tick-tock* of the sun-shaped clock until the urge to scream had passed.

"You and your folks getting used to the deep freeze?" Lyle had asked her the first time Rina came over to watch a movie. He'd ushered her into the blessed warmth of the back landing and automatically covered her frostbitten ears with his giant hands. "It'll only hurt for a minute. Then you'll have no worries."

Meanwhile, Toby was coming up the basement stairs two at a time. "Dad, let go of her head," he'd said.

"Leave them alone," Sharon called from another room.

With a gentle rub of his thumbs, Lyle released her. "It'll only hurt for a minute."

As if suddenly shy, Toby stopped on the top stair. "Dad's an idiot," he said, "but he means well."

Rina stood awkwardly in her new clunky boots and puffy parka, wondering what she was doing there. Then she'd noticed her ear lobes no longer stung.

There was only a pleasant, steady heat. "No worries," she said.

Afterwards, it would become her mantra. "Let's not worry, you and me, about later," she'd say. "No worries, right? No worries, Toby."

And for months, Toby had seemed content with this, to let her cling to him as they made their way through the parking lot, the other miners standing and staring, wiping their noses in their sleeves and shaking their heads. Until one June night as he was dropping her off.

"Where are you going to live again?" he asked.

Rina knew her father was inside, one eye reading his newspaper and the other watching the clock. She reached into her bag and got a cigarette, took her time lighting it. "Hmmm?"

Toby threw his head against the back of the seat. "Live," he repeated. "Where you going to live in the city?"

Rina held the smoke in her lungs, counting to ten in her head. "At the campus residence," she said casually, as if this were a conversation they'd already had. "Where else?"

"Okay," he said, "you don't want to talk about it. I get it. What else shouldn't we talk about?"

Rina had flung the cigarette out the window and then dove into his chest, reaching under his jacket and untucking his shirt, pressing her palms against his stomach. She'd known that her days of carefree goodness were numbered, but the strange, nervous anger in his voice still hit her hard. When he recoiled from her cold fingers, she'd pressed harder and whispered: "No, I know, I don't want to talk. I know. But please, Toby, I'm sorry. Please."

There, in the safety of the white truck, her hands warming against his skin, she'd found herself longing to climb right inside of him. She imagined disappearing somewhere into the wide, strong shelter of his rib cage where she would sleep for days and days.

"Okay," he'd said, stroking the silky hairs on the back of her neck. "Whatever. No worries."

When Rina didn't return from the house, Toby kicked the foot of the picnic table. "What's your problem?"

Ally looked down at her untied runners and shrugged.

For a long time, Sundays had been her favourite part of the week. Up until last year, she and Ruth had usually stayed in their housecoats all day, watching whatever old movie happened to be on and eating dinner out of a can. Only once, when she was ten, had Ally asked why they didn't go to church like almost everyone else in town.

"That stuff screws you up," her mother said, and Ally had let it go, not wanting to ruin their lazy hours together. All through her teens, Ally had savoured these preciously boring Sundays — until one day she'd begun to notice the way Ruth smelled before she showered, or the way she clacked the spoon against her teeth when eating ice cream. Then Ruth had begun to lash back at what she called "the look."

"You should go live with your father," she said. "You can learn that look from the master."

That's when loafing with Ruth had been replaced by loafing with Rina and Toby.

Just last Sunday Toby had said, "One time it snowed eight feet in one day and we got stuck in the school. We had to sleep in the gym and they kept giving us cookies and fruit punch to shut us up until finally, about five in the morning, I puked it all up."

Rina had looked at him blankly.

"No, but then after," he'd gone on, "after I puked, one thing led to another and everybody else started, and then it started to snow again . . . "

That's when Ally had raised her arms in victory and danced on top of the picnic table. "The whole gym reeked," she'd shouted, though actually Harry had still been around then and kept her at home because of the forecast. "We called it Puke-Ed class."

Now, when she looked up at Toby again, there were tiny beads of sweat along her hairline. The little creases in her pink forehead seemed to plead with him.

He picked up the air rifle and began methodically loading the pellets again. "You know we're just saying, Al, just keep an eye on him and don't believe everything he says. Don't be stupid. You and Ruth have a business to run. That guy who used to work at the dry cleaners, his junkie brother came home and stole everything. Remember that? He even took a box of those metal hangers and stuff like forks and spoons and shit."

"He took the cat, too," Ally said.

Toby planted his feet firmly in the gravel and brought the rifle to his shoulder. "That stupid cat that was always on a leash?"

Ally craned her neck and pretended to strain and tug. "Yeah, it would wind itself around a tree until it was stuck and then make this pathetic, choking meow all night."

"Fuck, that cat was stupid," Toby said.

Ally blinked away drips of sweat as his shot *thwakked* against the tin foil. Here, alone with Toby, his face so focused and calm, talking like they always did, she desperately wanted to tell him about what her cousin had looked like in his sleep the other night.

While Adam had dreamt of frantically digging the old woman's grave, Ally had stood barefoot in the hall on the way to the bathroom. She'd watched his eyelids flicker mysteriously and his legs grow hopelessly tangled in the afghan, unable to decide whether it was funny or awful to a see a two-hundred-pound man curled up on his side like an unborn baby doing the dog paddle.

Ally had no memory of her own night terrors, when Harry was still with them and she would wake up screaming at nothing her three-year-old self could express. As she'd gotten older, the dreams she remembered usually involved everyday anxieties that were mostly a source of entertainment. "Last night," she might say to whomever she was hanging out with at the time, "I dreamt that you and I were dancing in our bra and panties in the gym and everybody in the bleachers was booing us except for this one old guy who kept whistling and yelling, 'Take it off, baby!' It was brutal."

Yet the other night, she hadn't been able take her eyes away from Adam's stricken face. It was as if she were spying in her own house.

Afterwards, she'd wanted to tell him about what she'd seen, tell him how ridiculous he'd looked, to share the joke and get him laughing. Except he always left the apartment before lunch, striding wordlessly through the store and not coming back until the middle of the night. And whenever she came near him in the morning and peered for signs of life, he rolled over and pushed his face into the backrest in case she didn't get the hint.

Toby would listen, Ally thought, and he would get it and he would tell her what it meant.

But instead, Rina came out with a tray of ice cubes and began chasing him through the yard. Her friends lost themselves in each other and Ally had no choice but to keep her incomprehensible cousin to herself, to close her eyes and drift away to that place of secrets where the company of others gave no comfort. A place she had no real interest in and didn't understand. A place where you can be right beside someone and still alone.

This time, her daydream was a real memory, polished to a warm glow in her mind.

Weeks before, at an unofficial graduation party held just off the highway, sheltered in a cave-like clearing where students had celebrated for generations, Toby had given into his old friends' razzing. "Toby, man, where've you been," the young miners had said, "you're turning all soft and womanly on us. Come over here, we got something to show you."

For two hours he was gone and Rina sat fuming beside on a log, smoking and drinking straight gin. "This party is shit," she told Ally. "Who needs this? We come here and sit around in the dark, but for what? This whole place is shit. A shit lives in shit."

Ally had gotten happily drunk. Rina's self-conscious swearing seemed funnier with each beer. The bonfire and the sound of laughter echoing off the rocks made her feel warm all over.

But when Toby finally returned, he and Rina had disappeared into the bush and Ally stood up unsteadily, searching the dancing firelight for another group to join. Then one of the miners was suddenly sitting on the log where Rina had been. "They leave you here all by your lonesome, Al?" he asked.

The next thing she knew, Ally was following him into the darkness and there was nothing but hands. There were fingers in her mouth and around her neck, reaching into her jeans and pinching hard at her breasts. Something was wrong, there were too many bodies crushing up against her, crushing the air from her lungs. She flailed blindly, scratching and pushing until she was free, until she could stumble back towards the flickering light.

She found Toby sitting cross-legged on the ground with Rina's head resting in his lap. She looked like she'd just been sick. From out of the bush, a guy Ally didn't recognize stepped across Toby and Rina with drunken confidence.

He waved his hand towards Ally. "You can fucking have that one," he said to Toby. "She's kind of fat anyway."

Toby pushed himself straighter, but didn't get up. "Hey, watch your fucking mouth."

Later, when he pulled up in front of Ruth's store just after three in the morning, he put the truck in park. Then with Rina passed out against the passenger window, her lovely, flushed cheek mashed against the glass, he reached back and took Ally's hand. He didn't speak, or turn, or look back at her in the rearview mirror.

And later still, while Toby was helping Rina into the house under Merik's silent, judging gaze, Ally stood on the curb, wondering why he hadn't said anything to her. She'd gotten out without even saying good night, was still quite drunk, yet she was sure it had really happened — him in the front seat, her in the back, he'd held her hand tight for maybe two minutes, until he'd gently pulled away and put both hands back on the wheel.

RED WHITE YELLOW BLACK

5

RINA WAS NINE when the first shells landed in the streets of Sarajevo. The explosions woke her up in the early hours of the morning and she immediately ran to her parents' room.

When she was little, she'd done this regularly in the middle of the night — run down the hall, her bare feet cold on the tile floor, and joined Merik and Slavenka in their bed. As only a child, regularly included in grown-up company yet indulged like a little girl, her sense of injustice came early. Why should she who was so obviously small and weak, she'd wondered, have to sleep all alone in the dark while adults got to be together?

"You shouldn't encourage this," Merik would say to Slavenka as Rina nestled in between them. "It's best the child learn to sleep on her own."

Her mother would always let her stay. Born into a prominent family that could trace its roots back to ancient times, offering up generation upon generation of professors and composers, artists and judges, Slavenka often pouted over her husband's demands for "what was best." She could never make herself crawl out from beneath the down comforter and lead her daughter all the way back to her room, where she'd have to sing hoarsely in the chill while her husband snored as before. Plus she loved the intense, childish heat of Rina's tiny body cupped against her own.

"Hush," she'd whispered so many times, running her slim, pianist's fingers through Rina's hair, damp and curled with sweat. "Everybody go to sleep," she'd say, as if Merik were the one keeping them awake.

The night shells landed in the street Merik was already sitting up when Rina arrived in their doorway. He was searching for his glasses on the night table and his hair stuck up like wings over his ears. Even as the floor vibrated beneath her feet, Rina almost laughed.

Most times, she stood in awe of her father. He was more of a blur than a presence, rushing out with his bag and his newspaper to the important world outside their house. It was only first thing in the morning that he seemed real. In the manner of a busy man who gets too little sleep, Merik's eyes would be small and creased, his robe badly knotted, and Rina got into the habit of watching him shave. She would sit on a small wooden stool in the corner and watch his face emerge from the sweet-smelling lather. Every time a trickle of blood suddenly appeared beneath the razor, Merik would plunk a finger-full of lather onto her nose to let her know it was okay.

When the rolling thunderstorm of shells woke them up, rattling the windows and the small stool in the bathroom, it wasn't quite morning, but as her father fumbled for the lamp in the dark he still looked quite ridiculous in his boxer shorts. He squinted near-sightedly in the half-light. "Get dressed in something warm," he said. "Right now. We're going next door."

Slavenka remained where she was, lying with the comforter pulled up to her chin. She covered her ears and shook her head back and forth. "They have lost their minds," she whispered. "My god, they've finally done it."

It was this, more than the vibrating floor or Merik's terse instructions, that finally frightened Rina. Her mother was about red, red lips and music, not cowering beneath the sheets.

Still searching for his glasses, Merik spoke sternly to his wife in a way Rina had only heard before from a muffled distance. It always came through a door, late at night, after they'd been drinking wine at a party.

"Stop these dramatics, Enka," he would say. "You're frightening the child."

"This is madness," her mother whispered. She kept her hands over her ears as she sat up and her feet dropped to the floor like a rag doll's. "Madness."

Then Merik shooed Rina away with a firm swat through the air. "Get dressed," he said. "Now."

She raced to her room through the dark, shaking hall, so fast her nightgown strained against her knees.

Years after, that first night in the neighbour's cellar would come back to Rina in brief snippets rather than as a logical series of events. There was the dull ache of stubbing her toe against the piano bench as her family made their way through the blackened living room. There was the sinking sensation as the rotting wooden stairs down to the neighbour's cellar bent beneath their weight. There was the persistent "*psss, psss*" between blasts as their neighbour, an old widow with six cats, searched for her pets.

"Come, come," Merik had said, in what Rina still thought of as his doctor voice. "We won't take shelter in your cellar while you're up risking your death."

Unlike the adults, the cats — soft and lithe against the dank concrete — had paid attention to Rina, vying for warmth in her lap. Beneath the harshness of a bare light bulb, she had not dared to interrupt or interfere. She didn't point out that it was not fair to leave her out of the conversation just because she was a child. Instead, she clung to the cats' fur and wished away the grown-up voices. First the widow, gossipy and quick: "I hear they're in the mountains, all around. Tanks, machine guns, snipers. They say their headquarters are in the ski jump lodge." Then Merik, even slower than usual: "This can't go on. Now they'll have to intervene. They'll not let them take a defenseless city." Then Slavenka, strange and quiet: "They have lost their minds."

Rina's childhood world of boring violin lessons with her great-uncle and sunny afternoons on the ski slopes, of tea and sweets at the neighbourhood bistro, and secret languages with her school friends, would give way, in a matter of weeks, to a life denied the basic requirements for human existence. The city's beauty, its mountain fastness, would become its trap.

In a constant barrage of shelling and sniper fire, soldiers who had once shared restaurants and theatre seats with their victims, ringed the city and cut off supplies of water and electricity, food and medicine, fuel and hygiene products. Rina's plastic toy chest became a container to collect water from nearby drainpipes. Windows became deadly shards of broken glass. Merik became an expert in makeshift prosthetics.

No one saw more of the horror than the city's doctors, but Merik's gruesome work at least gave him purpose, let him do as he was trained. It was his time at home that was hardest.

Sometimes, he'd become irrationally nervous during a break in the bombing, as if silence itself had become dangerous. With no electricity, there was no way to distract himself with books and he would usually stay at the hospital late into the night, until almost too tired to stand.

One evening, after the city had spent more than seven hundred days under siege, he skinned and cooked a rabbit they'd been raising in a cage. Slavenka had refused to do it.

"You're still stubborn," Merik said, trying to tease her like he used to. He put the plate of stew in front of her. "Look, it's the finest meal you've smelled in months."

But Slavenka wept more bitterly than when her last house-plant had died. "This is madness," she mumbled. "What are we doing here?"

Earlier that afternoon, as she'd waited at the relief agency truck, a shrunken old man had leaned against a wall, in line for milk. Slavenka had quickly nodded to him as he let her cut in and then waited impatiently for several minutes, thinking of her only daughter all alone in the apartment, in this madness, when a commotion sprang up near the back. She'd turned around and seen a group of students struggling to carry the man's stiff, dead body away.

Careful not to lose her place, she'd watched and yet felt nothing — no surprise, no pity, no regret. It wasn't until she was on the way home, rushing through the ruins of the central square, old newspapers and garbage blowing against her legs, that she'd begun sobbing uncontrollably. Stumbling, she'd dropped the precious bottle of milk.

Later that night, with the rabbit stew in front of her, Slavenka was unable to explain to her husband or to her daughter why there was no milk and why she was weeping uncontrollably into her plate.

Merik pushed Rina's supper in closer towards her. "It's good," he said.

Rina was hungry, yet her mother's sniffling left her with no appetite. If Rina had hated cleaning the stinky cage, the rabbit was still a welcome diversion during the endless hours stuck in the house with no visitors. She'd given it a name and passed idle time by lying on the floor and sprinkling grass over her stomach, giggling as the rabbit nibbled around her belly button.

The rabbit's flesh steamed beneath Rina's nose, and Merik stared. He held his knife and fork in mid-air, waiting, looking tired enough to pass out in the stew.

First Rina took a bite, then Merik, and finally, Slavenka.

Not long after they arrived in Winnipeg with nothing but four small suitcases, Merik settled into the absurdly wide streets and flat commercial strips with blank acceptance. When he was informed it would take two years of upgrading before he'd be eligible to practice medicine, he didn't have the energy to be outraged. Slavenka, on the other hand, became prone to dramatic emotional swings.

Some days, she was unable to get out of bed and face the ugliness — not the high-rise apartment with its old-curtain dinginess and older-carpet smell, not the haphazard roadside snowbanks blackened with grit and exhaust, not the tastelessly flashing pawn shop signs of their West End neighbourhood. Other days, when the ladies' auxiliary of a nearby church would bring an ironing board or radio or other small token of support, Slavenka would weep quietly into their shoulders and claim her faith in humanity restored. Afterwards, she'd pace the dingy lobby like a caged tiger waiting to pounce, convinced that her family's future lay in becoming friendly with every tenant in the block.

Several times, she cornered a neighbour as they picked up their mail and invited them for coffee — and it never failed to be a disaster. Guests quickly became uncomfortable with Slavenka's limited language skills and odd formality, while she, embarrassed by the few chipped mugs she had to serve with, would find herself inwardly critisizing their greasy smell, their badly cut hair, their lack of table manners.

When the town of Franklin came calling, offering Merik his own practice if he hauled his family hundreds of miles North, Rina's parents jumped at the chance for a fresh start. Within five years, Merik had learned to speak the new language of his exile with barely a trace of an accent. He encouraged his patients to call him just "Dr. Mark" and introduced Slavenka as "Sylvia", and that was good enough for the townspeople. They mostly managed to overlook that there was something cool even in his friendliness, or that when he spoke it was like he was looking right through you.

"The one thing I know," he'd say in the quiet manner of an educated man used to being listened to, "is that the human body is the same wherever you go."

Slavenka insisted on being his office receptionist with her usual, fleeting zeal. She picked out a desk for herself and ordered a hands-free telephone headset. She lasted nearly five weeks, until she grew frustrated by how quickly his patients spoke on the phone, bored by the walls of files, irritated by the conversations about everyday ailments.

"You're not meant to type," Merik finally said, stroking her cheek as if this was what he loved most about her. "I'll hire someone. It's better this way."

After that, Rina watched her mother retreat, no longer even pretending to show an interest in Merik's talk of building a new house, spending most of her time watching the day-time soap operas. On her way in or out of the house, Rina would often pause for a moment while her mother summarized the wild intrigues and doomed love affairs, as if mindlessly reading off a shopping list.

"That one is having an affair with the dark one's daughter," Slavenka would say, or "His brother is taking over his business and his wife is dying, but he doesn't know."

So Rina was surprised when her mother suddenly got it into her head to invite Toby to dinner. The day after Ally's outburst in his backyard — *I'll bet he'll still be here after you've buggered off*— Slavenka asked why they'd never had the miner over for pepper steak.

Rina couldn't think of a lie fast enough. "You never asked," she said on her way out. "You want him for dinner, he'll come for dinner."

"This week," Slavenka called after her. "This week he should come."

Toby couldn't have said exactly what made him so uncomfortable at Rina's parents', but the house itself didn't help. A split-level with crumbling stucco outside and bare walls inside, it seemed only half lived-in, as if a whole year hadn't been enough time for Rina's family to unpack.

"I heard the doctor's going to totally level what's there," his father Lyle had told him, "and build a mansion, with a screened porch that wraps around the whole damn thing. Four thousand square feet, they say."

Three times, Toby had waited for Rina in the dim, tiny landing of the split-level, with its twin set of narrow stairs disappearing up and down, and three times Merik had let him in and then retreated back up the stairs. Each time, he'd turned at the top and looked down. "She'll be here momentarily," he'd said, and then just stood there, cleaning his glasses.

The first time Toby visited, Slavenka had appeared from the basement and barely acknowledged Toby as she squeezed by him with a laundry basket. But the third time, she'd brushed passed her husband at the top of the stairs and come all the way down. She'd touched Toby's shoulder, moving in close enough that he could smell her perfume, an earthy blend of musk and vanilla. She was shorter than Rina, but curvier, and he could feel her breast against his elbow.

"Enjoy, yes?" she'd said. "You have fun."

After Rina extended the dinner invitation, acting strangely shy, almost embarrassed, Toby went around in a kind of daze that wasn't like him at all. Down in the mine, he lagged behind for the first time since finishing his training. "What's fucking with you," his supervisor asked him, only half-joking. "You smoking something?"

Not long before he was to arrive at Merik and Slavenka's, he lost track of the time. It had been a beautiful afternoon, his day off, and there was nothing like a good, hard ski along the relatively flat road that marked the eastern edge of the mine grounds. When he got home, his mother Sharon was already ironing his white shirt.

"Jump in the shower," she said, as if he'd been considering just going as he was. By the time he arrived in Merik and Slavenka's doorway, he was nearly a half-hour late. When Slavenka answered the door, he was out of breath, his hair still wet.

She was wearing slim-leg jeans and a yellow v-necked T-shirt, and looked like she was about to laugh at him. Instead she took his elbow and rubbed her thumb reassuringly against his freshly-pressed shirt. "Well, you are here," she said. "Come in, come in. We won't bite."

As she led him into the dining room, her perfume was lost amidst the spicy cooking smells, but her breast pressed reliably soft and round against his arm. Merik stood at the head of the table, cleaning his glasses with a small cloth. He looked older than Toby remembered, with tiny, half-moon shadows under his eyes. The table was covered in fancy dishes and wide-mouthed wine glasses that made the bare walls looked even barer.

Rina was nowhere in sight.

"Sorry I'm late," Toby said.

Still holding his arm, Slavenka pulled back a chair and guided Toby down by the shoulders, as if afraid he might run away. "This is nothing," she said. "You people eat so early, almost in the afternoon. For us, it is more what, how do you say it, more lazy? At home, we would eat sometimes not until ten at night."

Merik held his glasses up to the light, then carefully slid them over his ears with both hands. With just his index finger, he slowly pushed the glasses up along the bridge of his nose and stared down at the table, concentrating hard, as if he could see right through the wood to Toby's shoes, the expensive, giant-tongued runners he and his friends all wore.

Toby wondered why Slavenka hadn't given him a chance to take them off.

"This is our home now," Merik said, still standing and staring, "and we welcome you."

Toby's shoulders were suddenly cool and bare as Slavenka disappeared into the kitchen. He could hear the *whir* of a hair dryer coming from the bathroom down the hall, and thought of all the times he'd watched Rina drying her hair in his own basement. It was like she would get lost in the warm, steady noise for what seemed like hours, still going even after her hair started to feel brittle.

One time, he'd teased her about the amount of time she spent in the shower, and she'd grown strangely serious.

"Do you know what it means to have an itchy head?" she'd asked him. "When we came to this country, I stood in an aisle full of shampoo bottles and I cried like a baby."

The *whirring* stopped and Rina appeared, brushing a fly-away strand of hair from her face. She sat down across from Toby and gently kicked his runners beneath the table. "She made pepper steak. You'll like it."

Toby wished he could reach over and brush the stray hair away himself. His fingers would linger against her cheek, trace the soft outline of her earlobe until she tilted her head into his hand.

"What's with you?" the other miners had shouted at him over the roar of the furnace and he'd had no answer. All he cared about was that she was finally here, right across from him, kicking his feet beneath the table.

Merik went to the window and closed the blinds. "At this time of summer," he said to nobody in particular, "the sun will shine right in your eyes as we eat."

Toby nodded, trying to mind his manners as Rina's toe worked its way up his ankle and rubbed slowly, sock to sock. Merik kept his back to them as he spoke.

"We've been in this country maybe five years," he said, "and still the sunshine amazes me. Winter and summer, it can be sunshine for weeks. Not one drop of rain."

Merik had become an expert at talking about the weather. That and food were always easy topics with his patients.

"Everywhere you go, you have to eat," he would often say, and though he knew nothing of hockey or ice fishing, there was always a joke about his wife's cooking. "You think the chili gives you heartburn? You haven't eaten my wife's stuffed peppers."

"But what good is the sun in the winter?" Slavenka shouted from the kitchen. "It does nothing. It's still freezing outside."

Merik stared out the window through the partially closed blinds. Rina kept her big toe snug against Toby's ankle, but looked right passed him to where her father stood. "Toby does the biathlon," she said. "He's created his own trails and everything."

Merik could recall seeing Toby along the roadside. It had struck him as an odd pastime for such an ordinary-looking boy. He had a hard time imagining the young miner struggling on the long skis while all the others on snowmobiles roared by, going fast enough to impale themselves onto a tree branch, spraying a blizzard of snow into his face.

Merik turned back towards the table and folded his hands slowly like he did when delivering good news to a patient. "Did you know, Toby, that the biathlon started as part of the military? There were regiments of soldiers on skis and they were the best snipers. Come winter, no one could match their speed and precision."

Toby nodded, though he'd never heard this before. "It's a blend of endurance and skill," he said.

Merik picked up a fork and pointed it at Toby. It was a gesture Rina hadn't seen since she was little and there'd been dinner parties with many grown-ups, all laughing and arguing.

"There has even been cave drawings of early humans hunting on narrow planks of wood," Merik said. "All the way to prehistoric times, Toby. Think of that."

Slavenka appeared, expertly carrying several dishes. She arranged them one by one on the table. "Our city, one time it hosted the whole world," she said. "All the winter sports were there. Now it is nothing. It is rubble."

The phone began to ring.

"That's enough," Merik said. "We're having a nice dinner."

By this he meant he'd been managing to put from his mind, just for tonight, that February morning after he'd delivered Toby's sister's baby. Merik had already been on his way to another call when Toby's father Lyle had chased him down the hospital hallway.

"Thanks doc," Lyle had said, his cheeks flushed and wet. "I'm the grandfather. I can't believe it. It's not like anybody planned this, and it never hits you until it hits you, you know." Then he'd grinned as if embarrassed by his tears and patted Merik's stomach with the back of his hand. "But don't worry about your Rina. My boy's not stupid. Don't worry about that."

Rina's father had stood speechless for a moment, not sure how to respond to such crudeness.

"Yes, yes, I'm sure," he'd finally said, before hurrying away.

"How much time is she spending with the miner?" he'd asked Slavenka later.

"Let her be," she'd replied. "It's only for awhile. We drag her up here and she's making the best of it. Let her be."

And so Merik had let it go, too tired to challenge her, wanting to believe that just this once his wife was seeing things rationally, unselfishly, that the future would take care of itself.

Now, he watched as Slavenka paused with the last covered dish in mid-air, like she might dump it on his head.

Without a word, she carefully placed it with the rest and left the room again.

For four whole days, Ally had held off calling Rina. Instead, she'd eaten little packages of pudding in front of the television until she felt sick. She'd waited in vain for any sound of Adam on the stairs. She'd watched Ruth order, then re-order the lentil bins.

"If you're not going to help, get out of my face," her mother had said.

Twice, Ally had woken up as Adam stumbled into the dark apartment in the middle of the night, and found herself trying to imagine his movements. Now he's throwing his clothes in a clump on the floor; now he's swatting the lumpy old pillow; now he's wrapping himself in the afghan and drifting off to sleep; now he's starting to mutter and paddle in his dreams.

Over and over, she imagined Toby sitting in his truck in Merik and Slavenka's driveway, waiting for Rina to get ready, until Ally herself would appear as if from nowhere. She would lean her head into the open window and Toby would say, *Get in. She could take hours in there.*

After they were out of town and on the highway, Ally would run her fingers through his hair and they would laugh like they did about the stupid cat on the leash, like they were sharing a secret joke.

There's something I have to tell you, she would say, like she always did, and Toby would stop laughing and stare straight ahead, eyes on the road.

Her imagination went on like this until eventually Ally opened the cupboard and saw the last of the pudding packs was gone.

When Rina answered the phone, it sounded like she'd been running.

"Where were you?" Ally asked. "You sound out of breath."

"Nowhere," Rina said. "Toby's here."

"At your house?" Ally asked.

"Yeah," Rina said. "We're just eating."

Ally tried to sound casual. "That's a first. How's it going?"

"Fine," Rina lied. "It's good. We're having pepper steak."

Hearing her friend's voice, Rina suddenly realized how much she'd missed her. *I'll bet you'll bugger off before he does,* Ally had hissed, out of the blue that sunny Sunday afternoon in Toby's yard.

But Rina wasn't ready to give it all up yet, to say so long to no worries. She wanted to scream again, but not in anger this time. Already, she could feel the twist of fear in her stomach.

"Toby's got some paint," she said. "He found some new spot up towards the swamp. We'll get some beer and go up there some night maybe."

She knew Toby had meant just the two of them, but she didn't care.

"Whatever," Ally said quietly. "I'm easy."

When Toby came out of the bathroom, Slavenka was standing with her back to him in the dim hallway, watching her daughter talk on the phone.

At the high school graduation ceremony in June, Rina had received a small scholarship and Toby had acted like a proud father, snapping picture after picture. "Look," Slavenka had said to her as they smiled for the camera. "Your miner thinks he's a big-time photographer today."

Now, as he turned awkwardly to squeeze past her in the hallway, Rina's mother said to him: "Look, my girl is so beautiful . . . "

Toby stopped and automatically followed Slavenka's gaze, as if they'd regularly met like this, he and Rina's mother, shoulder to shoulder, shooting the shit outside the bathroom.

There, in the late evening light, long legs dangling over the armchair, phone cradled in her arched neck, sat someone who'd seen death, man-made and cruel, fall from a clear, blue sky. Someone who could no more escape her past in this place of hushed, endless winters any more than Adam could.

Yet there no were visible signs of this, not one physical clue. And all someone like Toby could do was nod dumbly in agreement: she was so beautiful that all he wanted was to touch her golden skin, to feel her long legs around his waist, to hear her say his name.

Slavenka hugged herself as if she was cold in her yellow T-shirt. The smell of her perfume was stronger now. "She must leave us, you know."

Bugger off, Toby wanted to say. *Bugger off, bugger off, bugger off.*

All he knew was that he wanted to ask Rina to stay.

That was it, that's what was with him. It was stupid and pointless, but he could feel it in his throat like a thirst, keeping him from answering Slavenka, and making him feel like an idiot.

6

AFTER TELLING ALLY WHY he'd finally gotten on the bus, Adam stayed away from the apartment, losing himself in the town's hidden corners and undeveloped stretches, moving about like a plastic bag in the wind.

With the entire business district a single, four-block strip that mostly shut down after supper, the best places to lie low were random pockets of wilderness. Sometimes he veered off the rarely used sidewalks and crawled down dangerously sloping paths into deep, leafy crevices littered with the telltale signs of a private party — broken glass, condoms, charred wood. Sometimes he walked near the marshy pair of lakes that split the town in two, riding one of the bikes he found left unlocked, and then tossing it in. Once, as the back wheel of a ten-speed disappeared in a series of ripples, the late sun and endless puff of smoke had turned the water a soft, hazy gold, reminding him of a picture he'd seen once on a classroom calendar. When the midday heat grew too much he'd find a corner carrel in Franklin's compact public library, where he'd eat a giant bag of pretzels lifted from Co-op and mark whichever book he'd grabbed with his swirling tag, working page by page with methodical swiftness.

He got into the habit of sneaking along the mine grounds well after dark, trying to see how many rocks he could throw at the cooling-system pipes that sputtered and sprayed over a man-made lake before the security guard woke up and stumbled out with his flashlight. His all-time record was twenty-six.

In many ways, these wanderings weren't unlike his last few months in the city. Steering clear of his usual hangouts, avoiding his connections while growing increasingly desperate for a hit of something to take the edge off, he'd mostly found himself in a series of mid-priced hotel bars and fast-food restaurants with people he didn't know and who didn't want to know him. There, he'd tried to talk his way into free booze and burgers with a disturbing lack of success. There were small moments of triumph, like when he'd scored two cases of beer from the back of a delivery truck in broad daylight and drunk them one by one alongside the deserted rooftop pool of a high-rise. But his dead brother and his friends and all the people he knew were always there at the edges of his anonymity, rattling his nerves, destroying any chance of numbness, until finally he'd been sold out and left with no choice but to run and run far.

Toby was just finishing his shift, the smell of Slavenka's perfume still lingering in his nose from the night before, when Adam stepped into the street without looking where he was going. Moments before, just as he went to grab a bag of day old buns from the bakery, a truck had rumbled by and the girl at the counter looked up. Her eyes had opened wide, slightly bloodshot after an early morning of kneading dough, and as he escaped through the screen door, it was like those eyes, wide and tired, could see right through him and his knapsack.

The next thing he knew a horn was blasting and a guy in a suit behind the wheel was shaking his head. Adam brushed passed the bumper, nodding casually as if saying hello, and just kept going, not letting himself look back towards the bakery.

The guy in the suit rolled down his window. He'd spilled hot coffee in his lap. "Hey chief!" he shouted. "Watch where you're going."

Adam stumbled over the curb like a little kid. For years, he'd travelled in packs, walking two or three abreast, just daring anyone to say something once, just once, to make their fucking day. But it had never happened, in the middle of the afternoon, in the middle of the street. In an instant, Adam felt an outrage so pure he found himself marching back to Ruth's in broad daylight.

When he arrived, he stood outside for a minute, watching the two women go about the business of closing for the day. There was something in the way they brushed passed one another, so absorbed in their menial work — emptying the garbage, sweeping the floor, wiping the bins — that made him glad he'd come.

He strode through the door like it was nothing unusual for him to show up in the afternoon and hopped up onto the cash desk. "This town is fucking racist."

Ally looked up from tying a garbage bag and stared dumbly.

Ruth kept sweeping. The day's last customers were drifting in and out, and after the lazy, sleeping giant of the last few weeks she wasn't prepared for Adam to march in like he was Vincent himself, kicking his feet against the desk to get her attention. It was like she was back in her brother's chaotic, crowded kitchen all those years ago, when they were still speaking and her husband Harry was still around.

"What have we got here," Lucille had said while shifting one of her wailing infants from arm to arm, "we got nothing. We got screwed."

Harry had nodded uncomfortably while Vincent clapped him on the back and poured another drink.

"To getting screwed!" her brother had said, raising his glass jovially.

Now, she couldn't even look at her nephew. "Yeah? Well, welcome to the real world."

The shop bell tinkled and Ruth automatically smiled in greeting. Adam watched her scurry over to the one of the fat librarians who wrinkled her eyebrows every time he came in the library.

"That's all you have to fucking say?' he asked.

Fatty the Librarian looked over in surprise.

"I'm sorry," Ruth said to her, patting Fatty's arm as if she needed comforting.

She walked slowly over to Adam, coming so close he could see that her mouth, with too much lipstick and too many little lines, was actually quivering.

She spoke quietly: "I'll tell you what I have to say. How much longer do you plan to treat my place like a flophouse? Maybe you can tell me that."

Adam knew then that he'd gone too far.

He knew once and for all that he was no longer the same kid who'd figured out early on that his mother Lucille was most affectionate late at night, after the noise and mess of his brothers had died down, who'd easily latched onto those who could protect him in the confusing, suffocating walls of the school and the familiar, threatening streets of the neigh-bourhood. He wasn't the same man who'd mastered the art of seducing the wounded, needy young women who hung around their apartment, who'd instinctively understood the key was to treat them tough like they'd come to expect, with rare and spontaneous acts of gentleness thrown in.

But now, his aunt, this woman who'd seemed prepared to absently buy his lies and let him be, stood trembling in anger before him. And his cousin, who already knew too much, who seemed like a puppy, eager to please but with a good sharp nip, was now turned away from him, smiling weakly at Fatty with pink-faced embarrassment.

Adam suddenly hated himself almost as much as hated the racist bastard shouting slurs from the safety of his locked car. He hated himself for stumbling like a little kid over the curb, afraid to turn back towards the baker's X-ray eyes, with only a knapsack full of stale buns to strike back with. He hated himself for speaking the truth, the simple fucking truth this time, yet somehow getting it wrong even when he was right.

Adam's ancestors were the first humans to live where the city of Winnipeg, and the town of Franklin now stand. These ancestors were blessed by what seemed like endless spaces of field and forest and river, yet cursed by an unpredictable and unforgiving climate. They saw themselves as part of nature, largely content to simply accept and honour life's mysteries. But the ones who arrived from more temperate climes had already lost all interest in such acceptance. Instead, they were spurred on by a double-edged sword — the urge to explore and to conquer any mystery they came across.

By the time Adam's father Vincent was born, then, much of the old nomadic and mystical ways of the hunters had been lost. As he'd made his way down the birth canal, his mother Mary had no idea what was happening to her or how she should feel. She was caught between the practical rights and traditions of natural childbirth and the new fluorescent lights of a sterile nursing station. Mary was part of the first generation to be lost in a kind of limbo, caught between the civilized materialism of the cities and the ritualized freedom of the hunt.

It was here, just over an hour from Franklin, in a motley collection of half-finished houses and half-wild dogs at the end of a gravel road which Ally could barely remember and Adam was just starting to, that Vincent had grown into a man, and his sister Ruth had faced her terrible choice.

It was the morning of her seventeenth birthday and Vincent hadn't been home for two days. As she lay awake most of the night, Ruth had convinced herself that her brother was sitting frozen solid somewhere after playing some stupid trick on his girlfriend Lucille, and then passing out behind a snowbank at the edge of the endless bush. When Ruth finally made her herself get up and stumble from the room, still half-asleep, she found their mother standing at the window, giggling into her hand.

"What's so funny?" Ruth asked.

Her mother Mary whirled a finger by her ear. "Vincent's got bloodied up but he's feeling no pain," she said. "He's weaving around all over the place out there, pretending he's an airplane. He's like his father. Crazy."

Mary had at least been a love-match for Vincent's father, an older, married neighbour who liked the way she swayed when she walked. After dark, he would bring her moose meat and potato chips and then later, she would have to stuff a blanket in her mouth to keep from moaning too loud with pleasure.

Ruth's father, on the other hand, had been a police officer from far away, tall and young and important in his new uniform, here one day and gone the next. He'd shared nothing with her mother, not history nor meat nor even his name, simply took what he needed from an uncomplaining woman who happened to be handy on a winter night.

Seventeen years later, Ruth looked out the window and saw Lucille riding Vincent as if he were a horse. There was vomit in the snow and Vincent's cheeks were chapped red. When they fell to the ground, they held tight to each other and rolled and rolled until they looked almost frozen together, a giant snowball of arms and legs and hair in the cold morning blueness.

Ruth shivered in her flimsy T-shirt and felt a surge of protectiveness.

As she'd grown lovelier by the year, her black hair even blacker against her pale ears, men had begun to smirk at her with desire and her mother had grown more distant. But Vincent would take her gently into a brotherly headlock. "Don't worry, little sister. Any of those wrinkly bastards climb on without permission, I'm on them."

Even after Vincent had met Lucille, he would still invite Ruth along, grabbing her by the elbow and leading her along in encouragement. "My little sister needs a stiff one," he'd say.

"He's bleeding," Ruth told her mother.

Mary only shrugged like she always did, slow and dismissive, still giggling.

"What do you want?" she asked. "It's better to laugh than to cry, eh."

Mary had spittle at the corner of her mouth, and her black eyes were sunk so deep into their sockets Ruth couldn't read their expression. Ruth turned away, but not in judgment, not like Ally would years later when she noticed how her mother's arms jiggled in the heat. When Ruth had looked at her mother, she felt nothing but a hollow hopelessness in her gut.

She'd gone back to the bedroom they shared and crawled under a blanket that had grown thin with use and remembered it was the day she turned seventeen. She was seventeen and wanted to take her own life. The rifle was no more than six feet away, loaded and leaning against a rusted ironing board in the closet. But just remembering the blood she'd seen leaking from Vincent's eyebrow had been enough to make her stiffen with nausea.

So the next day, Ruth hitchhiked to the mining town where she found work in the government office cafeteria, and pursued Ally's father Harry — just arrived and freshly dressed from the city — with the patient determination of a bobcat.

A year later, when their mother Mary died, Vincent howled in pain until Lucille rocked him in her arms like a child, but Ruth did not cry. She had already become the Ruth that Ally would know and whom Harry would leave.

After Adam walked out of the shop, he didn't go back to the apartment.

This time, he stuck to the back lane of the business strip, flanked by haphazard loading zones and abandoned cardboard boxes on one side, and the tiny, toy-littered back yards of mining company housing on the other. Somewhere along the way to Ruth's that afternoon he'd begun to anticipate the possibility of a real meal after days of living off bags of snack food. That such a meal would not be forthcoming, and that it was his fault, made him even hungrier. The smell of other people's dinner wafting from kitchen windows was torture.

Clinging to the business side of the lane with its stench of sun-soaked garbage bins, he smoked his last five cigarettes one after the other. He almost choked on a mouthful of dry bun.

He punched half-heartedly at his own stomach. But nothing he did seemed to help.

Just past the Co-op, near a string of abandoned shopping carts, a dog appeared from nowhere and darted into Adam's path, forcing him to stumble for the second time that day. The mutt was missing half its left ear. It was skinny and dirty and sniffed Adam's shoes as if they were covered in gravy.

Adam took a swing at the dog with his knapsack. "Get lost."

But the animal was intent on its smelly business and for a moment, Adam too was led by his nose. The smell of matted fur and rancid dog breath overcame all the competing odours of the alley and Adam was suddenly small again, tickling a stray's furry belly as his father went on and on, slightly slurred but unusually commanding and serious.

"You boys, you'll learn," Vincent said. "You got enough worries without fighting each other. Those fuckers will try and keep you down, because they hate us and everything about us. You'll see. They'll try and keep you down."

Then, from sometime later, he heard the voice of his little brother Leonard, not long before he died. "Our old man, he's a fucking joke."

Leonard was engraving the number "16" on his forearm with a kitchen knife, in honour of his birthday. All the guys in the apartment stood over him, amazed by how the little bastard didn't even seem to flinch. "Where's all that talk, talk, talk got him?" Leonard asked. "None of that shit matters."

He held up the bloody knife. "This is what matters. Right here, right now. He's a fucking joke."

Now, Adam kicked at the dog's snout, but it only yelped playfully. It grabbed his shoelace in its teeth and yanked hard, knocking Adam off balance. He landed on his tailbone and the remaining few puffs of his cigarette went flying. With his free leg, he drove his heel into the dog's ribs and lost his balance again. This time, his head hit the concrete with a *thunk*. The dog let out a high-pitched whine and disappeared behind a rusted-out minivan.

"What the hell you doing?" a voice shouted.

A miner barbequing in his backyard had heard the commotion and now stood alongside the van, waving his hamburger flipper in the air. The dog wasn't his, but he sometimes fed it scraps. "You pissed or something?" he shouted. "Take that shit somewhere else. I'm making supper for my kids here."

Though Adam's light-headedness had turned to full-fledged dizziness, though his elbow was bleeding, though he knew his last cigarette still had to be smouldering somewhere close, he was up in an instant and running hard, leaving his knapsack behind to be flattened by some delivery truck. He ran until the dull ache in his stomach turned into a searing pain in his lungs. Until he got out of the alley and onto the main road that leads down, down, down to the lakes and the bus depot and the highway out. Until the voices, real and remembered, were drowned out by the persistent pounding in his head.

Until he saw her across the street, carefully leading a shopping cart over the cracks in the sidewalk as if it was a small child.

It was the old lady from the bus. She was wearing the same clothes — stretchy pants and shirt that were exactly the same washed-out orange. Her white hair was still so thin and stringy you could see her scalp from across the street.

Adam crossed the road and followed her at a careful distance, trying to match his pace with hers. She would speed up now and then, only slow to almost nothing, as if to taunt him. After a few minutes, she turned up in front of a small brick bungalow. The slabs of the sloping sidewalk were uneven and she had to struggle to keep the cart upright. It seemed to take her hours to get to the door.

The lawn was covered with barrels and boxes and pails, each growing a different-coloured flower. Near the basement window a small plastic donkey pulled a wagon. Months before, Adam would've noted that the crappy lawn ornaments were a sure sign the owners probably hid money in cans and curtain hems, but now he only stared pointlessly into the front window, squinting as the early evening sun reflected back at him. He couldn't make out a thing inside the house.

The old woman rested the cart against the front steps, then began lifting her bags — first the plastic one on top, then the paper one underneath. She set them each on the grass with great care. She shuffled up each step — right foot, then left foot, then pause, right foot, then left foot, then pause. She dropped her keys and made a small noise as she slowly crouched down to get them.

By the time she disappeared into the house, Adam's bruised elbow had begun to throb.

"You'll learn," he remembered his father saying, throwing the ticklish dog a piece of smoked meat, "you'll see."

But he didn't see. What the fuck do you do when even when you're right, you're wrong? The only thing Adam knew was that the old woman was alone. If someone else were home, they would've helped her with the groceries.

He shielded his eyes from the glaring reflection of the window. At his feet, a perfect circle of bluish stones surrounded a small tree. He picked one up and closed it in his fist.

He could see her face as she opened the door. There would be a brief glimpse of recognition in her face, followed by surprise, then dawning terror. She would stumble from room to room, sobbing that she did not know, how could she know where they kept things, it was her niece's house, the one who worked at the mine — she was only an office worker, sixty-five words a minute, don't you remember? He would feel her skull give in, the same fragile temple that had bounced off his shoulder as they rode over the prairie and into the forest, no match for the bluish rock. He could hear the *thud* and then her shortening, nasal breath, and then nothing.

"Can I help you?" a women's voice asked.

When the old lady's niece came up the walk, she had no idea that by leaving work early with a slight cold she might have spared two lives. She would never know what the desperate-looking young man had wanted, or why he fled, cutting across her manicured lawn, running fast. Days later, when she noticed a gap in the circle of rocks around her apple tree, she would make no connection.

7

THAT NIGHT, Adam ran from the small brick house until his lungs could take no more, then stumbled into the snack stand at the bus depot. But it was no good. The bored, pimply sales clerk blinked at him from behind his glasses and Adam's body felt oddly useless, heavy and jittery at the same time. With his pockets still empty and his backpack gone, he escaped into the growing darkness.

With no food or cigarettes to sustain him, he found himself wandering across the road towards the lake, just as he usually did, as if he was drawn by its cool, late evening sheen. He followed the water's edge, first along a sturdy boardwalk that had been built in honour of the town's fiftieth anniversary, then down a gravel path that grew narrower as the porch lights of lakeside houses grew fainter. He wandered further than he ever had before out along the mysterious edges of the lake, until he was stumbling over roots and rocks, growing increasingly blind in the thickening bush.

The day's heat remained, dry and relentless even in the distant moonlight. As he swatted low branches from his face, sweat drizzled down his temples as if to tease his growing thirst. Still, he trudged on, barely aware of the comforting breeze that rushed through the brush and blew mosquitoes into confusion.

It was just before midnight when he reached a steep rock face that would let him go no further. He stared blankly at the dark, impenetrable wall, then turned around and let himself fall back against it, as though testing its strength. He slid down into a crouch, in defeat, not even groaning when his swollen elbow collided with a rocky outcropping. He was past the point of hunger now, his insides craving only the obliterating rush of nicotine.

Although the centre of town was just across the water, the night was darker than he'd ever known. There was only the rustling of leaves and the whine of a mosquito by his left ear. Whether his eyes were open or closed, it was still the same black nothing.

Cradling his elbow, Adam remembered a late-night movie he watched once while nestled against Lucille's round hip. It was set in the heyday of his ancestors, and near the end of the movie, a young warrior had been taken out to a barren, desert-like place and left there for days until he began to see crazy things: men with antlers, birds with teeth, eagles that turned into trees.

Adam had turned his face into his mother's ample waist and Lucille had reached between the cushions for the remote control and switched off the TV. The streetlights outside cast dim shadows in the dark room, but her teeth shone white as she smiled at him and brushed her fingers through his hair. "Why didn't somebody give that guy some food, eh," she said. "You don't eat, you go sick in the head."

The way she'd said it, so sleepy and matter-of-fact, had made him laugh out loud even as the haunting images still lingered. Later, it seemed all the old traditions were nothing more than a joke.

"I'm going on a dream quest," he liked to crack, while on his way to getting high or drunk or into the pants of a new girl.

"I had a dream last night too," Leonard said once, still copying Adam, always trying to talk big in front of his older brothers. "It said, hey, all you big warriors, forget the arrows and the fucking dreams. Why don't you get yourselves some fucking guns?"

Now, Adam sank down until he was sitting on the hard ground. There, in the nothingness, he saw a front door open silently, watched Leonard lean in like he sometimes did when he wanted them to hurry the fuck up and get going. But his brother's eyes were blank, his hair matted with blood, his hands hanging useless at his sides.

Leonard fell with a wet *thud*, half-in, half-out of the doorway.

Adam covered his ears, but the *thud* remained. Suddenly, all he wanted to do was sleep. When the roar of a semi-trailer traveled across the water, he let himself fall over onto his good arm and curled up on the ground as if in his afghan cocoon.

For hours, he lay in an uncomfortable half-sleep, small stones or twigs digging into his ribs, the odd bug flying up his nose, while the memories darted through his mind like a bird caught in a barn. His lips burned in the fishing shack. The pink, squirming gopher flew through the air. The old man whittled on the step.

That night, the old man came to him again and again, moving with slow purpose, faceless behind a mass of wrinkles, sauntering into the bush with his rifle over his shoulder while the dogs circled in a frenzy. There he was, skinning a rabbit in the blood-stained dirt, cooking outside on the small gas stove even in winter, Vincent laughing as they passed. Just as dawn began to break, the crows and meadowlarks noisily announcing the new day, Adam opened his eyes and was sure the old man was there, moving through the dewy, sheltered half-light as the wind laughed in the treetops. But the crazy old shit didn't seem to care. He paid no attention at all, he just kept moving with slow, secret purpose.

Adam didn't wake for good until shortly before eight, just as the amber shimmer on the lake began to hint at the day's coming heat. When he sat up, he was all alone and felt like he'd been on the losing end of a street fight. Every inch of him ached in its own way. In the end, it was severe thirst, his throat so dry it was painful to swallow, that finally got him up and forced his stiff, wobbly legs to stumble back the way they'd come.

The undergrowth that had seemed so dense the night before was softened by sun filtering through in shimmering shades of gold. All Adam really noticed, though, were glimpses of water through the leaves. When the sloping path turned to gravel, he nearly ran the remaining distance to the boardwalk. At the lake's edge, he got down on all fours and cupped mouthful after mouthful, letting the coolness drip down his chin. He drank until he had to lean back on his heels and stop for breath.

That's when across the still water, beyond the reedy grasses and scrubby bush, he saw the smoke rising weightlessly from the tall stack above the smelter. The smoke changed the colour of everything—the clouds, the houses, the water—giving them a muted, sickly hue. Adam opened wide, as if trying to exhale the smoke he'd just drunk. How had it come to this? he wondered. How long had it been since he'd eaten real fucking food?

It was even harder getting up the second time. He rose unsteadily and continued down the boardwalk, lulled by the hum of morning traffic and the soft whoosh of water against wood.

Once in town, he moved like a sleepwalker, until half-a-block away from Ruth's store he slowed almost to a stop. She was out on the sidewalk sweeping dust from the top of the awning. He'd somehow forgotten that she'd be there, her bitter question still unanswered — *how much longer was he going to treat her place like flophouse?*

Before she could look up, he veered into the street and ducked into the souvenir shop for cover.

For days, Adam had avoided this shop like no other place.

Lingering near the door, he surveyed the place for any food he could lift. There were sounds of life somewhere in the back, but the shop looked empty, the cash register deserted. Business was slow this time of year.

His expert eyes scanned little pieces of a past that was his, but not his, all for sale at the right price: plastic toy figures of bears and wolves and half-naked, muscular hunters; intricately webbed wall-hangings that promised to catch the buyers' dreams while they slept; large tribal drums stretched with hide and smaller ones covered with vinyl. Some of the merchandise was brought in by elderly women from reserve lands nearby, looking to make a fair dollar for their painstaking handiwork. But that was more than most were willing to pay and the majority of shelves were filled with mass-produced imitations.

A distinct smell pervaded the whole room, dense and earthy and vaguely familiar. As Adam surveyed the bounty, he felt a spurt of energy in his limbs. He wanted to kick down the display of saskatoon-berry syrups, smash to smithereens the fancy little bottles tied with bows. He wanted to clear the shelves with broad sweeps of his arms, hear the dull split of wood and smash of glass beneath his heels. He wanted to rip at things until his hands couldn't rip anymore, then dump the bin of hatchet-shaped cigarette lighters near the cash register. He'd light first the wood, then the bark, then the hides, until even the plastic had no choice but to melt away.

A toilet flushed and a woman, the owner's wife, Ally's first grade teacher, appeared from behind a curtain. She started in surprise and took a step back. "How long have you been here?"

That smell was deer hide, Adam thought. The crazy old bastard had reeked of propane, and smoke, and deer hide.

Across the street, Ruth stepped out onto the sidewalk with her purse. Adam watched her disappear from view, then took his outrage and left the souvenir shop as silently as he'd come.

After Adam had barged in, calling the town racist, and then split, Ally hadn't interrupted her mother's pointless sorting and counting in the back room. She hadn't immediately called Rina to ask her what she thought. She'd simply gone through the motions of closing the store so they would be ready in another fifteen hours, when she would go through the motions of opening again.

The next morning, as she flipped open the store blinds and turned on the same radio station that had been playing all day, every day, since she was a child, she imagined her cousin showing up again just like he had that first Saturday — swaggering, smiling like he knew a secret.

He would come from behind her in the apartment, without a sound, and playfully whisper, *Long time no see, Cuz.* Then he'd turn to Ruth and casually say: *I was feeling better, so I thought I'd get out and see the place. But I missed your blueberry jam.*

It's not my blueberry jam, Ruth would say. *I bought it at the Co-op.*

Yeah, he'd say. *But I still missed it.* Then Ruth would go back to her receipts without a word and he would slide a cigarette behind Ally's ear. He'd grin wide enough to show his gap and slump down beside her on the couch.

After Adam's outburst in front of the head librarian — a bingo friend of Ruth's, and the wife of Lyle's boss — Ally's first instinct was to get as angry as her mother had. She'd felt the defiance of a lifelong Northerner, defensive and territorial when need be, something she usually reserved for her father.

When Ally was six, she'd visited Harry's new townhouse in the city for the first time. The walls were freshly painted bright white, the carpet still unbelievably cushy, and Harry had sat beside her at the new kitchen table. Ally had been able to see her legs through the glass top, and when she pressed down with her thumb, little fingerprints appeared.

"Your mother has it wrong," he'd said, hands clasped in front of him like a teacher's pet. "It's just that town, I couldn't breath. The stack just keeps spewing and spewing. It's a godforsaken place, Alison . . . "

Ally had tried to tune him out, carefully making the shape of a flower with her thumbprint. His words made her uncomfortable, even frightened, and the chemical smell of newness seemed unfamiliar and foul. She wanted to go home.

She wanted to go home and never come back, and just like that, before she was old enough to read, Ally's allegiances had been set. Honed over the years by Ruth's sheer determination, spurred on by Harry's ineptness as a father, she would come to define herself by the cutthroat success of the mine, the resilience of hardworking people, the brutal yet beautiful surroundings. And this loyalty to the isolated town drove the wedge between her and her father ever deeper, while creating a reliable bond with Toby.

Whenever Rina complained about the cold or pollution, Ally and Toby would team up against her. "Don't be such a sucky city girl," Ally had said one frigid March night as they shuffled into Sharon and Lyle's back landing. "A little cold never hurt anybody."

Rina had snorted. "What are you talking about? I can't feel my fingers. Maybe thirty minutes in this and you are frozen solid."

Toby took Rina's mitts and blew warm air into her palm. "A team came up for a volleyball tournament once," he said in between warm breaths, "and they wanted to go snowmobiling. Do you remember, Al? They rented all this gear in the city, the heated helmets and the snowsuits and everything and lugged it up with them and then they wimped out because it hit forty below."

"Because they're not crazy," Rina said.

"No, just listen," Toby went on. "On their way back, there was a bit of a blizzard and their bus stalled and they had to wait a couple of hours before somebody could come and change the air filter. When the guy showed up, they were all shivering and crying and worried about freezing to death when all that gear was just sitting there under the bus, taking up space."

Ally and Toby, eyelashes still white with frost, had nodded knowingly at Rina as they let her stand over the heat vent, the three of them still in their parkas, breathing hard in the warm, cramped space of the landing.

But that was before. Before Adam came. Before Ally stayed up at night listening for a stranger who was supposedly family and who paddled furiously in his dreams.

When Adam came in the store, she was bent over with her back to him, cleaning out an empty candy bin. She was breathing hard and her T-shirt had come untucked to reveal the chubby, pink roundness of her waist.

"Hey Cuz," he said.

Ally straightened up and the blood rushed from her head. It took her a moment to decide it was actually him and not her mind playing tricks. With the real Adam before her, she felt a surge of disappointment. "You look like hell," she said.

He slowly moved towards the stairs, like an old man, and grabbed onto the railing.

She threw the sticky cloth back into the bin. "Why did you say our town is racist?"

"Because it is," Adam said. "And Auntie Ruth's the worst. She's a fucking traitor."

Ally just knelt there, staring. "You don't even know us," she finally said.

Adam held on hard to the railing. For the first time, he felt on the verge of collapse, as if just the sound of his cousin's voice was slowly making his suffering more real. She worked in the traitor's store like a good little girl. Her whole fucking life she'd lived with these bastards and still had no clue. No clue whatsoever.

"Forget it," he said. "Listen, I need to crash."

Ally settled back on her heels as if preparing for a long chat. "Toby's got a bunch of paint. We're going up to the rocks tonight. You want to come?"

Adam paused, trying to remember who Toby was. He wondered how long it had been since he'd held a paint can in his hand. For weeks, he'd been surrounded by lame graffiti and all he'd managed to tag were a few crappy library books

His cousin gazed up at him, clueless and inviting. "Yeah, maybe," he said, already halfway up the stairs. "Wake me up later."

Ally watched him go, too surprised to bother him with anything else.

About forty minutes north of town, a cliff rose up alongside the highway in steep, ragged steps. Toby led the climb, expertly swinging a beer case in one hand and steadying himself with the other, while Ally scrambled to catch up. Rina followed, and then Adam, who kept his eyes on the view of her legs stretching just above him, the crotch of her jean shorts gaping invitingly.

Here and there, scrappy brush grew out of crevices like stubborn acne invading the rock's smooth, metallic sheen. The further they climbed, the smaller Toby's white truck got. They had to reach for jagged outcroppings and loose roots to keep their footing.

"You think you could've picked somewhere a little more out of the way?" Ally called up to Toby.

He was in no mood for Ally's big mouth. He kept up the punishing pace, his free hand growing bloody as he grasped for rock and wood. When Rina told him she'd invited Ally along, he'd said nothing. He'd swallowed his disappointment and told himself there'd still be other nights. But Ally was one thing; her cousin was another.

When Toby and Rina had arrived at Ruth's, Adam was still asleep. Ally had stood over the couch like a magician preparing to make her cousin rise up and float in mid-air. After a minute or two, she'd poked him in the shoulder. "You've been asleep for almost twelve hours. Are you coming or not?"

Adam had winced and shielded his eyes from the light.

"We've got paint," Ally said. "Remember? You said you wanted to come."

Ruth had been at the kitchen table, surrounded by receipts and dirty supper dishes. She'd stared at Adam like she wanted to throw the adding machine at him

"Give me a minute," Adam had said. "I'm in my panties here.

Now, Toby couldn't help wondering if time really was running out. He kept remembering that other time on the rocks, after six months of waiting for her, amazed that someone so obviously sexy as Rina would draw back just as things were heating up.

"It's okay," he'd said over and over, trying to keep the momentum going. "I've got protection. It's okay."

"I am sorry," she'd always said. "I know. I'm sorry."

But that last day of May, when the stiff breeze had lost all its chill, they'd gone to his usual place just before the airstrip, a climb he'd done dozens of times with friends he barely saw anymore. It was a favourite painting spot, a towering wall of rock rising from a small plateau about fifteen feet above the highway, and someone had jokingly covered his name with a giant question mark.

He'd spread a blanket over the pine needles, anchoring it from the wind with his knees. It was the first time he'd seen her in summer clothes, her arms and legs bare in the open air. As he ran his hands all over her, feeling every little bump and contour through her cotton sundress, thin as a nightgown, she'd reached for his belt. There was no chance of his parents walking in, or of voices intruding from the kitchen above.

"Are you sure?" he asked.

Then she'd pushed her tongue between his lips and he caught her fingers in his and together, they undid the tricky belt buckle.

Even before he'd known his A-B-Cs, Toby had understood that two names joined by a plus sign spoke of that strange adult world of love. Romantic messages had littered the rocky landscape his entire life, and after that May afternoon, he'd found himself ready to join in, ready to declare himself like so many before.

He'd got the paint cans. He'd identified the perfect spot. And yet he'd let their night alone together be hijacked by Ally and her asshole cousin.

"Did you hear me?" Ally asked. She'd volunteered to carry the backpack of paint and was huffing now. Without even looking, Toby knew her face must be all sweaty and pink. "How'd you even find this place?"

He didn't bother to turn around. "Last time we got a moose I saw a way up."

After a few minutes, they reached a sloping plateau no bigger than Ruth's kitchen. The rock face rose up like a castle wall in front of them, its blue-grey denseness awash with gold in the late sun. Silvery-green moss stretched across the rock like a spongy carpet, lush enough to sink your toes in.

Ally threw her load to the ground and took the case of beer from Toby. She began passing out bottles like an eager hostess, her damp T-shirt clinging to her back. "Drink up," she said. "We're not carrying this shit back down."

Adam made a beeline for the rock face as if determined to inspect his canvas. Toby watched Rina settle down on a spruce stump and inspect her nails for damage from the climb.

"These aren't screw tops," she said to Ally. She tossed the bottle onto the silent, mossy carpet. "You want us to open them with our teeth?"

Ally pulled Ruth's bottle opener from her pocket and held up her arms in victory. "Just thought I'd scare you." She picked up the bottle and aimed it at Rina. "Any explosion and you're getting it."

But when she cracked the cap, there was only a half-hearted fizzle of foam. Ally got out a cigarette and threw the package at Rina. "Pass it around," she said.

Toby watched Rina expertly light up and exhale into the treetops, her throat pale and exposed in the shadow. When she threw him the pack, he made no effort to catch it and the cigarettes slid perilously close to the cliff's edge.

Adam held the bottle against his burning face. The beer was lukewarm. It was absurdly quiet except for the hushed rustle of poplars way down below. There wasn't even the sound of passing trucks.

He turned to Toby. "You hunt moose up here?"

Rina studied her nails and Toby took a long gulp of beer. "There's a swamp down there," he said, gesturing back towards the narrow path. "It's a watering hole."

Adam nodded as if he had a clue about such things.

"Toby's a really good shot," Ally said. She poked Adam in the shoulder with Ruth's bottle opener. "He could take you out some time."

Rina crinkled her nose as if about to snort.

Adam went to the bag and pulled out a paint can. He shook the can hard, listening for the satisfying clink of the mixing ball. "Maybe we could make a deal," he said to Toby.

Rina picked at the label of her bottle. Toby watched her, and Ally waited. It was quiet except for the *clink-clink-clink* of the little metal ball and the gentle *hush* of the poplars.

"Tagging's my specialty, eh," Adam said. "You take me hunting, I'll do something for you here. Anything you want."

Toby shook his head. "It's not hunting season."

Adam stopped in mid-shake. "Don't give me that shit. All this land, it used to belong to my people. I don't want to shoot a whole fucking herd or anything."

"What are you getting upset for?" Ally asked. She handed him her cigarette. "Take it easy."

Toby looked down at Rina's sandals, at the tiny scraps of paper littering the primitive plant growth. He had no idea how to respond to someone like Adam in front of someone like her. It had never really bothered him when the other miners teased him about being a mama's boy. Or when his father only half-jokingly accused him of chickening out when things got ugly behind the net.

But now, Rina blinked up at him from the shadows. And Adam held up the paint can, cocky and challenging. "You going to pay the fine if we're caught?" Toby asked.

Adam sprayed purple paint into the air. "I do this, you take me."

"You pay the fine," Toby said.

Adam made a small purple "x" against the rock. "What do you want?"

Toby shrugged as if he hadn't given it any thought. There was no way he could tell the truth.

Ally settled down cross-legged at Adam's feet. "Toby was here."

Rina exhaled to the sky again. "That's original."

But Ally didn't come back with a quick retort like, "you have something better Lady Scholarship?" Her face turned the same ugly, blotchy red as it had in Toby's back yard — *I'll bet you'll bugger off before he does.*

Rina reached down and fingered the spongy moss. It had all gone bad after Ally's cousin arrived, she thought. It was because of him that she'd begun to grow irritable with Ally, had just embarrassed her friend like a taunting schoolteacher. It was because of him that her Toby now stood like a silly little boy taking on a dare. If Ally hadn't brought him along, everything would've still been all right. Ally's cousin was like a cancer, taking advantage of the innocent, eating away at everything that was good.

Rina leaned forward, elbows on knees. "Let me ask you, Adam, do you even know how to hunt? And while you are answering questions, why don't you tell us what exactly are you doing here? We'd all like to know."

Ally twisted around, her face still blotchy. "I told you. Somebody snitched on him."

But Adam needed no such defense. Ruth's treacherous face earlier that night, looking at him like he'd just shit in the peanut bin, was still vivid and fresh in his mind.

He turned to this new accuser, who was leaning forward just enough that he could see the beginnings of her small, high breasts. He wanted to shove the bottom end of the paint can between her big, lovely lips. "I was born here," he said. "All of this land should be mine. What are you doing here? Eh? You're a fucking foreigner."

Toby took a step forward: "Fuck you. Who even asked you here?"

"I did," Ally said. Her words were defiant, but her pink, crinkled forehead seemed to plead with him, like always.

Rina felt Adam's eyes fixed on her chest. Fear began to infiltrate her anger like an invisible, odourless gas. She knew this look of defensive hatred all too well.

She ripped out a fistful of moss and considered filling her mouth with it like a gag. If she started screaming now, she wasn't sure she would ever stop.

"During the war," she said, "a bomb hit our zoo, and some animals lived and they escaped into the burning city, with no one to feed them or save them. Tigers and zebras and peacocks. They said that there was even a polar bear in the river."

Her voice trailed off, as if even she had begun to doubt what she was saying. "It was so hot and he had nowhere to go."

It was quiet again except for the relentless poplars and the soft *hiss* of Adam starting to paint. Ally didn't say a word. Toby didn't move a muscle.

He wanted to go and kneel beside Rina, brush the hair from her face. But he couldn't move, as if he were afraid she might shrink away and there would be no going back.

"One time," he said, just for something to say, "when the forest fires got too close to the buffalo reserve, they loaded them all onto trucks, but two escaped. They hung around in the bush for three days until some kid spotted them near the campground. When he went and told his parents, they didn't believe him."

Rina tried to smile. Adam was already finishing a strangely curving purple "T" that almost danced off the rock. His arm moved with a kind of grace and fluidity that seemed to have a mind its own. He was adding blue now, and yellow. When he moved onto the "b," she could see that the "o" was quite beautiful — perfect and round and bright.

Before he came, Rina thought, she never had to speak of such vile things.

Adam kept spraying, lost in his work, as if he hadn't heard the sweet-ass girlfriend's story about a polar bear roaming through a bombed-out city, swimming down a warm river, waiting to die.

8

DURING DRY SUMMERS, like this one, the endlessly chugging smokestack inevitably loses its status as the only game in town. In late July or early August, formless, moistureless clouds move in, turning the normal haze over the sun almost opaque, showering down the thick stench of thousands of trees disappearing into ash.

A flash of lightning, a careless camper, a simple chemical reaction — that's all it takes for miles of dense woodlands to go up in smoke. And the fires aren't picky, they don't discriminate. A stretch of towering spruce trees that's grown undisturbed for more than a century, a clump of young aspens just setting in new roots since the last blaze — nothing is immune.

Just as Adam was finishing the "s" in "Toby was here," an electrical storm moved in from the south. Normally neutral clouds began breaking down into opposite charges and this unstable energy, the clash of positive and negative, lit up the growing darkness above the treetops.

Toby craned his head back and clapped his hands together. "This could be a good one."

Rina sat on the stump, shivering in the heat. She knew it was probably harmless from this distance, but with each silent flash, more brilliant by the minute, the screams lurking in the back of her throat grew more restless.

"I'm done," Adam said, throwing the empty paint can into the bush. "I'm fucking out of here."

"It's nowhere near us," Toby replied, his head still thrown back. "There's not even any thunder."

"So stand here all night," Adam said. "I'm fucking out of here."

After Toby had dropped off Ally and Adam, and he and Rina were finally alone, he pulled over just before the turnoff to Sharon and Lyle's. "You coming over?"

Rina didn't say anything. By then, the familiar houses and neat little yards of the new residential district were a dazzling lightning show of blinking silhouettes.

"You know," he said, "the safest place to be right now is in this truck."

"I think maybe I'm getting sick," Rina said. "My nose feels stuffed and my head feels all heavy."

Toby nodded, as if he'd suspected this all along. "I can hear it in your voice."

"Maybe I should go home," she said.

When he pulled into her driveway, he put his hand on her thigh like he usually did before pulling her towards him. But he hesitated slightly, as if he was doing it for the first time. Normally, Rina would've wanted to grab for his T-shirt and bury her face in his chest, tug gently at the curly little chest hairs with her teeth until he laughed in surprise. Instead she opened the door and stepped out into the silent storm.

"I don't want to infect you," she said.

The next morning, Rina sat behind her parents on the way to church. The storm had given way to breezeless, muted sunshine, but the fear remained. For much of the night, she'd lain awake, unable to comfort herself, unable to stop thinking about Toby's sudden shyness about touching her, or Ally's odd silence on the drive home, or the unexpected beauty of the graffiti.

"What do you think?" Slavenka asked Merik, flipping down the sun visor to check her lipstick. "What will our Rina be?" During the week, Merik insisted they practice their adopted language even at home, but on Sundays she was free to be fluent in her native tongue.

"Maybe she'll become a diplomat," she went on. "She learns languages just like that."

Merik yawned. "People always need doctors."

Slavenka snapped the little mirror on the visor shut. "Don't push her, Merik," she said. "I always said that all you need to worry about while a student is three things: you meet inter-esting people, you read the classics, you find your passions."

Rina closed her eyes and tried to ignore the language of her childhood. After she'd won the scholarship, her parents had begun to plan and tease in a way she hardly remembered.

"She's going to live in the residence," she'd heard Slavenka announce while on the phone to her sister back home in the rubble, "but will probably not choose a subject major until next year at the earliest."

It was as if just by going to school she was bringing back to them that precious home now lost, the place of academic debates in sidewalk cafés, of lofty ambitions and learned ideals, where the tragic absurdities of civil war and the hard realities of Northern mining towns weren't yet real.

Merik pulled into the church parking lot and playfully patted his wife's shoulder. "That's fine," he said. "I'm just saying don't rule out the sciences."

Inside, Rina went through the motions of worship as if sleep had finally come to her. These were rituals she'd always known, easily exported across centuries and countries and oceans. She was barely aware of her parents on either side: Merik shuffling dutifully, up and down, up and down on her left, repeating the chants with his low, clear voice; Slavenka kneeling on her right, as if oblivious to her fellow worshippers, softly murmuring into her hands. Rina was barely aware of placing the dry, tasteless wafer on her tongue just as she had a thousand times before. At the moment the congregation began to stir, shaking hands, chatting about smoke and fires, she brushed through the crowd and escaped out the heavy wooden doors onto the parched lawn.

Outside, the air was thick and eerily pale and all Rina saw was a disturbing reflection. Her past and future lay hidden behind ashes and dust, and here she stood in the increasingly murky present, feeling the suffocating tug of fear in every breath she took.

"Here you are," Slavenka said. She was holding a tissue over her face. "You should stay inside. This is bad for your lungs. You don't want to get ill right now."

Rina considered asking her mother what she spoke into her hands every Sunday, and if it gave her any comfort. She would ask her in their native language and Slavenka would really hear her for the first time in years. Her mother would hear her as strong and clear as the lullabies they used to sing while rocking Rina's doll to sleep, perfectly pitched and sad and lovely.

But Merik was already there, taking them both by the elbow and leading them back to the red truck.

"This smoke will be bad for the asthmatics," he said.

Toby called just as Rina and her parents got home.

"How are you feeling," he asked.

"I'm okay," Rina said. "No worries."

"Are you sure?" he asked. "I can hear it in your voice. You sound stuffed up."

"No worries," she said. "I'm okay. Should I come over?"

"You should stay in bed," he said. "You have to nip summer colds in the bud. One time my sister starting sneezing in August and it turned into pneumonia."

Rina paused, caught in her own lies. How could she argue with him about this? She would have to stay at home listening to Slavenka sigh and Merik rustle the paper while her Toby practiced in the yard, so still and powerful one minute, so sweaty and laughing the next.

"Are you sure?" he'd asked that warm spring night on the rock.

Merik and Slavenka would've been devastated to learn that Sharon and Lyle left their children alone in a basement bedroom. Where Rina came from, sex was not merely a natural act but a complex ritual weighed down with the baggage of religion and war. For months, Rina had backed away at the last minute.

But that night it had all been so good, the breeze and his hands playing lightly over her. She'd pushed her tongue into his mouth and then she'd felt the ground hard against her back, a tree root rubbing against the lower part of her spine. With the first pain, she'd grabbed for the blanket and come up with a fistful of pine needles instead. She'd squeezed and squeezed, and just as the pain became both so awful and so good that she didn't know if she could bear it for another second, it stopped.

"I'm sorry," he said. "It was so fast, but you make me crazy."

She'd laughed out loud — so loud Toby might've been hurt if he hadn't been so utterly content. His breathless apology had made her feel so safe she was almost giddy.

"Do you hear me?" he asked now. "Drink lots of juice and I'll call you later."

Rina almost laughed again, his concern was so sincere. And something wonderful struck her. She knew she'd studied hard and must go and find her passion. But she did not have to leave him. She didn't have to face the city again all alone. Toby could come with her.

"Yes," she said, remembering that as they lay side by side in the breeze he'd pulled the pine needles from her palm one by one, kissing the tiny wounds as he went. "Lots of juice."

When Merik was a small child, his mother had taught him that if he spilled salt on the table, he must immediately snatch some up and throw it over his left shoulder.

"You want bad luck?" she would say with a look of concern that made him quiet. "Do you want your father to go off to who knows what? That's all we need right now."

He'd grown up in a mountain village where generations of shepherds had tended their flocks while watching for signs of trouble approaching from the southern coast below. One of his first memories was of being woken near midnight and led through the dark to church, where there was nothing but a sea of candles as the villagers began to walk once, twice, three times around the building. When Merik had been handed his own candle, the wax dripped hot against his skin and he tripped and stumbled in the deep ruts, but did not cry out. All above him the night was ablaze and the light was filled with low, chanting voices and the wet stench of spring as he marched along, proud and sleepy.

If he hadn't been born during a great wave of opportunity, when a shepherd's son was seen as the perfect specimen for social development, Merik would have stayed there to become a man. He would have learned the sloping paths so well that he could have made his way home through the sweet-smelling twilight with eyes closed and stick held aloft, growing old enough to pass on the trappings of battle legends and ritual. As it was, he pushed all this to the back of his mind like a handful of smooth stones left in a pocket, forgotten and untouched as he methodically studied the workings of the human body; as he poured through thick books on learned subjects; as he met Slavenka.

When he first saw her, she was wearing a plain white peasant blouse tucked into her blue jeans and round, black-rimmed glasses perched on top her head. Her lips were as red as the poppies that grew along the low slopes of his childhood.

"I think I left this on purpose," she said, reaching down for a folder of sheet music on the café table. "I must perform this afternoon, but I don't like this composer much. When they write down the old folk songs and adapt them, something is always lost. Yet my cousin, a musician with records sold all over the world, makes a good point. He says if they don't write them down, no one will ever hear them but us. It's a terrible dilemma, don't you think?"

It took Merik no time at all to fall for her. In their early days, he would stand back in awe, watching an outrageously self-assured young woman sing out old poems in a brand new lecture hall outfitted with all the latest in technology. When she glanced at him from the stage, the young medical student was sure he was experiencing the perfect balance between passion and reason.

But the untouched stones of his childhood were always there, and when the siege took hold and the glorious city of their courtship became a prison, Merik was not completely surprised. What came as a shock was how it all ended for them.

One night, not long after they'd eaten Rina's pet rabbit, Slavenka stood waiting for him at the door though it was well past midnight.

"We must get out of here," she said.

Merik had just spent fourteen hours on his feet, cleaning wounds with old shirts. He could barely find the energy to speak. "I don't know how," he said.

But as soon as the words were out, he knew they were not what he meant to say. He'd meant that it was too dangerous.

"There is a way," she said. "This is madness."

"It's too dangerous," he said.

Slavenka crossed her arms over her chest as if she were cold. "We're going," she said. "Rina and I. I've been talking to people who can help. I've given them money. We go the day after tomorrow."

"I'm needed here," Merik said, still in the doorway. "This is our home."

Slavenka closed her eyes and shook her head. "This is madness. We're going. You can come if you want."

Merik struggled to breathe, like when he'd been a child walking with his father up and up and up the mountainside, until the tiny flowers turned to snow. "Further?" his father would ask, knocking Merik's shoulder in challenge. And all little Merik could do was nod stiffly, over and over, as if convincing himself that there was no choice in the matter.

He'd nodded at Slavenka.

"All right," she'd said. "Day after tomorrow."

Years later, on an otherwise peaceful Sunday morning, after he'd left bullet wounds behind and become an expert on frostbite and asthma, Merik's chest would tighten in much the same way. He was reading the paper in his church suit when Rina came into the kitchen.

"Toby's coming with me to the city," she said. "I'm going to ask him to come."

Merik put down his paper and saw Slavenka standing at the sink, hugging herself as if cold. In this at least, they were united. For both of them, real life was still about symbolic beauty and rigorous debate. Though long buried in rubble, the valley city of their youth and courtship — with its delicate balance between tradition and tolerance, passion and reason, friend and foe — remained as precious to them as it had ever been.

The miner seemed a hardworking and honest young man. But how could they allow it? The boy had neither the education nor the inclination to even talk about the things that were most important in this life. Since they'd run away, Merik had compromised much in his efforts to adapt to his new life. He drew the line at his only daughter.

That afternoon, Ally arrived at Toby's as usual. She was surprised to find him sitting alone on the back steps, fixing a loose wheel on his summer skis.

"Rina's sick," he said.

Ally chewed on the nail of her pinkie, internalizing what this meant — it would just be her and Toby today, alone.

Toby spit into the grass. "This smoke is shit."

Ally nodded, still chewing. "The smoke is always shit."

"This is the worst," Toby said, gathering up his tools. "I can't stand it. My little nephews are downstairs. Do you want to come inside and play?"

Still nodding, Ally pulled her finger from her mouth and let him lead her from the choking heat of the yard into the cool dampness of the basement. Lyle was on the floor struggling beneath a pile of three little boys, shouting that he promised to never, ever break out of jail again.

"Toby's the monster! Toby's the monster!" the biggest one shouted.

Ally stood there at the foot of the stairs, still adjusting to the dim light and sudden mayhem. Toby immediately got down on his hands and knees and began biting at the boys' legs. When Lyle came rushing to his grandsons' rescue, Toby wrestled his father onto his back.

"Wait!" Toby shouted. Lyle lay spread-eagled on the floor, huffing. The boys jostled to climb on their uncle as if he was a pony. Toby growled over at Ally. "She's the monster! Get her!"

In a matter of seconds, Ally was on her back and they were all tickling her until she gasped for breath.

"Enough!" Lyle shouted.

Then only Ally and Toby were on the floor. She lay flat on her back and he was curled up against her, his knees nestled into her waist. Her shirt had come untucked and his hand rested on her bare stomach.

"You are so ticklish," he said. "I thought Rina was bad, but you are the worst."

Ally closed her eyes. She was breathing so hard that Toby's hand swayed up and down on her pink belly. Since he'd dropped them off the night before, since the moment she woke up in the morning, she'd wanted to ask Toby if he'd heard the story about the zoo animals. She wanted to ask him why they never asked Rina about that stuff.

But not now. After years of Ruth's select, pointed words and Harry's self-conscious silences, all Ally wanted was to bask in the sound of Toby's gentle voice, like a hot bath on a cold night.

Toby pressed the back of his hand against her cheek as if checking for a fever. "You're burning up," he said.

Then when one of the boys jumped on his back and together they rolled away with a roar.

While Ally remained blissfully still, Toby's touch still warm on her skin, across town Adam woke to find Ruth standing over him in her housecoat, holding a cup of coffee with both hands. Her hair was loose and messy around her shoulders, and with no make-up on she looked more tired, but younger.

Adam raised his eyebrows in question, and Ruth immediately turned away. She began banging about the kitchen as if in a great hurry.

"It's fucking hot in here," Adam mumbled. He threw the damp afghan aside and made his way to the bathroom. Even his underwear felt clingy and wet.

"Thanks for the update!" Ruth shouted. He could hear her loud and clear through the bathroom door. "If you happen to know how to fix flophouse air conditioners maybe you can stick around."

Adam splashed himself with cool water, paying no attention to the small puddle he was making on the floor. He picked up a towel Ally had discarded on top of the hamper and wiped his face, which seemed to be leaking traces of muddy blood. He dabbed at his nose and blew into the white towel. Sure enough, there were traces of blue and green and red, but they were mostly washed together in a dull, putrid grey.

Adam smiled to himself. It had been ages since paint had lingered in his nostrils and beneath his nails. And it had been ages since he had a real plan. But the night before, he and the miner had made a deal. They were going to head out into the bush to hunt just like the old man. Which meant Adam had to find a way to stick around this dump full of traitors.

When he came out, the sofa-bed was made up and Ruth was watching television. A blonde woman in a tight T-shirt was demonstrating how a special blend of herbs could reduce wrinkles in as few as twelve days.

Adam took a couple of cigarettes from the pack on the table. He lit them both and passed one to his aunt. "I'm going hunting with that miner," he said. "Our people should know how to do that shit."

Ruth took the cigarette, but kept her eyes glued to the screen.

The back of Adam's knees were already wet with sweat again and he could feel his left one begin to dance. Why had he thought that would work on her? he wondered. What kind of person stares at you while you're sleeping and then ignores you because of a stupid flashing price on a screen?

Adam stepped in front of the television. "He also said he could maybe get me on the night shift. Just as a casual or something."

Ruth squinted her eyes and exhaled. She wasn't consciously aware of how much she missed the way she and Ally would sit together on Sundays, watching old movies with happy endings. All she knew was that it was Ally's fault that she was stuck here all alone with Vincent's son in her face. He was blocking the part of the screen that she knew said, "Call now to get a special gift, absolutely free!"

"Have you even called Vincent?" she asked, still squinting.

"Have you?" Adam asked.

Ruth got up and carried the overflowing ashtray to the garbage. She'd tried to quit seven times in the last ten years, always failing after only a few weeks. Since Adam's arrival, she was smoking more than ever, keeping the cigarette dangling from her lips as she lifted or sorted or wrapped. She'd begun to hear Vincent's needling voice again coming from somewhere across the room: *Ruthie needs to relax, somebody get her a butt. Anybody got a butt? Here you go, Ruthie, that a girl.*

"I can help out around here," Adam said. "I can lift shit."

When Ruth began nodding unenthusiastically into the garbage, he knew that he'd won.

By the time Ally got home, Adam and Ruth were sitting on the couch together, watching television.

Adam held up his hand in salute. "Hey boss."

At the commercial, Ruth got up and threw some soda crackers in Ally's lap. "There's your supper," she said. "He's got three weeks to find something or he's out."

The next morning, Rina came by the store for the first time in days. Ally was on her hands and knees behind a row of bins, scraping at a wad of gum someone had flattened against the raisin container. Adam was sitting on the cash desk, kicking his heels in a steady rhythm.

The air conditioning was on the fritz and Ruth had propped open the shop door with a brick. Rina entered without a sound, breezily pushing her sunglasses to the top of her head. When she saw Adam, she stopped so suddenly that her feet slid forward in her sandals. She had to steady herself against a display table.

Adam grinned wide enough to show his gap. He kicked possessively at the counter, eating sticky caramel popcorn that had clumped together in the heat. Her whole demeanor had shifted right before his eyes. She'd gone from cocky to awkward in a matter of seconds. Now she just stood there, neither coming nor going, as two firefighters in their orange coveralls appeared in the doorway behind her.

Adam watched their eyes pass over Rina. They obviously hadn't expected to find the miner's sweet-assed girlfriend in their way.

At the sound of shuffling work boots, Ally popped up as if from nowhere. All morning, she'd been torn between her daydreams — Toby would rest his hand on her tummy and she would say, *I have something to tell you* — and her cousin's distracting presence. Adam had even started calling her "Cuz" again.

Rina stepped aside to let the firefighters by. "It's hot in here," she said.

Ally got to her feet, wiping the sweat from above her lip. "No shit."

She threw the scraper to Adam, who made no attempt to catch it. It hit the counter and landed with a *clang* near Rina's feet. "Are you feeling better?" Ally asked.

Rina shrugged, still in the doorway "Toby exaggerates," she said. "These summer colds, they're not as terrible as he says."

Ally nodded absently. For the first time, she couldn't think of anything to say to her friend. She went behind the cash desk and slapped Adam playfully on the shoulder. "There's a job for you." She tilted her head towards the firefighters. "All you have to do is point a hose. Guys are usually pretty good at that."

Adam poured the last of the popcorn straight into his mouth, and spoke through the sticky lumps: "They wouldn't want me."

He eyed the miner's girlfriend, standing with one hand on her hip as if posing in a catalogue. Except she wasn't smiling. Girls like that, Adam thought, they always arch their backs just a little and then get pissed when you look at their ass.

He jumped down from the counter and dodged at Rina, coming so close that she took a step back out the door. "You really want to know what I'm doing here?"

Rina stared. "It was stupid of me to ask," she said. "I don't care."

Adam smiled. "I torched a dry cleaners."

The firefighters, who'd been filling bags of mixed nuts and chocolate macaroons, looked up.

Adam snapped his fingers in Rina's face. "Poof. Gone."

For years, he'd travelled in packs, trolling back lanes, setting small fires in decrepit garages and dumpsters as a kind of bonding ritual, a handy way to create solidarity through mutual, pointless risk. But the dry cleaners had been after-wards. After Leonard's death, when the smell of gasoline had seemed like an old friend and Adam did things for no reason at all.

The miner's girlfriend looked at him just like she had the night before, when he'd wanted to shove the paint can between her lips and punch it right through her pretty little head. He walked over to a bin of sunflower seeds, taking his time, and grabbed a handful. He cracked a seed between his teeth and spit the shell near Rina's feet. If his quest for numbness had been futile, his outrage made him strong.

"It was built on an ancient burial ground," he said. "I was just taking back what fucking belonged to me."

Ally moved closer, speaking low so the firefighters wouldn't hear. "That sounds like bullshit."

Rina took another step out the door, a scream tickling in the back of her throat. Once she'd sprung her decision on her parents, she'd told herself that everything would be all right. Merik and Slavenka would come around. And as for Ally, the one who'd rescued her by shouting "hey foreign-girl" in a schoolyard, that too would be no worries. Ally would not be upset to lose two friends at once if she was a co-conspirator. It would be all right as long as Ally was the first to know.

But Rina hadn't expected Adam to be there, sitting in wait. As soon as the firefighters approached the cash register, she took her first chance to escape. "I can't stay," she said to Ally. "Call me later."

So as Adam clung to his outrage, finally ready to hunt down a dying world that still lingered in the trinkets of a souvenir shop, the chaos stayed close enough to whisper in his ear. High on the rock, as the storm flashed overhead, he'd tried to focus on his task, to make each letter as fluid yet symmetrical as the last. But the lightning bore down on him and his knee grew restless. He'd felt the vast, storming universe, where unstable charges grown up in the earth's ever-shifting atmosphere pull and push dangerously with no regard for the existence of warm bodies below.

For Rina, the lightning had come like a flash of memory. Each jolt seemed to remind her of something before the war that only came to her in dreams now.

Long ago, Merik and Slavenka had gone off on holiday and left her in the mountain village for the first and only time. There, repelled by the ripe smell of her grandmother and quickly bored with feeding the sheep, only one thing had really broken through the monotony and homesickness.

The year Rina turned six, the battle legends were gaining steam all over the region. The shrivelled remains of a fallen hero, preserved for more than six centuries, were making their way to every city and every village. And on a warm spring morning with a slight drizzle in the air, Rina and her grandmother had walked down to soggy mud road to wait.

"Your parents should be here," her grandmother had said. "The young people, they forget and marry who they want."

But Rina paid no attention. There were people, young and old and in-between lined up ten-deep along the muddy trenches. All heads were turned in one direction, as if a giant wind had come and forced their necks around. Rina followed their eyes, up the sloping road and the narrowing mountain path until she spied a small group of men, tiny in the distance, struggling through the misty green with a large box on their shoulders. As they made their way down, she saw there were others, too, coming around the curve. They moved together like a long, black snake slowly winding its way down into the crowd.

"Your mother would not understand," her grandmother had said. "She has known none of this suffering. But maybe you will. You watch, you watch the tears. This martyr, this is who your father is, and this is who you are. It's good you see this, because one day you may have to choose."

But she barely heard her grandmother's words, for as the snake of people got closer, Rina saw they were all holding their arms up to the wooden box as if begging. All the crowd, young, old and in-between were wet with rain and sobs. Close and closer they came, wailing and raising their arms when suddenly someone lifted Rina up so she could see the procession as it passed.

The box was decorated with spring flowers and inside was the body of what must have been a man once, long ago. His skin was dark brown and wrinkled like a prune. She was almost close enough to reach out and touch his shrivelled face but she wasn't frightened because she knew all the people were there, holding up their arms. As she cried with them, great, choking sobs, she knew they would not let her fall.

She didn't dream of it until afterwards, after polar bears swam down the river, after they'd run away in the night. In the sad Winnipeg apartment, the black snake would make its way down the green mountain and when she woke, she would shake with the memory of such power and beauty and danger in the distance, coming closer.

Later, Toby would watch her twitch and murmur as she napped, amazed that this girl was there beside him in his parents' messy basement.

The minute he saw her as a gorgeous mystery, it was love.

BODY SOUL MIND SPIRIT

9

༄ Just as Rina was leaving Ruth's store without telling her friend what she'd come to tell her, Toby was stepping into a crowded cage full of men. Standing shoulder to shoulder in their matching coveralls and steel-toed boots, they waited for the brief jerk, then the groan of the cables as they descended the south shaft, travelling thousands of metres below the surface — down, down, down into a sunless place where time is measured in eons instead of years. As usual, the men joked roughly with each other as the cables groaned, trying to forget they were only a small group of mortal men who had no business travelling through the ages.

One of them nudged Toby in the stomach with his safety glasses. "Hey lover-boy, you fucking awake today or you planning to sleep at the controls?"

When the cage jerked again, Toby automatically filed out with the others like he had so many mornings before, the miners moving as one person into the low, dimly-lit tunnel that stretched like a horizontal vein through the body of rock. He slipped on his heavy gloves and slapped his hands together.

The dull sound ricocheted against the rock as the men began to disperse in either direction.

Toby realized he still hadn't said anything back. "Don't you fucking worry about me," he called. "I can move more rock than you with my fucking eyes closed."

The first time Toby went down the shaft, he was ten years old. He'd stood in the middle of the cage, stiff and terrified, chewing the inside of his cheek until it bled.

"Don't worry about that little bit of shaking," Lyle told him, resting his hand on his son's shoulder. "These cables are about as strong as they come."

Yet it wasn't the fear of falling that bothered Toby. It was the sense of being swallowed alive, leaving the wind and the sky and the lunchroom with its snack machine further and further behind until there was nothing but walls — walls that left no room to stretch your growing legs, no air to take a good, deep breath.

When the cage opened, Lyle turned on the cap lamp of Toby's oversized hardhat and led him by the hand through the dim cross-cut to where the men were working. There, far below the packed snow and solid layer of permafrost, Toby suddenly felt too warm in his winter sweater and his fear receded immediately.

He stood in wonder, watching a team of sweaty miners methodically move a mountain with their noisy equipment. These were men Toby knew — they'd sat at his kitchen table, he'd played in their yards — but here, in this underground world, he didn't recognize them at all. Indistinguishable in their protective gear, each huddled in a filthy, moaning machine that still glared yellow and bright against the blackened tunnel, these men were changing the face of the earth together, dumping load after load into a pit where giant pieces of rock seemed to disappear without a sound.

"That's the ore pass," Lyle said, pointing at the hole. "Everything gets crushed there at the bottom, then we bring it all up again. That lifter with the shovel there, it's worth more than a million."

But Toby hadn't been in the mood for a lesson. His fear was still fresh, the bitter, iron taste of blood still in his mouth, and this only seemed to add to the elation of his discovery. To him, the mine looked like a hidden sandbox for grown-ups.

Over the years, Toby would never grow used to the cramped, groaning cage, but his job of ore train operator, or mountain-mover, was all he'd ever wanted and it suited him well. He wasn't like his father Lyle, who'd worked his way up until he was supervising the surface smelter and who saw managing his men and managing his family as the two great pleasures of his life. Toby didn't really mind the sweaty monotony that his work demanded. In this way, he took after Sharon, who could contentedly sort legal files for hours on end, surrendering herself to the perfect order of her task.

Within weeks after his training, Toby had settled into what he thought of as *the zone* — the same as when he was skiing at full tilt. With his blood pumping, his muscles pushing over the snow in a mindless rhythm, it was like his body was in perfect control. His mind grew magically free and clear and hours passed like minutes. Sometimes, he'd find himself multiplying numbers or repeating nonsensical phrases to himself. Within six months underground, lulled by the muffled crashes and deep vibrations of the tunnel, he'd begun going over the alphabet backwards while at the controls, over and over until he could stand up and repeat it to the men in the lunchroom. He'd come to be known as an unflappable worker who got the job done and was good for a laugh.

It wasn't until this past spring, after Rina had cried out beneath him high on a plateau, that the zone had become more and more elusive and his team more and more impatient. "Hey, Alphabet-Boy," his shift boss had shouted just the day before, "you still not done there? You think your mama's going to come and haul that shit up for you?"

After his shift, when he finally emerged into the soft evening light, Toby could hardly bring himself to check if she was waiting there.

A stiff southerly wind had blown all afternoon and it was even smokier than when he'd asked Ally to come in and play. In the distance, all details were lost in the haze, but the pose — legs slightly apart at attention, hair freshly washed and flying in the breeze — was unmistakable. As he got closer, Toby saw she was wearing the same sundress that she'd worn that late May afternoon. When she leaned back against the high metal fence, the cotton blew between her legs and he could make out the bony outline of her knees. He kept going until they were close enough to touch, but didn't.

"Come with me," she said.

Toby grabbed onto the mesh of metal over her head and leaned in until he could've licked her nose. *She's here*, he told himself, *like always, wearing the dress that's as flimsy as a nightgown.* "Okay," he said. "Where we going?"

"No, come with me," she said. "To the city. Come with me."

He brushed a strand of hair from her face. Toby instinctively understood how to enjoy a moment, uncluttered by what came before or what followed. Just like that, all his doubts were left buried deep in the ground and elation washed over him like a gloriously hot shower. "Of course," he said. "Anywhere. Yeah."

It wasn't until they were snug in the basement and she was lying on his childhood bed as always, staring up at the water-stained ceiling tiles, bent knees swaying back and forth to some silent music, that he dared ask a question. He stood over her, fresh and clean and gripping the towel around his waist as if suddenly self-conscious about his nakedness.

"Really?" he asked. "You're serious?"

Rina grabbed the towel and pulled him down to her. His soapy smell almost made her weep. "Please," she said. "Yes, please, really."

Then he struggled to pull the thin dress over her head, catching her elbows in the fabric, but she didn't laugh. Instead she clung to him, entangling her legs in his, as if she'd never wanted him so much. Before he knew it, he was in the zone, letting his body take control, soothing her into a steady rhythm, her words playing over and over in his head — *yes, please, really.*

Later, as Rina slept, Toby got up and put on a pair of shorts. After they had sex, he was usually content to watch her murmur while she slept, but this time was different. This time he suddenly felt the urge to move, and before he knew it, he was taking the stairs two at a time and stepping out into the yard.

The wind had faded into nothing more than a light breeze and the smoke had thinned in the cool dusk. Stretching out his arms as if playing airplane Toby wandered shirtless and barefoot onto the dew-covered grass and breathed in the night. He recognized the chill in the air — it was an August chill, gentle and subtle, and the dusky sky was an August sky, richer than July, a blue so deep that the stars shone brighter against it.

He could hear the reassuring *whiz* of semi-trailers passing by the edge of town, one after the other, just as he'd heard them in bed when he was little. How many times had he slipped contentedly into sleep with the window open and the night still so blue, listening to the lonely hum of the highway mix with the voices of his older sisters and their friends as they lazed on their backs in the darkening yard, chewing on grass stems and making silly wishes upon the first star?

Now, with Rina murmuring in his bed, the lovely, familiar night only seemed to add to his agitation. If he stood still much longer, his tired limbs might begin to tremble uncontrollably, his resting heart explode right there against the white stucco garage.

Toby grabbed the key to the garage from its hiding spot beneath the eavestrough and let himself in. He found a pair of old runners he hadn't worn since high school gym class and strapped on his summer skis.

Cracked asphalt was no match for the smooth, silent rush of snow under freshly waxed skis, but any chill Toby had felt against his bare skin was gone within minutes. He raced along the flat stretch of road that bordered the mining grounds, pumping his limbs with the rhythmic, extended motion that was now second nature. He pushed himself until he could feel the pull in his lungs and the breeze in his ears. By the time a sport-utility vehicle rushed past, throwing up bits of gravel and honking in recognition, he was back in the zone. *Yes, please, really*, Rina's voice said over and over, *yes, please, really*.

The young men in the SUV were childhood friends Toby had shared classrooms and hockey rinks with, and who couldn't help but see him as a bit of traitor now. For years, they'd all been a team, lacing up their skates in dimly lit change rooms that stank of sweaty leather and wet rubber mats, facing opponents from surrounding communities as the pride of a whole town rested on their shoulders.

Toby had showed some promise in his ability to handle and shoot a little black puck, but the truth was, he'd never felt any great passion for the game. He'd never relished the messy, slashing confrontations deep in behind the net, the strident, half-crazed calls from the fans. If he felt fleeting moments of collective exhilaration or defeat, he'd never quite matched the other players' intensity, their preoccupation with reliving who had done what, at which line, after which whistle.

Instead, all his life, Toby's dreams had been dominated by a sense of solitary speed. Over breakfast, he would tell his sisters all about the latest chase in his dreams, always running or skating or falling or climbing, never sure if he was moving away from something or towards it.

"You must be tuckered out after all that," Lyle would say, and that was the signal for the girls to begin chasing their little brother around the table.

In his final year of high school, Toby had flipped to the sports channel one boring Sunday afternoon and seen his first biathlon. The vision of lean, foreign men flying gracefully across the snow with rifles on their back got under his skin like nothing else before. It struck him as both utterly strange and familiar at the same time. He was used to hunting with Lyle, crouching for hours in the October dampness waiting for that one perfect moment to take a shot. But the biathlon was a race and Toby instantly wanted to feel for himself the same hard-wrought speed, the perfect stillness before the shot — and then off again.

He responded to his friends' honk by waving a pole in the air, but his concentration never wavered, the breeze in his ears never slowed. At that moment, he couldn't have been further away from the constant banter on the team bus, or in the mine's lunchroom, or at his parents' kitchen table. He couldn't have been further away from the cage, the earth swallowing him down, down, down as the men jostled and joked.

For Toby, there was nothing like being on the trail, especially in winter, when the silence of his steaming breath cutting through ice crystals gave way to the sharp *pop-pop-pop* of the rifle. Each time a snowmobile passed, it was always the same — some shout of encouragement that went all but ignored except for the brief, practiced wave of his pole.

As he disappeared into the growing blackness, Toby's old teammates in the SUV could only shake their heads.

"That crazy son of a bitch," the driver said.

The one in the back leaned forward and threw a can out the window. "The chubby one is a goer. He's probably doing her *and* that Rina."

The driver continued to shake his head. "That lucky, crazy son of a bitch."

When Toby returned home, still shirtless and dripping in sweat, his father was making his usual salami sandwich for the night shift. Lyle couldn't help smiling, just as he'd smiled the morning his grown son had packed four donuts into his lunch bag. "Break any records?"

Though Lyle was just as baffled by his son's solitary obsession as anyone else in town, it hadn't bothered him much—he didn't expect to understand everything about his son anymore than he expected to understand everything in general. Years ago, when sitting for hours waiting for the rustle of a buck or the tug of a fish, Toby had sometimes asked his father why people ate animals or why people worked in a mine if they knew it could kill them.

"That's a good question," Lyle always replied, patiently, "that's a good one," as if this in itself was an answer.

Yet there were times when a mysterious wonder would overcome Toby's father, and no matter how hard he tried, he couldn't begin to express what it meant. Like when he'd held his first grandchild, gazing into the tiny face that was red and ugly as a beet and not much bigger. Or when he'd stood in the empty clearing that would one day be his family's cabin, utterly alone except for the cry of an unseen loon.

Toby drained the last of the orange juice from the carton, ignoring his father's question.

"We got cool-down tonight," Lyle said.

Just three years after he and Sharon arrived in Franklin, the smelter had been cooled too quickly, exploding into a wall of flames that left seven widows in its wake. But Lyle's faith in a world of steady progress and improvement hadn't wavered. Growing up on the coast, he'd learned early on that fishers were swept away and coal miners buried alive in the name of commerce, until there were no more fish to fish and no more need for coal. He'd learned how to accept that improved regulations always came only after an accident, better late than never; learned how to remain a loyal company man.

Toby put down the carton and wiped his mouth with the back of his arm. "You should stop working nights," he said. "You look like shit."

He watched his father carefully spread the mustard, then close up the sandwich and press the bread together with his palm. He could hear his mother's voice: *Why do you insist on squishing it like that? The meat's not going to run away.* It was the same as when she scolded Lyle for his behaviour at the rink: *Why do you get so worked up? You're like a different person out there.*

"You guys ready?" Toby asked.

Lyle stretched his arms over his head and yawned. "Oh yeah. We'll take her easy. 'Nice and easy wins the day.'"

Toby threw the empty carton into the sink. He was still sweaty, and with the kitchen window wide open, he was starting to feel the chill. He knew Rina was waiting for him, in his bed, and before the month was out, they'd be gone. But it didn't seem real, not with the flattened salami sandwich smelling up the room, not with Lyle lingering like he always did, trying to be buddies, talking shop.

"I'm thinking of moving to the city," Toby said.

Lyle tightened the lid on the mustard. "You going to leave your job?"

Toby shrugged, and Lyle motioned towards the landing. "She just left."

"What did she say?" Toby asked.

Lyle stopped making his lunch and looked at his son. "She said she wanted to walk home. I told her if she saw you she should give you a swift kick in the ass."

That night, Lyle had no time to dwell on Toby's news. He was too busy proving himself master of the furnace that spewed unforgiving fumes over the town, polluting its lakes and killing vegetation. It wasn't until after he and his crew had carefully tamed the smelter's explosive heat, after they'd boldly cleaned its slag-filled mouth with hoses so powerful they could knock a man off his feet, after morning had come and he'd finished his shift and climbed into bed beside his wife, that he would remember what his son had told him.

Sharon was waiting for him in bed. She never got up for work until he'd joined her, still warm from the shower. "How'd it go?" she asked.

Lyle fluffed his pillow the way he liked it. "Fine," he said. He lay on his back like he always did, resting his right forearm across his forehead and gently pressing upwards to open his sinuses. "Rina asked Toby to go to Winnipeg with her. He says he's moving."

Sharon sat up and turned to him, her nightgown twisting awkwardly around her waist. "Since when?"

Lyle adjusted his arm and breathed in with a long sniff. "Since last night."

"What's he planning to do?" Sharon asked.

Lyle closed his eyes. "How should I know? He's a grown man. We did it ourselves once."

"We were going for a job," Sharon said. "We had a plan."

Lyle rolled over onto his side even though he knew his left shoulder wouldn't like it. Dr. Mark had diagnosed arthritis a few months ago.

"You can keep talking, but I'm going to sleep," he said. "Just think, now we'll have somewhere to stay in the city."

Sharon didn't reply. It was getting late and she knew she should be having her coffee and toast already. But still she sat there, waiting for the sound of her husband's gentle snore. She knew she should be happy for her son.

If, for people like Merik and Slavenka, home remained a precious, unalterable idea, for Lyle and Sharon it was more like an actual space — tangible, but portable. Together, they'd simply up and moved to where the jobs were, where they could construct a roomy house, and buy what they needed to enjoy their leisure. From the time they arrived in Franklin, they focused on building a comfortable nest for the new family they'd created. It was a long, expensive plane ride to fly back East and they'd returned to the coast only a handful of times.

"We could redo the bathroom for the cost of the kids' tickets alone," Sharon liked to say. "We could get a new dishwasher for half the price of mine."

Once they were there, Lyle would bask in the familiar faces, enjoying his role as visitor in a place he knew so well. "I got the bill," he'd say to his cousin or brother or old workmate over breakfast at a local diner. "Next time you're out our way, you can pay."

Sharon would never remember how much she craved the familiar tastes and smells until she was surrounded by them.

"Oh, breathe that in," she'd tell her children, "just breathe it in. That's the smell of the ocean. I can taste the salt standing all the way back here."

Toby would lick his lips and nod, though he couldn't taste a thing.

All their life together, Toby's mother had been happy to be carried along by the tide of their generation — seek opportunity, honour your children, enjoy your rewards in this lifetime. So why wasn't she happy for her son? He was moving on to a place of even greater opportunity, where flowers didn't grow covered with a thin film of silt, where comfort might not demand such a high price. He would not remain rooted and dependent like her second daughter, so young to already be a mother.

Still, there she sat in her twisted nightgown, growing increasingly late for work, more unhappy than she'd ever been.

Across town, Ally was trying to show Adam how the cash register worked. Ruth had woken him at seven-thirty sharp by resting her alarm clock against his ear. His eyes were still puffy from sleep and he seemed more interested in the bin of chocolate-covered peanuts.

"Are you even listening to me?" Ally asked.

Adam licked chocolate from his fingers and picked up the phone by Ally's elbow. "Give me your little boyfriend's number," he said. "I want to make sure he doesn't forget our deal."

Ally stared. "Did you really burn down a dry cleaner's?"

He waved the phone in her face. "The less you know, the better, Cuz. Now what's the number?"

Since the day before, Ally had felt strangely anxious, like it was the first day of school. She wanted to know more about Adam, and yet she didn't. She wanted to talk to Toby, and yet she didn't.

Adam grinned at her as if he knew it was only a matter of time before his little cousin would do his bidding.

She grabbed the receiver. "*I'll* call him."

Toby was on the way to the fridge, still in his underwear, when Sharon handed him the phone.

"Hey," Ally said. "Were you awake?"

"Yeah," Toby said. "I just haven't had my juice yet.

He'd been expecting it to be Rina. The lines of communication in their friendship had been set early — Ally called Rina and Rina called Toby. Only once or twice, when there'd been some breech in the usual protocol, like when Rina's cellphone battery died and Slavenka left the kitchen phone off the hook, had Ally ever called him.

"You sound like hell," she said. "Were you out drinking last night or something?"

Sharon yelled something from the bathroom that Toby couldn't make out.

"No," he said. "I told you, I just haven't had my juice yet."

"Cool down go okay?" Ally asked.

Toby searched through the fridge for the carton of orange juice, then remembered he'd finished it the night before. "Yeah, I guess. As far as I know nobody got incinerated."

"That's always a bonus," Ally said. "So Rina's all better, eh? I've never heard of twenty-four-hour cold before."

After last night, Toby was in no mood for Ally's big mouth. He didn't want to consider that Rina might lie to him. He didn't want to care that unlike Ally, Rina never asked about his work, wouldn't know a smelter from a blasting box. He didn't want to think about how Ally had trembled shyly beneath him the other day, her round stomach so exposed, her eyes closed, as if blindly offering herself.

Not once had he thought of that strange dawn in the truck, with Rina's unconscious legs splayed bare beside him and Ally's soft, sweaty hand clinging from behind. Not once had he asked himself why he'd done it.

"Yeah," he said irritably, "did she tell you I'm moving?"

"Moving?" Ally asked, as he knew she would. "What do you mean?"

"I'm moving to the city," Toby said. "Rina asked me to go with her."

Adam poked Ally between the shoulder blades.

"Adam wants to know if you're still going hunting," she said.

Her voice was oddly flat, almost cold, and Toby instantly regretted what he'd told her.

"Why did you agree to such a thing?" Rina had asked him. "That Adam is a shit. He is bad news. Didn't you hear him? He is a shit."

But how was Toby supposed to explain to her what he couldn't explain to himself? Now, all he wanted was to erase the awful hurt from Ally's voice. To do whatever she asked of him.

"Whenever," he said. "I start split shifts on Friday, so I'm off Thursday."

Ally didn't reply.

"Tell him it's got to be early," he said. "I'll be there before six."

He could hear her breathing. It sounded like the way he used to gasp when his sisters would chase him and then pounce, tickling until all he could manage was a kind of wordless pleading.

"You got someone at the cash?" he asked.

"Yeah," she said. "I have to go, okay?"

As soon as Toby hung up, Sharon came in carrying a hot water bottle. "I think the little one gave me some kind of flu last night," she said.

She'd been running the bathroom tap to drown out her son's voice, trying not to eavesdrop. She'd wiped the toothpaste spots from the mirror and replaced the empty toilet paper roll. But this morning her mind kept going back to their second trip back East, to that brief, forgettable episode with the whale.

It was the first trip Toby would really remember and Sharon had watched a kind of nervous euphoria overtake her usually placid son. Gone was the boy who'd so happily sat in an armchair for up to an hour before bed, rubbing the dog's soft ears against his cheek like a security blanket. This trip, the angry lapping of the white-capped waves, the building-size boats that moved noiselessly through the water, the doting relatives that promised him he would love the horrible, snapping lobster floating in a bucket — all had kept him awake well past midnight, blabbering away, intoxicated by the novelty of it all.

About midway through their stay, the whole family had been strolling along a rock-sheltered, sandy coastline when they came upon a crowd. A whale, bigger than any moose Toby had ever seen, lay beached and dying on the sand.

"What's he doing?" he asked. "Why isn't he in the water?"

Lyle hoisted himself onto a boulder to get a better look. "That's a good question. Why do the crazy buggers do it?"

A young man standing nearby passed Toby his binoculars so he could have a better look. "We don't know why," the young man said to him. "We know it's probably no accident, whales are too smart. But why they would intentionally throw themselves up there, we have no idea."

Lyle nodded the friendly, patient nod of a seasoned local who's seen many a whale up on the sand. Sharon thought the young man looked lonely, and in need of a bath.

Lyle jumped back down onto the sand. "Unless we're planning on eating blubber, we should get going," he said. Toby's sisters had already begun making their way back up to the boardwalk. "I saw a hot dog stand back there."

But Toby didn't budged. He held the heavy binoculars steady in his little hands, unable to turn away from the giant mass that seemed to glow in the midday brightness.

"Give him a minute," Sharon said. "We'll catch up."

"Will they save him?" Toby asked.

"Of course," Sharon said. She knew it was only a matter of time before he grew cranky from hunger like his sisters. "They can rig them up and ease them back in. I've seen it done."

The lonely young man turned to her and stared as if she was somewhere between a liar and a fool. "It doesn't always work," he said, taking back his binoculars. Then Toby had looked from Sharon to the young man, back and forth, not sure who to believe.

Now, when she looked at her own grown son, all Sharon wanted was to assure him that she hadn't listened in on things that were no longer her business. But she *had* been listening, because her grown son's boxer shorts still hung loosely at his hips, just like when his sisters had chased him when he was little, grabbing him from behind by the elastic of his pajamas, playfully pulling him to the carpet. Because she remembered how he'd scrunched up his nose while chewing the rubbery lobster, telling his cousins about the flaky pickerel he and Lyle would catch from a hole in the ice. Because by the second week, he'd had enough and was ready to go home. Because when she thought of the foreign doctor's daughter with those lovely, unreadable dark eyes, she couldn't help but worry for her baby boy.

"What were you yelling about before?" Toby asked. "You knew I was on the phone."

"We're out of juice," she said.

10

∾ AFTER SHE TALKED TO TOBY on the phone, Ally became oddly sullen and Adam got the hell out of there, pretending he was going to look for work. But after a few blocks, he eventually circled back and found himself wandering into the souvenir shop once again.

The same woman was there, helping a bald guy whose head was so sunburned it had begun to peel. As they huddled over a pair of suede slippers, Adam approached a display case of trinkets and jewelry. Its sliding glass door wasn't completely closed and he could've easily wrapped his arm overtop the finger-printed glass and grabbed whatever he wanted. But he couldn't help feeling like the woman was eyeing him even as she blathered to Baldy about the painstaking beading techniques. Just like last time, all he did was imagine himself smashing things, punching the glass over and over until it turned to tiny shards of sand in his bloody hands.

By the time he got back to Ruth's around suppertime, Ally was already in bed. Her door was open a crack and he stuck his head in without knocking. "You got an alarm clock?" he asked.

She was lying on top of her balled-up bed covers. Without looking at him, she gestured towards the clock radio on her dresser.

He pushed the door open further and saw there were empty pop cans and discarded socks littered at her feet. The blind was drawn and he had to maneuver carefully though the dim, cluttered room, edging towards the glaring red numbers of the clock. "Who says you have to hunt at dawn?" he asked. "Who gets up that early? I usually don't get up until I have to piss."

But she didn't smile. "Toby's never late."

Adam studied the formless lump that was his cousin. After he'd blabbed to her about the snitch, and the torched cleaner's, he'd thought he was still fine, that she was cool. But he was beginning to wonder. "You're hot for the miner, eh," he said.

Ally closed her eyes and rolled over towards the wall. "No, I'm not."

"Yeah, you are," he said. "I've seen you."

"No, I'm not," she said. "He's not even staying here. He's moving to the city."

Adam picked up the clock and pulled, but the cord was wedged behind the dresser. He didn't want to talk about the city. Already, every time he visualized tying the bleeding buck onto the roof of the truck, he had to push Vincent's voice from his mind.

"That thing is the biggest fish that place ever seen," his father had said, many times, in many ways, but always the same. "It was there for maybe half an hour, no one around, when I felt the tug and I knew it was going to be a giant. A lure with a little yellow feather, that's all it took to outsmart the bugger."

It was always the same after he lost another job — the beers, and the drinking buddies, and the stupid mounted fish in the hallway.

"That thing is useless," Lucille had replied once, already yawning at two in the afternoon. "You just like to be a big shot."

Then Vincent had grabbed her arm until purple finger marks appeared. After his buddies had left, he'd cried in apology, and Lucille had cradled his head in her lap. "Look at your dad," she'd said to her boys. "He wouldn't even skin his own fish and he cried like a baby at his mama's funeral."

Adam and his brothers had looked at the floor and tried to smile.

Now, he tugged until the cord gave way and the red numbers disappeared. "You're hot for him all right," he said.

Ally rolled so close to the wall that her knees bumped. "Shut up."

Adam tucked the lifeless clock beneath his arm, assured he had nothing to worry about. It wasn't him she was pissed at.

Still, for the rest of the night, as Ruth remained glued to the television and he carried out his preparations — setting the blinking clock, pocketing a half-eaten package of soda crackers, envisioning himself dragging a buck by the antlers though the thick, scratchy underbrush with his dirty, blood-stained hands, double-checking the alarm — Adam kept feeling that he'd somehow had that conversation with Ally once before. It was like he was back in the old apartment he'd shared with his brothers, stepping over garbage and sleeping bodies all day and all night; tuning out the clamour of phones ringing and deals being made; listening to the muffled cries of a girl named Krista.

Night after night, he'd heard her through the wall, plagued by a mix of disgust and desire. One time, he'd bumped into her on the way to the bathroom and she'd lain down on the dirty floor right in front of him and pretended to purr like a cat.

"You're going to get a disease," he'd said.

"Am not," she replied, like the way Leonard had when he was four.

Adam had stepped over her. "You so fucking are."

"Shut up," she'd whispered, rolling towards the wall. "Shut up."

Just after midnight, a cold front moved in, drawing what moisture there was from the persistent heat, leaving the area thick with smoke but heavy with humidity. Something about it didn't seem quite right, as if you could smell dampened coals still burning at full force. Eventually, something would have to give.

The moment Adam stepped out into the pre-dawn hush, his T-shirt grew limp against his back in the muggy air. He noticed the first tepid grey light to the east and the dawn washed over him like a warm, drawn-out shiver.

Despite the insanely early hour, he was wide awake, acutely conscious of the new instability in the air, the eerie silence of the street, the first caw of a crow coming from somewhere nearby. He noticed how each breath filled his lungs with a kind of satisfying heaviness. He noticed the squatty, unassuming buildings of the strip, dwarfed by the metal giants of the mine grounds, now so familiar he could've seen it all in total darkness.

For a moment, there was the exhilarating, terrifying feeling that he was the only person in the world. Ally and Krista were forgotten. There was only him, and the ghost of an old man walking into the bush, rifle over his shoulder.

When Toby's truck finally approached, headlights glaring cruelly in the sickly half-light, Adam almost turned away from the noisy intrusion, closed his eyes to the unnatural brightness.

This was it, he had to tell himself. This was what he'd been waiting for.

As he pulled up in front of the store, Toby was surprised to see Adam already there. He'd been half-expecting to have to go upstairs and bang on the door until Ally showed up in her housecoat, her eyes still pink and crinkly from sleep.

Leaning across the front seat, practically lying flat on his stomach, he pushed open the passenger door. Adam climbed in and Toby held out a thermos. "Want coffee?"

Adam slammed the door and the cab light went out, leaving only the sickly dawn again. He ran his hand slowly along the dashboard as if assessing the truck's value.

"Coffee?" Toby repeated.

Adam took the thermos and set it awkwardly in his lap. He gazed blankly down at it, as if he had no idea what it was for. His left knee began to shimmy.

"The cup screws off," Toby said.

Adam acted like Toby hadn't said a word. He removed the cup and poured until it was almost overflowing. He took a sip, then made a face like he wanted to spit it out all over the new upholstery. "It's fucking hot!"

Toby pulled away from the curb, watching the cup teeter dangerously in Adam's hand. "It's a good thermos. It'll keep like that for four hours."

Adam didn't reply and Toby wondered if was going to be like this the whole way out. The humidity was overwhelming even in the air-conditioned cab of the truck and he could already smell the aftermath of a good downpour — along with the smouldering ash, there would be the sweetness of damp, sticky sap in the breeze. The rocks would be washed clean and slick and colourful.

Last year, when he'd worked nights for a while, Toby had liked to go outside on his break and stand in the gravel lot to watch the weather move in. While the town slept, he tried to predict what the day would bring, holding up his finger in the wind, charting the pattern of the clouds, until the silence became too much and he stepped back inside to join the crude, meandering banter of exhausted men killing time.

When the entrance to the smelter appeared in the headlights, he sped up, anxious to leave the endless mine yard behind, to speed past the broken line of chain-link fencing that hugged the town's entire northern border, to get out onto the empty, winding highway.

Just after he'd hung up with Ally yesterday, the phone had rung again.

"I just talked to the lady in the residence," Rina said. "I don't know if they will give us a double room, but we can get an apartment, maybe. There are lots this time of year, but maybe we'll have to go early so we can look around. There are some that I think are right there, on the campus. But we'll have to go early, like even next week, maybe, just to look."

Toby paused, still stuck on the explanation he'd rehearsed. "Yeah. Sorry about leaving you there alone last night. I lost track of the time ... "

But she hadn't let him finish. "No worries. Your dad said he would drive me and I said I have these things called legs. But you know what I thought of? I thought of how maybe there's a club in Winnipeg. Maybe there's a place for you to practice for real, with the real targets and everything. We can find out maybe next week."

He hadn't expected to get off so easily. Though he knew he should have told her about Ally's hurt silence on the phone, should have mentioned his plans with Adam, he couldn't bring himself to ruin it. "Absolutely," he'd said. "We'll check it out."

"Absolutely," she said. "Absolutely, absolutely."

It was a Rina that Toby didn't know, her words tumbling out in a jumble of nervous excitement. The evening before, she hadn't waited near the fence but had scurried up to him with a list of potential landlords in the city. She'd clung to him around the waist as they walked like one person with four legs across the gravel lot, talking so loud that some of the men had turned and raised their eyebrows.

This morning, as he'd scribbled out a note for Sharon saying he was off to scout new training ground, he found himself looking forward to the quiet, pointless banter of two men in the bush. Away from the clingy looks his parents had started giving him, like they were about to say something but didn't dare. Away from Rina's eager questions about one bedroom or two.

Adam propped the thermos between his feet, then rolled down the window and dumped out his cup. Though it was still too dark to see, he was sure he heard the coffee go *splat* against the shiny truck.

"When I was a kid, I thought coffee was disgusting," Toby said. "But at work you get used to it. You either get a taste for it, or fall asleep at the controls. It's like beer, you have to get a taste for it."

Adam struggled to put the top back on the thermos. Every time he tried, the cup seemed to screw on crooked somehow. "I guess that's the difference, eh?" he said. "You don't need to be slaving in a dungeon to want a beer."

Toby wasn't sure if this was meant as a cut. It was like the other night with the paint — the more challenged he felt, the more he needed to explain himself. "My dungeon days are over. I'm moving to Winnipeg in a couple of weeks."

Giving up on the thermos, Adam left the cup resting precariously on top. He didn't want to talk about the city. "Where'd you learn to hunt, anyway?"

As Toby merged onto the main highway, he opened the window a crack to breathe in the morning. It seemed like he'd always hunted, always known the location of the camouflage platforms, when to sound a call and when to stay quiet, how to squeeze the trigger nice and steady. He was cleaning his own rifle by the time he was twelve and a better shot than Lyle by fourteen.

"Don't you feel badly?" Rina had asked him once. "Don't you feel bad when you kill something? Why can't you just shoot the targets, with the air rifle?"

Ally had come to his defense, parroting what they'd been taught in school. "It's population control. Have you ever seen a starving moose?

Toby had poked her fleshy shoulder. "Have you?"

She'd turned even pinker than usual and poked him back. "You know what I mean."

Now, as rock and pine closed in on either side, Toby pushed both Ally and Rina from his mind. In thirty minutes, they would be wandering down paths that only the initiated could hope to navigate.

"They have a club down at the mine," he told Adam. "They have their own spots and ranges and shit. When he moved here, they took my dad out, then he took me out."

"How many rifles you got?" Adam asked.

Toby kept his eyes on the road. "How many do you need?"

Adam twisted around as if to see for himself in the struggling dawn. All he could make out through the back window was the dark, shapeless void of the mine grounds slowly receding from view. It went on and on, barren stretches of flattened rock and sooty earth, where nothing green had grown for decades. He'd rarely wandered this way, except to rouse the security guard with the rock toss. All he could see now through the back window was a monotonous scramble of dull grey, a barren wasteland from another planet.

Adam thought of the old man on the step, shaking the bright red blood from his hands. Had he really seen that, or had he added the blood himself? He was no longer sure, and didn't care. He settled back into his seat and saw the thermos had tipped over. A shallow puddle of coffee was dripping off the floor mat and onto the spotless beige carpet. "My people were fucking robbed," he said. "We've got to reclaim our ways."

It's what he'd said to himself on the way out of the souvenir shop, passing a waist-high bin full of tiny plastic figures — hundreds of miniature men in loincloths piled in a tangled mass of arms and legs — what he'd said as he stuck his hand in without stopping on his way out the door, shoving what he could into his pocket.

It's what he'd repeated to himself for the rest of the night. As Lyle would sometimes do to remind himself the mine was right — "we got the new procedures right here up on the wall. They're right here in writing. You can read, you can do the job right."

But it wasn't until after midnight, after Ruth and Ally were both snoring, that Adam had pulled out the mess of plastic figures from his pocket. One of the little men was running with a hatchet over his head. The other was sitting tall and straight on a black horse with no saddle. They'd obviously been painted fast, in a cheap factory in some awful part of the world where they had to crank out so many little men per hour.

The one that was running looked slightly cross-eyed.

Adam and Toby talked little for the rest of the way, each sensing that anything more might put the whole thing in jeopardy, each wanting to carry on for their own reasons.

At one point, Toby pointed off to the left. "Take a look back. You should be able to see it."

For the first time, Adam had noticed that the entire highway was like a winding tunnel pockmarked with scraggly bushes. It felt like he could reach out and touch the protruding leaves as they sped by. "See what?"

"Too late," Toby said, and Adam's handiwork disappeared into the distance, unseen. "That's where we were the other night. You'll see it on the way back."

Not long after, the cliffs on their right gave way to a dark mass of towering poplars and scraggly jack pine, and Toby eased up along a narrow, sloping shoulder. For a second, Adam thought the miner was going to turn directly into the wall of trees, but then a road appeared as if from nowhere, almost too small to even be called a road. It was narrower than the truck itself and as the miner sped up again, branches and leaves beat furiously against the windows. It was like they were being swallowed by the bush.

Toby sped up as the road grew tighter and more rutted, forcing Adam to cling to the door handle just to keep himself from flying into the miner's lap. He held on as if he could sense in his bones the vast emptiness all around — hundreds of miles of mature, boggy forest that could confuse even the most expensive global positioning system, or drive lost children into a kind of terrified frenzy, running away from the voices of their rescuers, deeper and deeper into the forest.

By the time Toby finally threw the truck into park, Adam felt sick and the road had completely disappeared. Trees were squeezing them in on all sides. Toby swung open the driver's side door, swept aside the leaves and branches from his face, and disappeared. Adam immediately followed out his own door, pushing away the crowding brush just as the miner had done. But his runners were still slippery from the coffee puddle and he nearly fell as he fought his way out of the cab.

Once on solid ground, the nausea faded, but not the foreboding. As he stood trapped between the half-open door and thick brush, the sounds of the forest began to swarm. Along with the odd solitary birdcall, Adam heard something else — a high-pitched, undulating, recognizable buzz.

Back in the city growing up, anything was better than the musty rental house and Adam had gladly spent the summer covered in mosquito bites. But this was something different. The noise was so loud it could've been coming from his own head, the sort of ringing that happens after a long drive when the engine is turned off and you've finally stopped moving. Here in the bush, the mosquitoes didn't seem like a nuisance but some kind of terrible, all-encompassing presence.

With his T-shirt clinging to him in the breezeless damp, Adam listened to the awful humming grow louder and louder in the leafy half-light. Soon, they were on him, covering every inch of exposed skin. They bit through his sweat socks and flew up his nose.

"What are you doing?" Toby shouted. "I'm back here!"

Adam stumbled through the bush, following the edge of the truck until he found Toby standing surrounded by gear in a tiny clearing. Two rifle cases were leaning upright against the back bumper.

After standing still for a moment, Adam began slapping himself and flailing like some kind of crazy puppet. Toby held out a khaki camouflage jacket like the one he was wearing.

"Forget that," Adam said. "I'm fucking sweating."

Toby threw the jacket at Adam's feet. "Put that on or you'll get eaten alive."

"What's that thing going to do?" Adam asked, still slapping. "A bear would rip right through it."

Toby stared for a moment, not sure what to say. He'd assumed that Adam had a clue. "The black bears around here couldn't care less about you. If one comes, just punch it in the face." He threw a can of mosquito repellant near the jacket. "It's the mosquitoes you can't get away from. They love this shit: hot, damp, no wind. Put on the camouflage and spray everything, even your shoes."

Adam did as he was told, spraying until all he could smell was fumes. He spat, just missing the truck's back tire. "A bear comes at me, I'll fucking shoot it."

"That's against the law," Toby said. "They're protected this year."

Adam grabbed one of the rifle cases and opened it up. "Screw that. It's self-defense." He'd never held a gun this big before, and the weight of wood and metal felt good in his hands, solid and cool. He turned it over like he knew a thing or two about rifles and was inspecting it for quality. Satisfied, he pointed the barrel near Toby's feet. "This thing loaded?"

Toby whacked the barrel aside, nearly knocking Adam off balance. "What, are you fucking stupid?" he shouted. "Knock it off. There's no such thing as an unloaded gun."

"You think I'm going to shoot you?" Adam asked, holding the rifle in the air as if surrendering. "Just wanted to know if the thing was loaded. Just asking a question."

Toby threw the knapsack over his shoulder and kicked the empty case towards Adam. "Put it back," he said.

He'd been trying not to think of what Lyle would say if he knew they were out here. *Hunting's a sport like any other*, his father had lectured over and over like a preacher. *You know what you're doing, you play by the rules, nobody gets hurt.* And talk of bears had reminded him of Rina, of that creepy story she'd told, as unbelievable as a fairytale. He thought of how she'd still be sleeping, murmuring like she always did, her hair falling across her face and into her mouth.

Toby wanted to get moving, to feel the spongy moss silently give way beneath him. "Grab the other one there," he said over his shoulder, and disappeared behind an old spruce trunk marked with faded orange paint. "We'll load up on the platform."

This was Toby's favourite time of the morning. It was a magical hour, when the grey, indistinct shapes began to reveal colour and detail. You began to notice that the aspen and birch trunks, lined up straight and black as prison bars, were now shining silvery white. You noticed that there was fern, all identical and green, growing low beneath the canopy, and that the giant spruce were not dark towers, but millions of tiny, delicate needles that blanketed the ground with rich, rusty brown.

Within minutes, Toby's careful steps developed a momentum all their own, as if his feet were independent from the rest of his body. With the forest held fast by the dense air and Adam swatting and swearing and obediently following at his heels, Toby felt himself approaching the zone. He didn't care if Lyle would've stared at him in disbelief, his own son no better than the poaching bastards who deserved to be strung up with a meat hook. He didn't care what Rina was doing, whether she was asleep or awake.

This was his game, this was his world, and he didn't mind sharing it.

"Just ignore the bugs," he shouted over his shoulder. "Flailing's not going to help."

It was almost daylight by the time they reached a small clearing where three huge spruce lay on their sides, their intricate roots eerily exposed in massive, circular mounds of upturned earth. It looked like a giant had strolled through the forest, plucking mighty trees like weeds and then discarding them. The weak light of the morning snuck through the forest ceiling where the great trees had once stood, and wild lilies grew in the empty craters left behind.

Toby threw down his knapsack and began silently removing his equipment. Adam stood at the edge of the clearing as if it gave him the creeps.

"Why you stopping?" he asked.

But Toby was already busy screwing metal pegs into a pair of tree trunks. He set a narrow plank between the waist-high pegs and hoisted himself up onto it so that he stood balanced between the trees.

Adam dropped his load of rifles to the ground and lit a cigarette, waving it around as if hoping the smoke might throw the mosquitoes off his scent. "What are you doing?"

Toby screwed in more pegs a few feet higher. "You shouldn't smoke in here."

Adam picked up the rifle cases and went closer. Just a few feet above Toby's head, Adam saw there was a plywood sheet set amidst the branches. "This is it?" he asked. "We're going to shoot out of a fucking tree?"

With four wobbly steps in place, Toby was already easing his way back down, blindly searching for each narrow plank with his toe. "You never been up on a platform?"

But he didn't wait for an answer. Once on the ground, he threw the knapsack over his shoulder, grabbed a rifle from Adam and began easily making his way up again, steadying himself with the rifle in his left hand, pulling himself up with the strength of his right. When he reached the platform, he threw himself up onto his stomach and shimmied around to peer back over the edge. "You okay?"

Adam was still on the second rung, clinging to one of the tree trunks with his right hand and reaching for the next rung with his left. The bark of the tree bit into his skin each time he tried to move.

"Slow and steady," Toby said. "Slow and steady."

Adam glared up at him, keeping his eyes off the ground. Overhead, the aspen leaves were as round as coins and the morning sky was completely overcast, dull and ominous. Sweat dripped into his ears while the mosquitoes droned. As he began to climb again, the planks seemed to bow ominously beneath his bulk.

"Slow and steady," Toby said again.

He pulled out the half-empty box of bullets from his bag and fingered their heavy smoothness, like he'd done since he was a child. He thought of Rina that Sunday afternoon, going on about the kinds of things Ally's cousin could've been into. *B and E,* she'd said. *Dealing. NFA.* He couldn't remember what the last one stood for, only that it had sounded funny coming out of her mouth. There were so many things she never talked about.

Adam appeared at the edge of the platform and heaved himself beside Toby like a beaching whale.

"Get on your knees," Toby said, practically on top of him. "There's more room for you to turn around."

"This fucking thing is for midgets," Adam said, still lying flat on his stomach, breathing hard.

"The bugs aren't quite as bad up here," Toby said, "but we can't stay long anyway. I figure we got two shots, maybe three tops. This time of year, there's NROs all over the place."

Adam scrambled to his knees. If it weren't for the knapsack jammed between them they would've been nose-to-nose. "What the fuck are NROs?"

Toby slid the rifle case from Adam's shoulder and began loading the gun with the easy confidence of someone who's completed a task hundreds of times and enjoys a small audience. It was like Sunday afternoons with Ally and Rina watching him practice.

"Natural Resource Officers," he said. "This has to be clean and quick."

He handed Adam the rifle and pointed south. "There's a little lagoon south about two hundred feet. Game go by here for their morning drink."

Adam set the rifle back down on the platform as if he'd suddenly lost interest and fished out a cartridge from the box. It was as cool as the gun barrel and soothed his raw, bark-ravaged palm. When he rolled it around, felt its weight and slick texture, the old man was suddenly back again, not whittling this time, but cleaning off bullets on the broken step. Adam could see the old man dumping them from a pail into the dirt and then wiping them clean with a rag, studying each one of them between his fingers, holding them up to the light, like the diamond appraisers in TV commercials. Adam could hear the clear, solid *clunk* as each one hit the pail.

From their perch above the clearing, he imagined a deer coming in from his right where the miner had pointed. It would appear from behind one of the spooky tangles of roots and earth. It would sniff along the ground, chewing at the flowers or the leaves or whatever it was they ate. Then its ear would twitch, its haunches tense.

Adam lifted the rifle into position like he'd seen on television and practiced aiming. But it somehow felt wrong, the gun slightly awkward and unsteady. He switched shoulders. He adjusted his elbow, gripped further up the barrel, then further down.

"You ever used a thirty-thirty before?" Toby asked.

There was a splatter of raindrops against the plywood.

Adam put the rifle down again and lit another cigarette as another drop of rain splattered against his cheek. There'd been no rain for weeks, and apparently one more fucking morning was too much to ask.

He rolled back off his sore knees and onto his haunches. He was getting tired of the miner's little hunter act. "I'm used to something that's easier to hide."

Suddenly, all that mattered was putting the miner in his place once and for all, no matter what the cost or consequence. He wanted to shock the shit out of the fresh-faced jock who Ally and the foreign one thought was so fucking special, to wipe that righteous, friendly expression from his face.

Screw the old man, he thought. *Screw everything.*

Adam stretched his cramped legs out straight and leaned back onto his elbows. He exhaled into the spitting clouds. "You want to know why I'm here up in this shithole?"

Toby got out another thermos, this one filled with cold water. "That's your business," he said. After drinking his fill, he offered the cup to Adam.

Adam waved it away. The key, he knew, was in the details.

"There was a disagreement, over some money," Adam said. "And we're at this girl's place, just sitting around the table, having a few. It's late, eh, but there's little kids there, not even in school yet, but they're running around when all of a sudden all the windows are breaking, glass everywhere."

It was raining in earnest now. A shallow puddle was forming near Adam's hip where the wood had begun to warp.

"My little brother goes flying out the front door," he said, "and we all follow him. But already, he's got five guys on him at once. They're beating on him with bats and I think, fuck that, and I go to the drawer where the girl keeps her panties. I go out onto the front steps there and it's dark, so I can't see very good but I can hear the bats — *whack, whack, whack.*"

Adam dropped his cigarette into the puddle. It fizzled out with a hiss. "I know I took out at least one of them," he added, "cause I heard it sort of rip into his gut. Then they all cleared out, dragging their wounded."

Toby tightened the thermos cap and nodded absently, as if he understood why you would keep a loaded handgun where children were running about, as if he'd heard the sound of a human gut ripping open before. After all, what do you say when you find yourself up close with a killer at your favourite time of the morning?

"We should shut up now," he said.

Then the forest, glistening with moisture, was still and silent.

As Toby knelt high on the platform with Ally's cousin, Rina rolled over in bed and told herself it was too early to wake up. She told herself that Merik and Slavenka would never carry out their threat to withhold all financial support if the boy went along. She told herself that the city would be different as long as her Toby was there.

She told herself there was no reason to fear a big-talking, tough-boy shit who burns down a dry cleaner's for no reason. Who paints letters that dance. Who saw things the others didn't.

11

JUST PAST SEVEN that morning, Ruth walked into Ally's room without knocking. "You slept in," she said.

But there was something about the way Ally rolled over to face the wall that gave Ruth a chill. It wasn't like her daughter to simply turn away like that, leaving only the back of her head, dismissive and unreadable. The little patches of pink showing through fine blonde hairs reminded Ruth of when Ally was a baby. There had been times, while nursing in the middle of the night, when Ruth would rub her baby girl's velvety, fragile skull and find herself weeping as Harry slept.

Ruth turned away. She began cracking the eggs for French toast, as if the smells of breakfast would be enough to lure her grown daughter back.

Just leave her be, she told herself. Leave her be like the month or two when Harry was still with them and Ally had woken up screaming in the middle of the night, shaking and inconsolable over some terrible visions that her infant self couldn't express. Harry had insisted on a visit to the doctor, who'd called it night terrors and said it was a common phase, and soon Ally started sleeping through the night again without notice or explanation.

But it seems the imagination can lie dormant for years only to grow up again with a kind of desperate vigour. After Toby told Ally he would be leaving, it was as if her daydreams took over. She retreated further and further, fighting any interruption or intrusion, going through the motions with customers, eating Ruth's cheesy mashed potatoes without a word. Like the nagging in her stomach that had begun telling her it was time for another cigarette, she let herself be drawn in, again and again, to the same silent conversation.

Toby would be standing in front of the store, the white truck packed with stuff at the curb. Rina would be waiting in the passenger seat, already asleep with a book on her lap, or not there at all, still waiting for him patiently at Merik and Slavenka's.

With Ally standing on the curb and Toby on the street, they would be almost the same height, which would make them laugh.

I guess this is it, she'd say, and he would lean forward and hug her for the first time, firm and friendly at the beginning, then longer, rocking a little as if there was music in the background. When they finally separated, still close enough that she could feel the warmth of his breath, she'd say, *I have something to tell you.*

Then she would go back to the beginning, playing it over and over in her head until Thursday morning dawned damp and sticky and the real world barged in again. Until real people, with their own private needs and desires, came forward and demand their due.

The phone had already rung five times before Ruth charged in to answer it. Ally sat slumped at the kitchen table, staring into her bowl of dry cereal as if she'd forgotten how to pour milk.

Wrapped in a towel, with her toothbrush still in her mouth, Ruth picked up the phone and glared at her daughter. She was already irritated before she even heard the voice on the other end.

"Ruth, it's me."

There was only one person who phoned at this hour and Ruth couldn't believe she'd already forgotten. She'd run to pick up as if she could have no idea who it might be.

For the six years she and Harry were together, Ruth had been the morning person, the one who sprang from bed while Harry groaned and pulled the covers over his face.

"Relax," he'd said many times, his voice muffled through the blankets. "What's the rush? All work makes Ruth a dull girl. Get back into bed."

There was usually a kind of teasing lilt in his voice when he said such things, with a confusing tinge of exasperation. So Ruth dutifully crawled back in and tried to lie still, "just lounging" as he called it. But rather than relax, she'd feel the panic growing, like when she was young and could not decide what to do — pretend she was asleep on the fold-out bed so no one would bother her, or open her eyes and join in the party, grab the bottle from Vincent or Mary or someone else and try to join in the dangerous laughter.

"I got stuff to do," she always finally said to Harry, and he'd sigh and roll over on his side.

Years later, when the early calls started coming, she found herself right back where she was before he left, still trying to figure out what he wanted of her. *Since when was he up at this hour?* she wondered. Was he toying with her? Was he trying to make some kind of stupid point?

Ruth dropped the receiver down beside Ally and went back to brushing her teeth. Still staring into her bowl, Ally picked up the phone.

"Hey," Harry said. "It's your dad."

Ally fished out a raisin from the cereal and squished it between her fingers, trying to imagine Lyle having to say, "It's your, dad," to Toby.

"Yeah, I know," she said.

"How have you been?" Harry asked. "We haven't talked in a while."

Ally answered the way she always did. "Yeah, I'm okay."

"Good, good," he said. "How's the store? Is it busy?"

"We haven't opened yet," Ally said.

It was always such a struggle, every single time, and the visits had usually been worse. When she was seven, he took her to an art exhibit.

"While you're out here, I figured we should do things that you don't have access to at home," he said, but after only half an hour, he'd grown tired of her fidgeting and led her by the hand out into a rain storm. "I have to pee," she said on the way to the car, and so they'd turned around and run back to the gallery, but it had been too late.

When she was eleven, they went to the zoo. "I've got my period already," she said, "I'm not interested in monkeys," and Harry had blushed and stammered, looking around to see who might've heard.

When she was fourteen, he treated her to ice cream and a lecture about smoking and the need for regular exercise.

"Mom smokes," she'd said.

"You can do better."

"Yeah," she'd said. "I guess you could too. I guess that's why you left."

After that, they didn't speak for seven months.

"Right, of course," Harry said now. "It's still early. These past few years I'm up by six, six-thirty. I must be getting old."

"Yeah, I guess so," Ally said.

Harry laughed, slightly high and forced. "But listen, I have some news, Allison. I'm getting married."

Ally flicked the flattened raisin across the table like it was a tiny hockey puck.

"Her name's Lisa," Harry said. "She has two girls, ten and twelve."

Ally listened to her father lick his lips like he always did when she made him uncomfortable.

"I want you to meet her," he said. "I thought maybe you could come out and visit. You haven't done that in a while."

Ally imagined herself in the city, imagined how Toby would answer the door of his and Rina's tiny apartment while Rina was off buying books for school.

What are you doing here, he'd ask.

My dad's getting married, she'd say.

Then he would hug her for the first time. When they separated, they would still be close enough that she could feel the warmth of his breath.

This place sucks, he'd say, *I can't find a job.*

Then she would nod and pull her fingers through his hair, tangled and messy in the stuffy apartment, like the time they'd driven home from the lake.

I have something to tell you, she'd say.

"Ally?" Harry no longer sounded tense and ingratiating, only impatient. "I'm talking to you."

"Are you planning to cheat on her, too?" Ally asked.

Harry sighed and licked his lips. "Aren't you getting a little old for this?

"Whatever," she said. "Forget it. Congratulations."

Harry sighed again, like a man defeated. "Okay. Listen, I've got a call on another line. But we'll talk about this later. You think about it, Allison."

Her father had no way of knowing that the old Ally — the one who smoked just to be included, who eagerly let hockey players feel her up, who cried again and again against Ruth's indifferent shoulder, who managed to save up all the bitterness that she possessed for Harry and Harry alone — had already retreated.

She was already back in the city apartment, with Toby's hair between her fingers.

"I'll think about it," she said, and hung up.

If Ruth's rejection of her people had been a mortal necessity, Harry's had been more youthful bravado. After finishing a business degree at university, he'd seen moving to an isolated, industrial town to take a mid-level job with the government as a very romantic thing to do.

It helped that his parents did not approve. They'd ensured their only son wanted for nothing, fully expecting that one day he would leave them, probably heading to some big metropolitan centre where he would reap the earthly rewards of the advantages they'd given him. But like many young men who've never wanted for anything, Harry couldn't help feeling that there was more. If the rules of Adam's culture had taunted and eluded him his whole life, Harry was free to either accept or reject his as he pleased. And unlike Lyle, Harry had been raised to believe that the rules were his to control, to question and to conquer. This left him with a restless sense of personal responsibility and entitlement. He wasn't sure what it was he was looking for, only that there had to be more, and that he would not find it in his parents' spacious, suburban home.

When he met Ruth, not quite a week after starting his new job, she was like no other woman he'd ever known. Serving him chili and beans in the cafeteria, her beautiful hair squished into a hairnet, she would barely look at him. Yet on their first date, her hair hanging long and shiny, she had taken him by the hand and led him to the bedroom like it had all been prearranged.

"You always do this?" he asked.

"No," she said. "You look nice, though. You look nice in that suit you wear. The navy one with silver buttons."

Within the first month, he decided that the women he'd known on campus were vain and coy and talked too much, and that Ruth was all he'd ever been looking for. He stopped calling his aging parents, who refused to even visit Franklin, and committed himself to a new life. He was going back to the wild, to a simpler, more natural world and by looking after Ruth, with her hard, dark eyes and pale, dishwater hands, Ruth who was noble and beautiful and who hung on his every word, he would fix everything that had ever hurt her and people like her.

It wasn't until Ally was born that the little things began to needle him. With a nursing baby already depriving him of a good night's sleep, her brother Vincent's calls at all hours began to wear on his nerves. Harry found himself badgering Ruth: "He's only dragging you down, don't you see what he's doing? We don't need this."

Ally was late getting potty-trained, still wetting herself at three, and the nights at home with dirty diapers and a blaring television seemed longer and longer, while the silent, empty winter offered no comfort. His office grew boring, sometime petty. He began to remember what it was like to eat at a good restaurant. He began noticing the way Ruth might use words she didn't understand, or how she might not even notice when her pants were stained.

When Ally was not quite five he went to the city for his father's funeral and couldn't bring himself to return. "I need time to think," he told Ruth over the phone. "I'm going to stay here for a bit."

"Who is she?" Ruth asked. "Tell me her name. I want to know."

"No, Ruth," he'd said, trying not to judge, to ask himself why she was always so damn linear. "There's no one else. I need to be alone."

Harry believed that contentment was always somewhere off in the distance, lurking around the corner of another, another house, another romance. Later on, it's what made him such a good software consultant, sincere in his promises that there was always a better way, where no time is ever wasted and no employee ever unproductive as long as you've got your eye on the future and the latest upgrade for a good price.

It was really only when he had no choice but to revisit his past that Ally's father ever felt out of control, utterly unable to set the agenda and make things right. As he'd picked up the phone to call his daughter that morning, the awful blankness of the dial tone had seemed to taunt him. It had been Ruth who'd won the day after all. Who'd convinced Ally that she'd thrown him out because of the cheating — in fact he'd already been in the city four months before Ruth showed up at his condo door at an inopportune moment. She'd made the decision, refused to speak to him, to talk it out, shipped his things off within days. Then she'd gone ahead and started her own business with some of his alimony and shocked him with its success.

She'd left him with no idea how he might get his own daughter to talk to him like a normal human being.

In the cramped bathroom of the apartment above the store, Ruth felt no sense of victory. When she heard Ally hang up, she splashed her face with cold water, letting it drip down her chin, her neck, her chest. It was the mirror on the medicine cabinet that seemed to taunt her.

"You shouldn't smoke, Ruth," Harry had said so many years ago. "You'll get those little lines. Don't wreck your beautiful lips, Ruth."

She'd taken this to mean he would be with her until she was old.

For the last few days, Rina hadn't even wondered why Ally hadn't called. She'd looked to the future without fear, allowing herself to anticipate her classes with the nervous excitement of a promising student. She'd left herself no time for reflection, only plans, plans, plans.

But this morning, while her friend went through the motions of opening the store, Rina lay awake in bed, not able to sleep anymore, not wanting to get up. She could hear Ally's voice from months before, just after they started hanging out in the store after school.

"Don't you wish sometimes you had brothers and sisters?"

Rina had sat on top of the counter, aimlessly watching the ebb and flow of customers tinkling through the door, in exactly the same spot Adam had sat the other day.

"I had a pretend sister," Rina replied.

Ally looked up from filling a bin and made a face. "Pretend?"

"Yes, her name was Olga," Rina said, straightening up her shoulders as if offended. "I would set her a place at the table or read her a story before bed, but I was only six years old. Now I can't imagine it. I can't imagine what she might be like or how I would be with her. It's too strange."

"What's to imagine?" Ally asked. "You'd be sisters. You'd tell each other stuff."

"It's not worth it," Rina said. "You would argue. She'd steal your things."

Ally shook her head. "You know, they say people who have pets live longer because they talk to them and stuff."

Then Rina began to laugh, because Ally placed such faith in "they," and because Rina felt like laughing. For the first time in years, with the customers coming and going, a feeling of well-being seemed to lap against Rina's legs, warm and surprising.

"Well, what about you," Ally said, "Olga is the best name you could come up with? That is *shit ugly*," and Rina had laughed even harder.

Now, although her bedroom door was closed, Rina could hear her mother getting into the shower, hear the echoing boom of the tub as the soap slipped from Slavenka's grasp.

Focus, she told herself. *Identify a list of enquiries to be made in order of priority: apartments for rent, bursary programs, biathlon clubs.*

But it was no use. Once again, Rina was the darling only child sitting beneath the formal dining table, wondering how the smart man talking waving his wine glass around could have such ugly shoes. She was the achingly bored ex-schoolgirl lolling on the floor with nothing but a doomed rabbit for a playmate, wondering how much longer her mother could hold on. She was the withdrawn teenager in a foreign classroom, wondering what she hated most about the inner city bullies, their careless rebellion or pathetic posturing.

As she listened to the gentle rush of Slavenka's shower go on and on, she remembered that first night at the pool hall when Toby's friend Josh had fondled Ally as he put on her parka.

"Why do you let him do that to you?" she asked later.

"What?" Ally shot back. "That's just the way he is. He's a prick."

Yet Rina hadn't pressed her friend for a better explanation, hadn't really wanted to know what boys like Josh had done to Ally behind the school, why Ally might blindly follow a group of drunken louts into the dark bush. She hadn't wanted to mess with the joking, foul-mouthed veneer, with the Ally who proved the world wasn't always crawling with hidden dangers.

The steady noise of the shower ended with a *clunk* and Rina turned her face into the pillow. She waited for the pat of Slavenka's feet on the cool tile. But there was no sound of any movement, only a faint hiccup that could've been a sob.

All along, Rina thought, the three of them together had been so good, so right because one of them had been there, ready to lay herself down like a bridge. Ally had grabbed Toby's hand, wrote Rina's phone number in blue ink while Josh pawed at her like a careless child with a toy. She'd laid herself down and let them cross over her.

And now, now that Rina was only days away from her future, now that the mining town was already becoming more memory than reality, she could see the last year with an absurd kind of clarity. She didn't need Toby to tell her Ally was not okay with their leaving. Alone in her bed, with her to-do lists out of arm's reach, she saw the signs plain as day: there was the time Ally had gone with Toby to the vet, for no reason; the time she'd pretended to strangle him then let go, suddenly, unusually shy; the time she'd broken their unspoken agreement to not talk about the future. *Any bets you'll bugger off before he does?* she'd hissed.

Clearly, somewhere along the way something had changed — Ally had decided she no longer wanted to be the bridge, but the destination. Which meant Rina was going to crush the one who'd rescued her first and there was nothing to be done about it.

So what was the point of knowing?

Later that morning, Slavenka walked cautiously down the sidewalk in her thin-strapped sandals, hugging her purse to her chest. The lung-wrenching haze had been consumed by a damp gloom. Her hair was still wet from the shower, clinging unflatteringly to her temples. She hadn't even bothered to hide the morning puffiness around her eyes.

The night before, growing tired of her fidgeting, Merik had given her a sleeping pill and this morning, even after she'd shut off the water, she'd stood naked and shivering beneath the dripping showerhead. It had taken her three tries to button her blouse so that each little pearl lined up with the right hole.

"How did this happen?" Merik had asked as he handed her the little orange pill. "How did we not know? What do you do all day other than care for our daughter?"

Though he did not say it, she knew he blamed her for every-thing — it was her fault Rina wanted the miner, her fault that they were here. He blamed her like he'd wanted to all along, since the night she came to him with her ultimatum. It was enough to make her wish that Merik was a shouting man. Then at least he would lash out at her and be done with it: "You, of all people!" he would shout. "Why did you bring us here if you knew you'd be miserable? Isn't it better to stay and to suffer in the place you love than to slowly whither in a strange land?"

As she made her way around the shallow puddles, her neighbour's bungalows, which could sometimes seem almost pleasingly uniform and bright in the sooty sunlight, looked only monotonous and silly in the drizzle. She remembered a time when they were still refugees in the Winnipeg apartment with lime-green paint and spotty linoleum and Merik had looked up from his medical books while she washed dishes in the summer heat.

"You look beautiful," he said solemnly, taking off his glasses and rubbing the bridge of his nose. He said it as if it weren't a compliment but an interesting fact from his textbook, and this had made her want to hold his face in her soapy, chapped hands, and kiss him passionately. The way he rubbed his nose had made her think of what he must've been like as a child, moon-faced and overtired and ready for his nap.

"Your face has filled out a bit again," he'd said. "You're as beautiful as the day I saw you in the café."

But stumbling through the rain years later, on what was surely a fool's errand, she knew none of this mattered anymore. All such vanity, all her proud, curious, vain energy had been left behind somewhere in the rubble.

By the time she arrived at Ruth's store and the little bell tinkled overhead, Slavenka was hardly aware of her soaked blouse clinging like wet tissue against her arms.

Ally was kneeling near the coconut bin, scraping another wad of gum from the floor when she saw her. For a moment, she stared past Slavenka, waiting for Rina to appear. Then she sank back on her heels in surprise.

The store was empty and quiet except for the scratchy voice of a radio announcer.

"You have been a good friend to my Rina, yes?"

Ally nodded uncertainly and Slavenka knew how she must look to the girl. The last time she'd seen her was at Rina's graduation, where she'd been the only mother wearing a hat. Her own mother had given it to her, a gorgeous plum-coloured straw hat that Merik had repeatedly cursed in its big round box during their long journey from home.

"She lost a classmate, did you know that?" Slavenka asked. "A girl just her age. This girl and her brother snuck out of the house. It was a sunny afternoon and they were playing under a sign, a store sign, when a mortar hit. She was killed and the boy, he lost a leg."

Ally stared dumbly at Rina's beautiful, dripping mother.

There was something about Ally's face, pink and expectant, a captive audience of one, that spurred Slavenka on. "We have lived through much, you see. Our relatives in the countryside, the women were raped over and over all as a group. They have a name for it. Gang rape, they call it. My beautiful country was reduced to barbarians — animals. If we were still there, we would be rebuilding from nothing. Here, Rina can have a new life."

Slavenka picked up a small bag of candy-covered almonds from a display table and balanced them in her palm as if weighing them. She knew that Merik would never forgive her. He'd thought she was braver than she was and she'd let him down because she was not like him, a mountain boy with no illusions. He would never had stood here so defeated, looking like he'd just been dragged from the toxic lake, hoping this gaping sales clerk might help them understand what must be done.

"Do you think she is serious with this Toby?" she asked.

Ally looked down at floor, as if the spell had been broken. Her round shoulders shrugged almost imperceptibly. "They're moving in together."

Slavenka nodded, following the girl's gaze. She could see a dirty patch of bubble gum still plastered to the polished floor.

"It's fine here, in this town," she said. "But things change just like that."

Her wet hair had dripped to form three perfect beads of water at her feet.

"They change," she said again, but this time in a language that Ally didn't understand.

After Slavenka left, carrying away the bag of almonds without paying, Ally couldn't get back to cleaning the gum.

None of Rina's past had seemed real until now, until Slavenka had told her these things while dripping strangely in the doorway, playing with the buttons of her see-through blouse. The polar bear in the river, the little dead girl under the sign, the atrocities. They had all really happened.

Still, all Ally wanted to do was go back to her daydreams. She wanted to lose herself in that make-believe place where everything was the same, but different, where the story never ended but was always left hanging.

I have something to tell you, she'd say. Then she would reach out and touch him in her mind. She would never say it, though, and he would never reply.

In all her imaginings their conversation never once went any further, as if she could not bear the possibility of that voice, of all voices, inflicting pain.

12

ADAM AND TOBY LAY FLAT on their stomachs on the platform, rifles ready, so close that their elbows touched. All that separated them was a silence as heavy as the humidity.

Even at the best of times, Toby rarely enjoyed this long waiting on the small platform — it was like the opposite of the zone. After a while in the same prone position, his legs always grew numb while his mind skittered here and there, restless and unsettled. It reminded him of being trapped at a school desk, with his math teacher scratching tediously against the blackboard. In math class, no matter how hard he tried to focus on the numbers, there'd always been something else vying for his attention — his teacher's bald head shining under the fluorescent lights, the thin bra strap digging into the flesh of the girl in front of him, the lavalike texture of the chewed pen in his hand. It was the same hunting in the early half-light with his father, not moving a muscle, bombarded by details — an October leaf floating to the ground like the gentle rocking of a baby cradle, an irregular rock in the shape of an animal, complete with mossy coat and pointed nose; the dull crack of Lyle's jaw as he yawned.

Usually, Toby dealt with this by closing his eyes and dozing off.

"I have to bring a deck of cards," Lyle joked to his men in the lunchroom, "or the kid fades on me. You should see us. When it's a frosty one, we leave on the mitts and throw down cards with our teeth."

But this time, Toby remained wide awake, trying not to think of what Adam had told him about the three toddlers, the glass breaking, the bats swinging, the guts ripping. He listened to the *plop-plop-plop* of drizzle against the plywood, the *see-saw* whistle of the meadowlarks that are always long gone by October, the shallow breathing of a killer just a foot away.

After a few minutes, the *plop-plop* rhythm gave way to the steady drone of a downpour and Toby rolled onto his side, thankful for an excuse to move. He pulled a couple of crumpled rain ponchos from his knapsack and tossed one onto Adam's back.

Adam got onto his hands and knees and sent the poncho sailing over the edge of the platform. "That's fucking useless," he said. "I'm already soaked."

Toby ignored him, wrestling with the wet vinyl to find the hole for his head. As soon as he managed to get it on, water began to drip from the edge of the hood onto his nose.

Adam grinned, feeling better than he had all week. High on the platform, with the loaded rifle in his grasp and the miner cowed and quiet by his side, the rain felt blissfully cool against Adam's back. He remembered how the old man used to walk through the rain like he didn't even notice, like he didn't give a shit if he was soaking wet or not.

He could see the old man from inside the old house, through a rain-splattered window that leaked in spring. The old man was sitting outside on the steps as usual, counting bullets, but that time, in the flash of the lightning, everything stopped for a moment, even the old man, who threw his head back and opened his mouth as if trying to drink the rain. The old man had remained like that, a statue, until the thunder rattled the windowpanes, and he'd begun to count once again.

Adam remembered Vincent's voice, remembered his father's large hand squeezing his arm reassuringly. "You shaking in your boots there, little man? Look at that crazy son of a bitch out there. Can't hear a thing."

When Toby nudged Adam in the side, Adam automatically pulled away, just as he had from Vincent's squeeze. He didn't want to lose sight of the old man, didn't want to lose that lone figure, mysterious and unperturbed, caught like a statue in the flashes. But something was moving in the drenched bush.

Through the glistening leaves, far to their right, the head of a deer appeared from behind the wreckage of an uprooted tree. It moved slowly, each step careful and precise, the legs looking too thin to support such a broad belly and stretching neck. It seemed completely absorbed by the little drowned flowers that were bent almost to the ground now, going about its business completely oblivious to the rain and the hunters lying in wait.

Still kneeling, Toby's gripped Adam's shoulder from behind. "Not the doe."

Adam ignored him, shifting the rifle against his shoulder as best he could. After a second or two, he found the deer in his scope. It raised its head from the flowers, ears twitching, batting its eyes like a flirt. Adam clenched his jaw, held his breath, thought of the old man on the steps, focused and unanswering.

"Wait for a buck," Toby said.

Adam squeezed the trigger and a *crack* shattered the drenched forest. Everything seemed muffled, as if Adam's eardrums had gone numb, and he watched the doe disappear into the bush, its thin legs amazingly fast. With its white tail and hindquarters flashing through the leaves, it almost looked like she was mooning him.

Toby scrambled to his feet, all his athletic grace lost in anger. "Don't you know shit? You kill a doe, you lose her fawns too. You wait for a buck. It's called preserving the hunt. It's called having a brain."

Adam kept his eyes on the bush where his rightful prey had vanished. He tried to think of the old man, always slow-moving and preoccupied, as if he knew a secret and didn't care if you were ever in on it.

What he really wanted to do was kill the miner. With just one squeeze, the forest would shatter and *crack* again. The miner would shut the fuck up once and for all, clutching his heart and sailing off the side of the platform like a stuntman.

He could do it, Adam thought, right now, he could wriggle around and do it, raising the gun's slick barrel straight up. He'd felt the power, could still feel the force of it against his shoulder.

In one swift motion, Toby grabbed the rifle from Adam. "I'm done," he said. "I'm fucking out of here."

Adam knew it wasn't too late. The miner was in good shape, but he was the bigger man. He could even see Ally's face when he told her.

I had to do it, Cuz, he'd say. *He had no fucking right. My people, your people, we've got to do it. You don't get it. You were raised by a traitor.*

But Toby already had already unloaded the rifles and slipped them in their cases, was already flinging the pack over one shoulder and the rifles over the other. Even with his awkward load, even with the raindrops coming so fast they bounced off the wood as if boiling hot, he went down the makeshift ladder with ease.

Once on the ground, he immediately turned back they way they'd come. "I'm done," he called over his shoulder. "I'm out of here."

Adam didn't answer. He couldn't believe he'd let his chance just slip away. He couldn't believe he was stuck here, weaponless and waterlogged, deserted by someone who could load a rifle in seconds but thought cops and robbers was just a game.

In that fucking poncho, he thought, the miner looked like the little girl in the fairy tale, the one the big, bad wolf wanted to eat.

On his way back to the truck, Toby's runners sank into the muddy path with a satisfying *squoosh*.

The asshole will follow, he told himself. *He's afraid of bears. Just watch, he'll follow.*

He didn't want to think about what had almost just happened, taking a doe out of season like the worst kind of poacher. Or about those little screaming kids who would've been no older than his nephews. He waded through the narrow, mucky trail as fast as he could, pushing leaves and thoughts aside like he'd done so many times before — like whenever Rina's past came up.

"My mother, she won't go if I don't go," she'd complained once as they'd sunned themselves by the lake. Merik had been scheduled to attend a conference in the city and Slavenka was pushing her daughter to come along with them. "If I stay, she's just going to walk around the house," Rina complained to her friends, "you know, what's the word, when you're all long in the face like a pouting child?"

Toby just shrugged, but Ally jumped in, squinting her eyes as she exhaled. "Moping," she said, "Moping around."

"Yes. Moping," Rina agreed. "But I'm still not going. Not until I have to."

"July in the city is terrible," Ally said. "The pools are all full of pee and there's no place to cool off."

Although he'd never been there in the summer, Toby nodded. When he thought of Winnipeg, it was always winter and he was always on an overheated bus with a hockey team of overheated guys. The wide, congested streets were always lined with snowbanks grown black with grit and the hotel room was always smaller than he'd imagined. On strange ice, he'd always found himself too wound up, making stupid mistakes and ending up in the penalty box.

"The city teams," Ally had said once, explaining the nuances of the game to Rina, "they hit our guys hard because they think we play rough. They want rough, they get rough."

As they lay in the sun that late June afternoon, Toby had rolled over on his side and rested his hand protectively along the curve of Rina's buttocks. Remembering how long it took to get out of the city clutter, through all the streetlights and billboards until you were into the open air, he rubbed a thin line of exposed skin that was starting to burn.

"You didn't like living there, did you?" he said.

Rina propped herself up on her elbows and grabbed Ally's cigarette. She took her time inhaling. "We were poor. It was only nice on the other side of the river, with the big houses and miles and miles of lawn. Back home, nobody had yards like that, even before the bombs."

But Toby didn't really hear a word she said. He was too pleased that she'd rather stay in town with a moping mother than leave him behind, too satisfied with his hand on her tan line. He pushed her words away, just like that holiday afternoon on the East Coast, when the young man with the binoculars had told him that the beached whale, its skin glistening in the sun like shiny metal, might not be saved. Back then, little Toby had stood for a moment, transfixed by the young man, surprised by his words of doom, suspicious of his unblinking, dispassionate face. Yet as soon as Toby's stomach had growled, he'd turned back to his mother, taken Sharon's hand and gone for lunch.

Now, he walked quickly down the soggy trail, occasionally wiping the driving rain from his eyes with the back of his hand, a young athletic man easily balancing his awkward burdens on his back. Within a few minutes, he was in the zone and Ally's asshole cousin was long gone. He was thinking of the cabin that Sharon and Lyle were planning to build along the lake they knew so well. Though it was still only a design on a piece of paper, Toby could see himself and Rina there in five or ten years. She would be reading a book, holding a pen lid between her teeth and underlining things, like he'd seen her do when she was studying. He would come in from chopping wood, nice and sweaty the way she liked, and he would watch her for a moment from the screen door, so serious and sexy, sucking the lid in concentration. Then they would be skinny-dipping at sunset, with the water shining as gold as her earrings and there would be a baby, the same age as his nephew, who would do the dog paddle, and blow spit bubbles, and make them laugh.

As he spied his bright white truck through the wet leaves, though, he had no choice but to face the facts. The asshole had not followed, had not come up the path from behind, flailing and swearing as he went.

Toby threw his gear into the bed of the pickup and secured a tarp overtop. He climbed into the stuffy cab that now smelled of stale coffee and wet carpet, and stared into the fogged-up windshield. There was no way in hell he was going back there to shoot the shit with a killer, and yet he wasn't ready to abandon someone in the bush.

He had no choice but to sit restlessly, trapped there as the windows of the truck began to fog, waiting for some kind of plan to come to him.

After Toby plucked the rifle from his hands like candy from a baby then disappeared into the washed-out forest, Adam had remained flat on his stomach, arms dangling over the edge of the platform as if preparing to settle in for a soggy nap.

Fuck the little red miner, he'd told himself. *Fuck his shiny truck, and his daddy's rifles, and his fucking rules.* He didn't need any of it. He'd been on his own before. All night he'd stayed by the lake, like his crazy people who would go for days, starving themselves and waiting for the visions to come.

But after an hour or so, the wind picked up and Adam closed his eyes against the driving rain. He could no longer blink away the water. Something pawed at his back, clawing through his clingy T-shirt and he scrambled blindly to his knees, swatting and flailing as he went. Twisting around, he found nothing but the upper branches of a scraggly poplar, bent by the wind and its own damp weight.

The truth hit him then like fist in the gut. This time was different. There were no lights across the lake. There were no houses with little manicured lawns just up the path. There was only him and the endless, blurry nothingness all around.

Beneath his angry resolve, fear crawled and slowly fastened into him as more truths beat down, relentless as the rain. He knew he'd forgotten about the kids until he'd said it out loud to the miner. He'd forgotten how they'd stood all in a row in their pajamas, matching orange drink stains above their lips. How when Leonard went *thud*, they'd laughed like he was pretending, like he was a clown tripping over his shoes. How the stupid girl, their mother, had screamed and so they'd all screamed too, as if it were contagious. How the littlest one, still in saggy diapers, had kept screaming and screaming even after the others had stopped.

"Fucking shut that up!" Adam had shouted. But even after the girl covered the baby's mouth, the screaming hadn't stopped.

Alone in the middle of nowhere, lost and half-drowned, Adam knew that the old man was long dead, probably rotting in the ground for years. He knew that visions could be bought for forty dollars in a back lane. He knew he didn't know how to hunt any more than Krista knew how to make those little beaded slippers. She didn't fucking need to know. There were always enough suckers ready to buy her stick-legged self.

It was at times like this, moments of impending disaster, that Adam would think of Krista, the one who always stood there any time of the day or night, her pockets full of money or drugs or both, waiting in the apartment hallway to be let in, holding out her gifts in exchange for entry. One time, she'd brought submarine sandwiches all neatly wrapped and stacked one on top of the other. After two nights of partying, Leonard had stumbled to the door to meet Krista with a growl. When he came back to the mattress where Adam lay sleeping, he stood over him, hurling sandwiches down on him until Adam stirred.

As usual, Krista laughed too hard. She kneeled at the edge of the mattress, her laugh grating like an untuned radio in Adam's hung-over ears, while he and Leonard tore at the wrappers, letting little bits of lettuce and onion fall onto the sheets.

"Where is everybody?" she asked. "Why you guys so hungry? You been partying or something?"

"Yeah, guess you weren't invited," Leonard said.

As usual, she just kept on, picking at the small scab on her elbow, anxiously chattering as if she might be cut off at any moment. "I been coming here since I was twelve. I don't need an invite." She pointed at Adam, then Leonard. "Hey, which one of you is older?"

Adam crumpled one of the wrappers into a ball and threw it at Leonard. "I changed his fucking diapers."

Krista let her finger drop, looking skeptical. "Then how come he's lived here longer?"

Adam got up then, went to the sink for a drink of water. He knew what Leonard was going to say. His brothers never let him forget about the times his teacher, Miss Lavalee, had come to visit Lucille and Vincent at home, determined to talk about their son's potential. And Adam had never forgotten the way the classroom smelled of Miss Lavalee even when she wasn't there. Or the way she chewed daintily on her nails when she thought no one was looking. Or the perfect loops of her writing on the chalkboard. Or the way she would sit behind the desk with legs crossed, bouncing her high-heeled shoe on the end of her toes. He'd never forgotten the inevitable look of disappointment on her face as she sucked on her lower lip, mascara fallen like dirty snowflakes under her eyes. Never forgotten how much he hated her for making him make her look that ugly.

"I fucked off school way before he did," Leonard said to Krista that afternoon, his mouth still full of sandwich. "This one, he was a little teacher's pet there for awhile."

Adam had stuck his mouth beneath the tap and lapped up the cool water. He knew his little brother was probably horny then, self-satisfied and full. More and more, all Leonard wanted to do was have sex, but the girls didn't like him much. He didn't know how to talk to them and his teeth were crooked, all pushed together like there'd been a traffic jam in his mouth.

So Adam walked up behind Krista and rested both hands gently on her shoulders. "So you tell me something," he said. "Why do you come to this dump?"

For once, she was quiet for a moment, startled to have a question directed her way. "Come to see you," she finally announced.

Adam knew that this was true, that she'd wanted him because he was the big man of the moment. The week before, he'd made the cops look like morons by stealing a car from right under their noses when they came to look into a domestic disturbance next door. At least a dozen people posing as curious bystanders had got to watch him as he did it.

With a look, then, he sent Leonard out of the room and settled back onto the bed. Within a few minutes, he and Krista were high and Adam wasn't thinking about the other men who'd touched her, or about Miss Lavelee's ugly face, or about Leonard's dejected, crooked smile, pretending he hadn't wanted her anyway. Adam had simply let himself sink into that place where there were only warm tongues and glazed, admiring eyes.

High on the hunting platform, with the poplar branch clawing persistently at his back, Adam would've given anything for just one toke, for just a few minutes in that place where all that mattered was tongues. But as he lay back in defeat against the waterlogged plywood, all he got was a sharp poke in the ass.

It was the toy warriors from the day before. Cursing, he burrowed into the pocket of his wet jeans and pulled them out. He still wanted to set them alight, watch the miniature feet and legs melt away into a formless, noxious pile. But he couldn't have kept his lighter going, couldn't have lit a joint in this much rain even if he'd had one. All he could do was toss the figures over the side, send them sailing through the downpour into the mud.

The little toys, he thought, those he could toss, but not the miner. He'd just let the miner grab the rifle and walk away, because when it came down to it, the only thing he could really do was lie.

Adam remembered how after Leonard's funeral, Krista had hunted him down at the convenience store. There'd been rumours that she'd been the one who double-crossed them, and she was no longer welcome at the apartment.

"Why weren't you there?" she asked, trailing behind him into the back lane. "I snuck in, you know, way at the back and you weren't there. How come? He was your brother."

Adam had kept going, trying to ignore her, but she kept on his heels, brushing her parka-covered breasts against his arm, whispering close in his ear, laughing too loud. "You know what I think? I think you're not so tough."

He'd swung around then and knocked her hard onto the ice. "I was there. I was fucking there."

Now, hundreds of miles from that inner city back lane, he was sure the bears were starting to circle somewhere, hungry after the long drought. He could see Krista's face as she'd sat like a rag doll on the ice, legs out in front of her, still laughing a little. He could see her licking the blood from her lips, lifting her arms and motioning to him to join her, and he knew if he'd bent down to her and wrapped his hands around her throat, squeezing tight with his gloveless hands, she would not have resisted, would have only looked at him with those glazed, pleading eyes. So he'd run, away from Krista, away from his blood brothers and his street brothers, away from everything, until he'd found himself here, sitting high in the dark forest.

As Toby watched minute after minute blink by on the dashboard clock, he grew more frustrated with himself. Too agitated to sleep, he gripped the steering the wheel with both hands like he was ten years old and pretending to drive, growing sweatier and sweatier in the vinyl poncho. He knew he should take the stupid thing off, but couldn't seem to make himself do it. Instead he watched the raindrops make their way across the windshield, caught between gravity and the growing wind, each one taking a different path. They seemed to have no purpose or reason for the course they took, colliding with other drops and then changing directions, just like that. He could never tell which way a particular drop would go, how it might gradually make its way to the lower edge of the glass then disappear from view.

One minute, he would decide that he didn't owe the asshole anything, that he deserved to rot up there. Yet each time he took hold of the keys in the ignition, Toby made a new deal with himself. Ten more minutes, then ten more, then ten more. And the longer he stayed, the more he began to not just feel like an idiot, but to truly believe he was one. Who else, he wondered, would still be sitting there waiting for a criminal who didn't want to come?

As he sat trapped in the truck, wide awake, without a plan, small things seemed to grow bigger in his mind. The drops of water, relentless and unpredictable as they washed over the glass. The little green dots on the clock blinking time. The L-shaped scrape on the back of his hand, still fresh from grabbing for a branch. The white skin of his knuckles gripping the steering wheel. The doubts that had been lurking beneath the surface for days.

"You can compete in the city, maybe," Rina had said a few days before, and he'd been flattered that she thought of it. "This could be your chance to get serious," she said, "to learn the history and the techniques, to really race in competition."

But it had been almost a week since she'd asked him to go with her, and he hadn't looked into it. He hadn't even told them at the mine that he was quitting. And what did that mean? What kind of idiot was happy training on his own for a competition that would never come? What kind of idiot doesn't go into work and give notice the minute a girl like Rina asks him to?

Toby punched at the horn with both fists, first short and choppy, then a long, irritating wail. "Who the fuck do you think you are?" he yelled, but there was no one to hear it but the rain.

Maybe girls like Rina were meant to leave, he thought, and guys like him were meant to stay. Maybe guys like Adam would always end up making fools of guys like Toby, leave them at a loss, hopeless and frustrated. Maybe he was no match for either of them.

"Do you remember that time," he'd said to Ally over a pool table last February, "when I got my tongue stuck on that metal sign outside the Co-op? It was really cold and I was maybe five and there was this icy snow that I decided to lick off and then *'aack!'* I'm stuck there. But your dad, he comes by and tells me to be calm and pours a cup of scalding hot tea over my mouth. So I'm screaming and screaming when my mom comes out and your dad's just standing there, looking stunned."

Ally had dared him to do it again that night and they went out into the street and he'd stuck his tongue against a downspout. Rina had gawked with her hand over her mouth, amused, but there was something about the way she stood, shoulders back and slightly apart from the pack that made it seem like she couldn't really believe she was here, in this freezing place with these crazy children.

When Ally returned with the warm water, she'd laughed until she was wiping tears from her eyes. "I didn't know," she spluttered, wiping her nose with her mitt. "My dad, he never told us. He never told us."

He'd been an idiot when he was five, Toby thought, and he still was one. Who else would do something like that to impress a girl like Rina? All it did was get Ally laughing like only she could, jumping up and down like a kid who's going to pee their pants. Maybe that's why he'd always felt so comfortable with her. Ally never seemed to mind acting like an idiot. She was just Ally, always there, ready to laugh at his jokes, ready to let him feel like he was better than he was.

Toby turned over the ignition and watched the windshield wipers spring to life. Why hadn't he thought of her before? It was Ally who'd gotten him into this and it was Ally who would get him out of it.

He turned the truck around in the narrow path, snapping small trees and squishing undergrowth as he went. His brand-new tires moved through the muck with ease as the branches swatted at the side mirrors with a satisfying spray. Shifting gears, clearing fog from the windshield with his fist, he gave the engine a little gas. Ally's cousin wasn't going anywhere and she wasn't either — she would be at the shop where she always was. But it was good to know the tires had been worth the money, good to feel the heavy vehicle forcing its way through at a good clip.

By the time he spied the shiny grey strip of highway through the bush, Toby could already see her as he walked in the store, her round pink face lighting up in surprise, then her arms dropping everything to come to him.

Across a rain-slicked surface steel met steel, and then steel met rock. The natural laws of force and motion declared themselves with an awful, wrenching *crunch*. Then there was nothing but stillness.

When Toby regained consciousness, a hand was reaching in and coming to rest just inside the window, beside a shard of glass in the shape of an iceberg. The windshield was now a spider web, intricate and beautiful, but all Toby could feel were raindrops against his left ear. The nails on the hand were chewed, the tips of the fingers a smoker's yellow.

"How you doing there, buddy?"

It was a gravelly voice, low and breathless. Toby wanted to laugh. "Never been better," he wanted to say. But instead, there was only the taste of tin and salt.

"They're coming," the voice said. "They said they're coming, buddy."

They're coming, Toby said to himself, *they're coming, they're coming, they're coming*. Ally always said "they," he thought, as if you were supposed to know who that was.

"They're coming," the voice said again. "Christ, you came from nowhere. Christ."

But Toby didn't hear him anymore than you might hear background music in a restaurant. His mind was still with Ally. He'd been on his way to her and now he wasn't.

There was something he needed to tell her.

"There's somebody back there," he said, his tongue strangely thick between his teeth. "In the bush."

Then there was a face near his, a fat man's heavy, panicked breathing, water dripping from a purple, bulbous nose.

"What's that?"

Toby closed his eyes and concentrated on the words. "He's still there," he said, "in the bush, on the perch."

When he opened his eyes again, the hand was still there. There was a wedding ring. Somebody loved the ugly truck driver.

"You don't worry. You don't worry about nothing. We'll look after him. Help is coming, help is coming, buddy."

Toby wanted to say something else but couldn't remember what it was. The world was flashing in and out now, like a strobe light in slow motion. What had he been thinking about? Something about the cottage, his parents' land, where he and Lyle had peed on the rocks to christen them while Sharon and his sisters laughed, pretending to be disgusted.

"This is ours," Lyle had said. "Christ, it feels great."

He'd been thinking of lying with Rina in front of the fire, naked under the striped flannel blanket that was always there and smelled like the sun.

Through the spider web, there were sweeping arcs of red against the gleaming rocks.

There were more voices, serious and calm in the distance.

There was the large hand against his face. "Hang in there, buddy."

The skin felt rough, yet warm and wet, like his dog's nose when she was old and feeling under the weather. Toby rested his cheek in the warm palm and closed his eyes again.

It's so dark, he thought, as his lungs filled with blood and grew still, *and so quiet.*

But that's good, because I'm tired.

PETROGLYPHS

13

WHEN THE POLICE CAME to the house, Lyle was asleep and Sharon was at the office running letters through the postage machine, sorting them into neat piles depending on their destination. Years later, Lyle would have no memory of opening the door in his bathrobe, of stumbling into his pants while the two officers waited silently in the landing, of riding through the rain in the cruiser with lights flashing. What he would remember was coming into the mailroom and seeing his wife's hands resting on the neat piles, her lips set like they sometimes would when interrupted mid-task, her eyes moving back and forth from one police officer to the other, until they finally landed on him, fierce and pleading. It would remind him of years before, when the delivery of their second daughter had gone into its twentieth hour. During the worst pains, Sharon had looked up at him and he'd felt a kind of anguish so raw that he'd had to step away and hide behind the striped curtain so he could catch his breath.

Neither Lyle nor Sharon noticed the rain starting to ease as Lyle fumbled with the lock on their front steps, neither thanked the police officer when he gently took the keys from Lyle and let them in. Neither were aware of how long they were back at home — minutes, or hours, or days — before Ally's knocking rattled their screen door.

A police cruiser had pulled up in front of the store as well. Ally had been sweeping up some rice when she saw Adam's hunched bulk emerge onto the curb. Bewildered, she had watched him cross through the store and start up the stairs.

"Hey, what are you doing?" she'd finally asked. "What happened?"

Adam had stopped about midway up, but hadn't turned around. The only thing moving was his knee.

"What did you do?" she asked. "Where's Toby?"

He'd started up the stairs again. "He had an accident. The truck is totalled."

"What do you mean?" she asked, louder. "Is he okay? Where is he?"

"No," he said. "I don't know."

"What do you mean?" she shouted, but he'd already disappeared into the apartment.

Ally had grabbed the keys to Ruth's truck from beneath the cash desk and raced through the rain-washed streets. She'd thought of Toby in a hospital bed, surrounded by stuffed toys and cards and balloons. It would be dark in the room, the middle of the night or early morning, and she would be sleeping upright in a metal chair beside him when she'd feel a hand on her knee. She would jump a little in surprise and he would laugh even though it hurt him.

What are you doing here? he'd ask.

She would shrug. *Where else would I be?*

Then he would leave his hand resting on her knee, and she would say what she always said.

When Ally arrived at their door, Lyle answered as if on autopilot: someone knocks, so you get up and you see who it is. But when he saw her through the screen, chewing her nails and looking like a lost sheep, his first thought was to send her away. "He's out," he wanted to say through the screen. "He's out skiing. He'll call you girls later."

He thought of his own daughters, who'd set up tents on the lake just the night before. They did this every year, the girls and their families getting together around the bonfire, an interim measure while the cottage was still in planning. Not long ago, he'd bought them each a cellphone in case of emergency, and this morning, as the rain had pounded the shingles overhead, he'd dreamt of them calling him up as they rode on inflatable beds down the rising flood water. "You've got to come, Dad," they'd cried happily. "It's such a rush."

When the police officers had offered to drive him there, Lyle had said, *no, no thanks, I'll get there myself.* Yet he had no idea how he would tell his daughters the unthinkable.

Ally pushed her way through, letting the screen door snap behind her. She walked straight onto the beige carpet without taking her runners off then suddenly stopped, as if an invisible precipice had opened up in the middle of the living room.

Sharon was curled up in an armchair, hugging her knees with her work pumps still on.

"How is he?" Ally asked, "Is he at the hospital? Why aren't you at the hospital?"

But Toby's mother didn't respond, like she was asleep with her eyes open. Ally turned back to Lyle.

"Highway 9," he said, He looked out through the screen as if the drizzle held some kind of clue. "What was he doing on Highway 9?"

"Hunting," Ally said. This was one thing she was certain of. "They were hunting."

Lyle kept shaking his head. "Not yet. Not for another month."

"I know, but they were," Ally said. "He went with Adam. This morning, they went."

Sharon sat up then, suddenly alert. This was the Sharon Ally knew, ready to jump up and let Toby know they'd arrived. "Loverboy," Lyle would always shout, "you expecting someone?" and so Sharon would roll her eyes, put aside the paper, go to the basement door. "The girls are here," she'd say, quiet and dignified, just loud enough for Toby to yell back "What?"

With her work skirt crumpled at her waist, Ally could see the dark shade of Sharon's underpants through her pantyhose.

"Adam who?" Sharon asked. "Who's Adam?"

"My cousin," Ally said. "He said the truck was totalled. Why aren't you at the hospital?"

Sharon stood up, a wounded animal unsteady in her heels. The girl's everyday presence in the middle of a nightmare made it hard to breath. The girl was here, the one whose father had left long ago, the one who always made popcorn in their kitchen like it was her own. But her baby was gone. The girl was here, alone now, because her baby boy was gone, and he would not be back.

"But what was Toby doing with him?" she asked. "What was he doing with that kid? He had no business with that kid."

Ally looked down at her runners, wet and gritty on the carpet.

"What was he doing?" Sharon repeated, almost a whisper now as she eased back into the chair. "What was he doing?"

Lyle stood helplessly, watching his wife curled up and silent once again, watching his son's friend breathe as quick as a frightened rabbit. When the phone began to ring, none of them moved.

It's the telephone, Lyle told himself. *You hear the ring, and you pick up the receiver, and you see who's calling.*

As soon as he heard her voice, he remembered how beautiful Rina was.

"Hi," she said. "Shouldn't you be sleeping? Is he making you answer the phone now too?"

Even when young, Lyle thought, Sharon hadn't been beautiful. But he'd loved her long, athletic build. He'd loved the way she would laugh at him, revealing that tiny, sexy space between her front teeth, loved the way she could hold her liquor.

Lyle swallowed and told himself to speak. *Someone asks a question, and you respond.* "There was an accident," he said. "He was in an accident. On Highway 9."

He could hear her breathing.

"Is he all right?" she asked.

Lyle shook his head. Then, "No. He's gone."

There was more breathing. "You mean dead?"

"Yes," Lyle said. "Dead."

There was silence, then a sudden, final *click*.

For a minute or two, Lyle kept the receiver to his ear, listening to the wailing buzz of the phone line. Years ago, during the long delivery, the nurse had given him a stopwatch and asked him to tell her each time a two-minute interval had gone by. Even while doing it, he'd suspected it was just to keep him out of the way, but he hadn't cared.

He hung up and went to the bathroom. When he came back into the living room with a couple of warm face-cloths, Ally was gone.

Sharon took one of the cloths from him and clenched it into an angry ball, like she was trying to squeeze water from stone. Lyle knew that he had to tell his daughters now, and the cellphones he'd bought them could not help him. His hard-working men at the mine could not help him. His steady, smiling Sharon could not help him. His strong, love-struck Toby could not help him.

This wasn't the maternity ward, and there was no striped curtain to hide behind.

In the dream-like days that followed, familiar faces drifted in and out with smelly casseroles, saying the same thing over and over the way Lyle's vinyl records had skipped when he and Sharon were young.

In between small tasks, he would find himself suddenly in the back yard, squinting and alone, with no memory of where he'd come from or why. Sharon would sit curled in the chair, listening to the everyday chatter that had been her life—open casket or closed, blue flowers or white—and feel herself falling in a dream where you never hit the earth, in endless limbo between the sky and ground, further and further away from the everyday voices of her daughters, from the mix of spicy deodorant and sweat that was Toby's T-shirts in the hamper, further and further from her little boy, his white teeth smiling in a grime-covered face.

In her grief and in her shame, Ally's imagination, freshly honed and powerful, would only serve to intensify her pain. After Toby's death, the old Ally was nowhere to be found. She would not go back for more of Sharon's quiet accusations. She would not look at Adam when they crossed paths in the bathroom doorway. She would not call Rina. Nothing mattered but the nightmare of "ifs" that had taken over her daydreams.

If she'd never asked Adam to go with them to the rocks. If she hadn't suggested Toby take him hunting. If she hadn't agreed to call Toby that morning. If she hadn't given Adam her alarm clock. If Adam had never showed up at their door. They all blended one into the other as the television blared and Ruth shuffled up and down the stairs and day turned into night.

Now and then, Ruth paused in Ally's bedroom doorway, but her offers of chocolate-covered raisins or jam sandwiches were always refused. Ally only rolled towards the wall as Ruth stood staring at the back of her daughter's head, exhausted from running things all by herself, feeling bent and useless and old.

"I'm closing the shop tomorrow, for the funeral," she finally offered.

Ally didn't even acknowledge the gesture, didn't seem to care that her mother was shutting down completely in the middle of the business week.

At the funeral, Ally was barely aware that Ruth stood stiffly at her side, sweating in the stuffy church. It was a beautiful August morning and the townspeople had piled into the nondescript brick building until there was no more room and they had to spill out onto the freshly mowed square of grass. Surrounded by faces she'd known her whole life, Ally might as well have been alone in the long wooden pew. When Lyle nodded distractedly in her direction, she kept her eyes to the floor. When the minister began his slow, gentle eulogy, when Toby's sisters got up one by one and spoke of their little brother, so playful, so loveable, so athletic, she barely heard their words over the whirring racket of "ifs" running through her mind.

It wasn't until near the end of the service, as she automatically got up to join the procession shuffling past the polished casket, that she noticed Merik standing off a little to the side. He was holding up the line and nodding slightly, as if giving his approval for the photographs on top of the casket — Toby with his dog at age five, Toby with braces at eleven, Toby with the silly furry collar at graduation. Rina's father was unmistakable in his freshly-pressed grey suit, his hair combed back to reveal the kind of broad, low forehead that is attractive only on a man. He was alone, and Ally immediately twisted around, scanning the crowd of grim faces.

Way back in the crowded foyer, she thought she saw the top of Adam's head, his black hair shining almost blue in the midday light, his bulk nearly overwhelmed by the mass of bodies straining shoulder to shoulder on the doorstep. But there was no sign of Rina.

As soon as the solemn miners carried Toby away in the shiny box, Ally reached for Ruth's purse. "I'm taking the truck."

Ruth unquestioningly fished out the keys, relieved to do this simple thing for her daughter, relieved to see her go.

When Slavenka came to the door, she still wasn't dressed. If Merik had stood out in his handsomeness, his smooth doctor's hands clasped over the perfect folds of his jacket, Slavenka's appearance was worse than when Ally had seen her last. The yellow silk robe hung limply around her shoulders. Her skin looked sallow against the bright colour.

She gripped Ally hard by the wrist and led her wordlessly up the stairs to Rina's bedroom. She knocked quietly, then opened the door halfway without an answer.

"Look who it is," she said gently, shoving Ally through. "It's your little friend."

With the curtains drawn, it took Ally's eyes a moment to adjust. Rina appeared to be sitting on the floor like a rag doll, leaning back against the wooden bed frame, staring at a glass of orange juice on a tray. Her hair was pulled back in an elastic and her ears looking strangely small and exposed.

At the sight of her friend, Toby's absence became real to Ally for the first time. Even though they'd always known Rina would leave, even though the daydreams had started, even though Toby had said he was leaving too, it had never seemed like it would really happen. But it was final now — there would never be the three of them again.

When Ally finally spoke, it was between sobs. "Where were you?"

Rina pushed the juice further away on the tray. "I'm bad luck. You should leave."

"I didn't even want them to go," Ally choked out. "It was a stupid idea."

"Who's them?" Rina asked. But she seemed more interested in picking at the plush carpet. "Was somebody with him?"

"Adam," Ally said. "Adam asked me to phone him, about the hunting, and so I did. But how was I supposed to know?"

Rina threw her head back and looked like she was gearing up for a good laugh. After she'd hung up on Lyle, she hadn't cried. When she'd told Merik and Slavenka that they didn't have to worry, that Toby was dead, her voice hadn't even cracked. And now, her friend's choking tears left her unmoved. The fact that Toby had kept things from her barely registered.

"It doesn't matter," she said. "Don't you get it?"

The sobs were coming too fast for Ally to respond.

"You should leave," Rina said.

So Ally obediently retreated, stumbled her way through a house she barely recognized, all her "ifs" drowned out. Now there was nothing but questions: How could you love someone and not be there to say goodbye? How could you be someone's friend and not tell them the most important things of all?

Afterwards, Rina remained motionless in the dim room until she noticed something on the tray she'd kicked away. It was a small orange pill no bigger than the tip of her pinkie.

"She needs rest," she'd heard Merik say on his way out the door in the morning, and she'd thought that it was her father who seemed exhausted.

Rina placed the pill on her tongue, leaving it until the bitterness became too much and she instinctively swallowed. With the acidic taste lingering in her throat, she reached for the purse that was still lying just inside the doorway, right where she'd thrown it so long ago, when she'd still been able to smell Toby on her fingertips. Lighting a cigarette, she leaned back against the hard wooden bed frame and inhaled deeply, waiting. First, the burning tobacco overpowered the sick, acid taste, then it travelled through her lungs until she was slightly lightheaded, but calm.

Let Ally believe she really thought she was cursed, Rina thought, let her believe that's why she'd skipped the funeral, why she was being so cold and quiet. It was easier that way, just another half-truth like all the others, delivered with a straight face to get through the day. Because now, Rina finally understood: what had happened to her in a place far away and what happened to Toby on some obscure highway had nothing to do with luck, good or bad. There was no magic at work. She always watched Slavenka pray, muttering into her hands, repeating the rituals over and over with such intensity, and wondered: why would this unseen presence up in the heavens give Slavenka's prayers more weight than any others? Back home, people who nearly lost their lives, who left a building just moments before it collapsed, whose earlobe was grazed by a sniper's bullet, would say that God had been watching over them. But why had God put them there in the first place? No, there was no magic. There was no handy, far-reaching explanation. Toby's death only confirmed what she'd suspected since that hideous night when the cats had meowed, pitiful and alert, crawling over her in their anxiousness, while the voices echoed in a dank cellar like the dungeon in a fairytale.

Though it could fool you some of the time, she knew, the world, at its heart, was cruel and petty. She had not wanted this to be true, had fought hard not to believe. But she could no longer deny it. There were no happy endings.

Rina doused the cigarette in her juice and climbed into bed. Within minutes, she was dreaming the dream, the one she'd come to know well, except for one small alteration over the last few months.

Lately, she was no longer a child, but as old as she was now, standing tall amongst the crowd lined up shoulder-to-shoulder along the road. Everything else was the same — she was still at her grandmother's, no longer bored, no longer homesick, straining to see what was creating such a stir.

As usual, the black snake moved through the hill of green and the people, young and old and in-between began to wail, some loud, some soft. Only now, when the snake slithered close enough to become people and Rina began to sense what their burden was, she didn't need to be lifted. She could see for herself, stand on her own feet amidst the amazing, relentless sway and jostle, could raise her own arms, almost reach out and touch it herself.

It was a body wreathed in flowers of every colour. Except this time, as Rina lay cradled in the deep, sinking rest of Merik's little pill, something else was different.

This time, it was Toby amongst the colourful wreaths.

It was his young face, fresh and clear and perfect as the flowers. There was no dirt from the mine. There was no sign of a fleeting temper on his brow. It was Toby, yet not Toby, so still and perfect and dead.

Rina woke before she could touch him, and found herself trembling not in fear, but in anger. Kicking the quilt from her bed, she wanted to lash out, to pull her pillow to bits, to bite at her tongue. But all she did was clench her jaw and lie helplessly.

How could someone like Toby be taken, all at once, with no mercy? How could something so beautiful and brief become an endless nightmare?

The door opened a crack. "Can I come in?" Slavenka asked.

Her jaw set, Rina didn't respond, and the crack grew to a gaping hole of light.

"You need to eat," her mother said. She stepped in and picked up the tray. "It's already past six. You need to eat."

Rina knew if she didn't reply, Slavenka would never leave.

Though it wasn't Sunday, she implored her mother in their language of lullabies. "Please, let me sleep. Leave me be."

When Slavenka came back into the kitchen, gripping the tray as if holding on for dear life, Merik was there, still in his suit from the funeral. All afternoon, he'd worn his white coat over his tie and dress shirt and patients had spoken of the retreating fires, their aches and pains, their memories of a boy who'd been famous for daring to ski in a snowmobile town.

"She hates us," Slavenka said.

Merik threw his suit jacket over a chair and went to the sink to wash his hands. "Don't be dramatic."

"How can you say that?" she asked. "Can't you see what's happening?"

"Yes, I can see," he said. "I can see you're not dressed."

Then the tray came crashing down and Slavenka after it, as if her body, the lovely source of so much admiration, had betrayed her too. She sank onto her hands and knees beside the broken glass.

Merik worked hard not to turn away in disgust. For their first anniversary far from war and fear, he'd splurged and bought her that yellow robe. He'd stood in wonder as she modeled it, prancing back and forth like a colt.

"You're sure yellow is the right colour?" she'd asked.

"Why do you always have to question?" he'd laughed. "Of course it's right."

When he took her arm now, calmly but firmly guiding her up, she let him lead her to the couch unquestioningly, took the little orange pill he handed her and dutifully swallowed.

He covered her with his suit jacket, then rested his hand on her forehead as if taking her temperature. One time, he'd treated an injured guerilla soldier whose machine gun had misfired. Torn between the duty to heal and the urge to kill, Merik had stitched the wounded hand with zealous care and precision.

"Hush," he said now to his beloved Slavenka, gentle and soothing over her pathetic, sobbing body. "Hush."

Later, after mopping up the juice from the floor, after sweeping the shards of glass into a paper bag, Merik got into his red truck and drove through the sloping streets of the town, with no idea where he was going or why.

He'd been moved by the funeral, the automatic gathering of the community, the sincere and united grief. As he'd followed the service, kneeling and rising as directed, filing past the coffin in his turn, he'd remembered why he did this every Sunday. Somehow, for a little while each week, it brought back a childhood long discarded, a village he barely remembered, where his parents had lived and died amongst the same three hundred people. It made him ashamed that Rina had been right, that some part of him had felt relief that the miner was gone. That he still felt it, even now.

After a half-hour or so, Merik pulled into the parking lot of the new hotel owned by one of his patients. He walked into the bar that he'd been invited to more times than he could count. It was a busy, noisy place, with a different sport playing on each of four big-screen televisions.

"Hey, Doc," someone said, "what are you standing there for," and he let himself be led in, penitent and ashamed.

The next morning, as Ruth handled the pre-lunch rush downstairs, Ally emerged from her bedroom and looked at Adam for the first time in days. He was on the couch smoking a cigarette, staring straight ahead at the silent, black television screen.

"Why weren't you in the truck?" she asked.

Her nose was so stuffed up it took Adam a moment to understand what she'd said. "He bailed. I wanted to stay."

Her eyes were swollen and ringed pink as a rabbit's. Snot ran unchecked into her mouth. Adam grabbed the remote and brought the television to life. "He left without me."

When Ally still didn't say anything, Adam turned up the volume and waited until he heard her bedroom door shut softly.

When he'd heard the sirens from his soggy perch, Adam was convinced the miner had turned him in. For a long time, he sat frozen by indecision, not sure whether to run like hell into the endless forest, or shout out desperately to the circling voices. In the end, there'd been no decision to make. When the searchers appeared in their bright yellow ponchos, he obediently came down and followed them through the rain, stumbling and practically limp with relief.

They stopped just before the clearing and told him about the accident. In the cruiser, they gave him a blanket as if it were cold out rather than muggy, and when they approached the highway, the one in the passenger seat with a big, tough-guy mustache looked back in concern.

The truck was still there, but there was nothing left to suggest it was the same structure of sleek metal Adam had admired just hours before. The violence of the crash had left it mangled, ugly and misplaced against the coppery, rain-washed rocks.

"He was conscious for a few minutes," the mustache said. "Hard to believe. But he went fast. He didn't suffer any real pain."

Adam knew he was trying to comfort him, that he thought he and the miner had been friends. "I barely knew him."

"What's that?" the mustache asked.

But Adam hadn't said anything more.

Afterwards, as Ruth acted busy and Ally pretended he wasn't there, the numbness he once longed for began to consume him. Though he knew his time at Ruth's was swiftly running out, he found himself unable to focus on his next move. He would see Leonard's body again and again, battered-in like the truck, and it was as if he were still stranded on the soggy platform, the water rising like a flood until he was treading up to his chin, every move and every breath coming more and more laboured.

On the day of the funeral, the deathly quiet of the apartment, once so soothing, had only seemed to mock him and he'd found himself following Ally and Ruth across the street and into the throngs of mourners. When he'd arrived, conspicuous in his jeans and T-shirt, the latecomers had been milling in the churchyard, straining through the heavy wooden doors to assess what space was left. *Go in*, he'd told himself, *let Auntie Ruth see you paying your fucking respects.*

But he remained lost in the crowd on the steps, halfway in, halfway out, remembering how it had been just a few months ago that his father Vincent had worn a navy blue tie, knotted too tightly and hanging too long, like a boy in his father's clothes. It had been a warm March day and Adam had hid behind a minivan in visitor parking, watching his mother get out of the shiny, black hearse. Vincent had already gotten out the other side, was already surrounded by the friends and relatives filing in by twos and threes, but Lucille seemed stuck. Her feet were already on the pavement, but she was still sitting inside.

Before Adam could reach her, the driver from the funeral home was already there. The driver was a stranger, yet Lucille was automatically taking his hand, letting him pull her up. When she saw her son, she let go and nodded as if she'd been expecting him all along. "Where've you been?"

Adam looked down, noticed her fat feet stuffed into high-heeled shoes. "I've been around."

"I didn't recognize him," she'd said. "In the hospital there. It didn't even look like him."

Part of Adam had wanted to get down on his knees right there in the parking lot, to grab onto her thighs and bury his face in her hips. Then he would refuse to budge, like when he was very small and didn't want to go to bed.

"When he was young, he was the cutest of you all," Lucille said. "Then his teeth went bad."

So Adam's mother Lucille had lost her baby boy, just as Toby's mother would. When Leonard had been small, he would suck his thumb until it was wrinkled and Lucille would pull it out, again and again, until she gave up and watched him run from her, even while he was still unsteady on his feet, but fearless, laughing, until she was laughing too. But unlike Sharon, Lucille had never let tragedy become a stranger. Unlike Rina, she felt no anger at its return.

Rina had taken her first steps in a world where every door seemed open and she need only grab the hand of those who loved her like no other and explore all that seemed beautiful, or tasty, or interesting, or amusing. The ancient city of Sarajevo had once been living, breathing proof of what is possible here on Earth and this intimate sense of what was possible was what would ultimately leave her so angry later on.

But Adam's mother had learned at an early age to expect little, to accept her insignificance and fret not, to take her pleasures where she could. She'd watched her father drink himself to death, watched diabetes take her mother away, limb by limb. She'd watched her husband Vincent move from job to job, looking for something he could not name, absorbing each blow, one after the other, always bouncing back to try again and again and again. She didn't know how he managed it, but over the years she'd accepted that she and Vincent would die without each other. His sister Ruth, watching them in fear and judgment as they'd rolled entwined in the bloody snow, had never understood this. She would run away, change her phone number, and never understand.

So whatever her disappointment in her boys, in her string of rental houses, in the world, Lucille didn't blame Adam for what had happened, didn't blame Vincent, didn't blame herself. Yet this wouldn't stop her guilty son from turning away, away from his own brother's funeral, away from his mother standing unsteadily in her high-heeled shoes.

"I have to get out of here," he'd said to her. "I'll see you later, I'll come by the house."

She didn't blame Adam, but that didn't keep him from sensing only accusation in her sad, matter-of-fact voice. Or keep him from flipping through the channels as Ally sniffled disgustingly in the other room, looking for something, anything to replace the *thud*, the mangled truck, the sight of Lucille stuck in the horrible funeral car as if too exhausted to haul herself out.

The accusation would float all around him, lapping like waves in his ears. *The others are dead,* it whispered, *and yet you remain.*

You remain, like the coward that you are.

Later in the week, after the traffic of helpful neighbours had slowed, Slavenka got dressed, and did her hair, and went to Sharon and Lyle.

When she came to the door, Lyle didn't recognize her, but he let her in and took her tangy-smelling casserole. It wasn't until she spoke that he understood, and wondered for the first time where Rina had been.

He brought Slavenka tea, and the way he handed it to her, carefully and eagerly, filled her with a kind of tenderness she hadn't felt for a long, long time. Not since she'd been young and romantic and generous. Not since she'd fallen in love with a mountain boy.

"He was going to go to the city, you know," Sharon said. "He loved her."

Though the tea was weak, she welcomed the hot drink.

As Slavenka had put on her lipstick before leaving the house, Rina had appeared at the bathroom door. "You always do this," Rina had said. "You never wanted to meet them before. Don't bother them."

But Slavenka had felt the terrifying heaviness again and she knew she must go, right then, no matter what her daughter said.

She sipped at her tea and smiled gently at Sharon. "Yes, I know. He was a fine boy."

Sharon's face crumpled then. "He was still a boy," she said, though she knew quite well it wasn't true. He'd been a tall, graceful man.

Setting her cup aside, Slavenka went to Sharon and crouched down beside the chair. "It is not for us to understand. It is not for us."

Sharon didn't believe her. There was no reason she shouldn't understand. But there was something about the woman's voice, strange and melodic, that soothed her. The minister, who she'd seen every Saturday at the meat counter, who'd she'd seen dance like a chicken at a wedding — his words had left Sharon empty. But there was something about the accent that made Sharon want to trust in it, to lean in and let this strange, sad, beautiful woman stroke her hair like a child.

"It is not for us," Slavenka said, over and over, "not for us," and for the first time in many years, she felt at peace.

14

TEN DAYS AND NIGHTS went by, but for those who'd loved Toby most it was like the world had become static. The sun rose and set along a distant horizon, the minutes ticked nearby on a kitchen clock. Yet the passage of time meant nothing. It was as if they had willed everything to stop as soon as they were aware that Toby himself had stopped — as long as they were alive, though, they didn't have much choice in the matter.

On a warm mid-August night, Ruth was at the adding machine when the phone rang. She glanced over at Ally, who'd been sitting over a cold piece of meatloaf for the last hour. Adam had disappeared into the bathroom right after dinner.

Ruth let the phone ring, her fingers flying over the keys as she continued to work her way through the pile of receipts. For years, she'd known she should do more of her bookkeeping by computer, but there was something about the way the little blue numbers instantly appeared, the way the paper roll steadily inched through the adding machine that she found too satisfying to give up.

On the eighth ring, she pushed her chair back and grabbed a slice of the meatloaf from Ally's plate. She was still chewing when she answered.

"Ruthie?"

"No," she wanted to say. "No." But the old name grabbed hold.

"How'd you get this number?" she asked.

"Your ex, there," Vincent said. "Harry. He's in the book,"

Ruth swallowed. "He gave you my number?"

"Yeah," he laughed. "I told him I was dying."

Before she could stop herself, Ruth laughed too. It was just like Harry to believe something like that.

"But no joke," Vincent said. She heard him swallow a sob. "We've had some hard times here, Ruthie. Our boy Leonard was killed."

Ruth felt the grip tightening. If Vincent's laughter could make her feel like she was twelve-years old again — still relying on her little brother to be kind, still ready to be sucked in, yet excluded at the same time — his tears were something else. That break in his voice was why she'd forgiven him over and over, helpless against his manic enthusiasm, his careless compassion and quick remorse. Helpless against all that made him such a popular failure.

Leonard? Ruth wondered. Which one was Leonard?

"I'm sorry, Vince," she said. "I'm so sorry."

Adam emerged from the bathroom, his hair freshly washed and slicked back like a gangster in the movies, and Ruth remembered. Her brother's son, not dead Leonard, but another one, was here in her home, unwanted and ungrateful.

"Adam is here," she said.

There was a brief pause. "My Adam? Up there with you?"

"That's what I said," Ruth replied.

"Shit, he's with you?" Vincent asked. He was laughing now, like he always did when he was confused. "All this time? Is he there, right now?"

Ruth watched Adam go to the fridge, one of her cigarettes dangling from his mouth like it had sprouted from his lip.

"Give a cig to Ruthie," Vincent had always said when they were young. "And she needs a drink. Don't forget Ruthie."

Ruth carefully placed the receiver on the kitchen table beside Ally and went to the couch. She fished out the remote control from beneath a cushion and turned on the television. "It's for you, Adam," she said.

Still empty-handed, Adam closed the fridge and looked to Ally for some kind of explanation. All he got was a blank stare.

A fucking night's sleep, he'd told himself in the shower, *a good fucking night's sleep is all you need.* But lately, it was like everything was conspiring to keep him awake: the whirring of the fridge, the rattle of the air conditioner, the staccato snorts of Ruth's snoring. It was always something, and the lack of sleep had started doing things to his brain. Just that morning, while still under the afghan, he'd imagined setting himself on fire. With a single match, he'd started with the hem of his jeans and then just stood and waited as the heat climbed upwards, until his clothes were all alight and the flames were licking at his eyelashes. Just a few minutes ago, while stepping out of the shower, he'd imagined slicing a hole in the bathroom window screen, then climbing out onto the ledge and diving head first, down, down, down until he was nothing but a *splat* in the back alley.

Adam looked from Ally to Ruth and back again, but neither would even make eye contact. It was like he'd already done it — like he'd already jumped from their lives and was nothing but a mess of blood and guts to be hosed off the pavement.

He picked up the phone and waited.

"Adam, is that you?"

"Yeah," he said. "Who do you think."

Vincent laughed — the same laugh as when the teacher had come to visit about Adam, smiling sweetly and saying she hadn't expected his parents to be home in the middle of the day.

"We knew you were somewhere," Vincent said. "But how'd you end up with Ruthie?"

Adam watched Ally take her fork and dig the prongs into her left palm. It left four evenly spaced indents in her soft flesh. "It wasn't hard," he said. "I looked her up."

Vincent laughed harder. "Right," he said, "right. You always have your ways."

Adam waited. Eventually, his father's laughter weakened into a small chuckle, then just a clearing of the throat. "But listen, your mom," Vincent said, "she's in the hospital, but she's okay. Just a little setback with the diabetes. But they say she's okay, just going to keep her a few days."

Adam thought of the last time he'd visited his mother in the hospital, when her round face had looked so small and dark inside the starchy white pillow. He thought of how with fire, it was nice and clean. There would be nothing left of you but ashes.

"You know, little man, the police have been around," Vincent said. "Somebody snitched on you."

Sucking out the last of his cigarette, Adam closed his eyes. *Just one fucking night's sleep*, he thought.

"Yeah, I know," he said.

"What did you do?" Vincent asked.

"It doesn't matter," Adam said. "It'll blow over."

There was a pause, but Vincent didn't press him. "You been back home?" he asked. "The old place?"

At first, Adam wondered what the idiot was babbling about. The old place? But then he knew: his father meant where the old man had sat on the steps. Where they'd rolled little Ally over and over in the tall grass.

"I hear they're doing better," Vincent went on. "Making some improvements. It's going to take millions, though, billions, to make up for the shit we've gone through. That land they gave us was worth shit. Less than shit. At least with shit you can grow stuff."

"I have no wheels," Adam said. "I'm fucking stuck here."

Vincent laughed. "Right, yeah. But you should go, sometime, just to see."

Though it was the whole reason that he'd called in the first place, Vincent didn't press his son any further. He didn't tell Adam about how when the medics had come and found his mother passed out from diabetic shock, they'd asked if she was drunk.

"Just help her," Vincent had said. "Just fucking help her."

Later, after three hours of staring at antiseptic yellow walls until she was stabilized, he'd pulled a metal chair up to Lucille's bedside. "You know what I was thinking?" he'd asked her. "I was thinking about the old place. Did you know my ma, she stayed there pretty much her whole life?"

Lucille had closed her eyes. The ugly tube stuck in her arm had put colour back into her cheeks. "I got my own troubles, Vince," she'd said.

When he'd got home to the empty house, he'd found himself thinking about the old days again, back when Lucille smiled so wide her eyes disappeared in the crinkles and his big sister followed him around. He'd tried to remember how long it had been since he'd spoken to Ruth — not since her man had left and she'd grown cold. Not since she'd lent him the money to make a fresh start in the city and it had not been fresh enough for her.

"Leave me alone," she'd said, "stop calling, you ruin everything, I'm better on my own."

"No wonder he left you," he'd told her then. "You never did know how to have a good time. He left you because you're a bitch." Then Ruth had changed her number, and he'd let her go rather than face such harsh words again.

But in the empty house, with his Lucille far away in some hospital and his boys nowhere to be found, Vincent felt more alone than when he'd worked a few months counting cars in a tiny booth along the boulevard.

"I'm not sure I can trust your numbers," his boss had said after a few weeks, with the same look of frustration and regret that Vincent's bosses always had just before they fired him. "They always seem low."

"Fuck that," Vincent had replied, "you think I can't count?"

But the truth was, he'd hated every minute sitting over the ledger, lost by himself in the steady hiss of traffic. He'd missed his friends, missed his Lucille, missed his boys.

As the low evening light closed in around the crumbling porch and the only sound was Adam exhaling his final puff into the phone, the empty house seemed to taunt Vincent. *What about those*, it whispered to him, *what about those you will hear from no more, who've left the party, who've gone quiet not just for a week, or a year, or a decade, but forever?*

Where Vincent had grown up, it seemed you were never alone. There was always someone to laugh and to fight with, to pass the time and share a bottle; to let you know you were alive.

"Put Ruthie on again," he said to his son.

Adam went and dropped the phone in Ruth's lap. "It's for you."

She picked up without turning down the volume of her show.

"Hey, Ruthie," Vincent asked, "you been back to the old place?"

"No," she said.

"I was thinking, " Vincent said. "Ma, she never really left there, did she?" He spoke quickly, like he knew this might be his last chance. "Me, I've moved twenty, thirty times, but I've never been back. And I was thinking, about that time we went berry picking and you got chased by that big ol' mama bear. You got in between her and her cub and she just came at you like you were supper. And Ma just started yelling and banging a stick against the ground and then I started, and the poor thing stops in her tracks and spins around like in the cartoons. We had a good laugh over that one. We had some good times, eh?"

Ruth didn't reply. She could taste the sharp, lovely sweetness of saskatoons, could hear her mother making a racket as if possessed.

"All you have to do is make some noise," her mother had said when they got home, teasing now, elbowing Vincent with a knowing smile. "It's not so bad to know some of the old ways. You're not eaten up, Ruthie, and we'll make some nice jelly."

Then Ruth had begun to sob and there was more laughter.

"Hush," her mother had finally said. "A black bear won't eat you. They'd want your bucket maybe, but not you. You got to take a joke, eh, Ruthie."

Although she didn't know it, this was the real reason Ruth no longer spoke to her brother. It wasn't because he'd failed to repay her hard-earned money, or even because she really believed he'd driven her husband away. It was because he did not remember what she remembered. When you're the one laughing, purple berry stains around your mouth, your mother elbowing you knowingly, it's hard to notice the one still trembling with fear even as she dumps her bucket into the washtub.

Every time her brother had been kind, calling to her to join in — *come on Ruthie, come on* — it had been utterly spontaneous. He had been thoughtlessly kind, and this meant he was not to be relied upon. Sometimes he saw her, and sometimes he didn't.

Now, just at the sound of his voice, Ruth felt an exhausting mix of longing and despair. "I'm good where I am," she said.

In his empty house, Vincent threw up a hand in frustration. Was it too much to ask to have one lousy conversation after so long? What had it been, ten years? Twelve? But he didn't press his sister, just as he hadn't pressed his son.

What kind of kid refuses to sleep? he'd often asked himself. There'd always been an intensity to Adam that Vincent found unnerving, like the kid was always watching him, waiting to hold a grudge. And yet he was also the one Vincent always worried about least. If Adam thought it would blow over, it probably would.

"Yeah, why live in the past, eh?" Vincent said. "It'll only bite you in the ass."

"He can't stay here," Ruth said.

"No, no, just for a bit," Vincent said. "You can do that, can't you Ruthie? You have a nice place there I bet."

"He can't stay," she repeated.

"Yeah," Vincent said, laughing again. "Ruthie you haven't changed, you know that? Not one bit."

He couldn't blame Harry for leaving her, he thought. Lucille could be hard as nails, but she didn't always spit them like Ruth. She didn't always judge like that. She could take a joke.

At the thought of his wife, her hand squeezing his just ever-so-slightly when they'd hooked up the awful tubes, Vincent felt his throat grow thick once again.

Poor Ruthie, he thought, *poor little Ruthie all alone.*

"You do what you can," he said.

As soon as Ruth hung up, Ally watched Adam march over to her, arms crossed. "I need the truck," he said. "Just for tonight."

Ruth started flipping channels as if he hadn't said a word.

"I want to go back to the old place," he said.

"It's too late," she replied. "You won't even get there before dark."

But she was already getting up, fishing around her purse, tossing aside gum wrappers and lipsticks.

Ally stared as Ruth handed him her keys, then bent over her cold meatloaf again. It was pretty much the same way she'd been sitting earlier, when Harry had called that morning. Only then she'd been bending over corn flakes, watching them grow soggier and soggier as the answering machine picked up.

"Uh, Ally, it's your dad," Harry had said. "We have to start making some plans. At this point, I'm going to assume you're coming down, but give me call. The sooner the better."

There was a pause, and then the muffled whisper of a woman's voice. "We'd really like you to be here," Harry added. "This is important. So call me soon, okay?"

Ally had waited for the *click*, then went and rewound the tape. Even the second time through, she'd felt nothing: no anger, no annoyance. Only the desperate confusion that seemed to be consuming her.

Now, Adam grabbed something from the cupboard above the fridge and made a beeline for the door. Ally picked up a slice of ketchup-smothered meatloaf with her fork. *What if I flung this against the wall?* she wondered. *What would it matter? What would it matter when the worst thing that could happen had happened? And what would her asshole-of-a-father possibly know about it? Even if he did know, what could Harry possibly have to say that would matter?*

Hi Allison, he would have said. *How're you doing?*

Not so good, she would have replied.

No? What's up?

My friend Toby was killed.

He would've paused then, flustered. *Oh no. Was there a mining accident? There was no news coverage.*

No, not the mine, she would've said. *His truck was smashed.*

Allison, I'm so sorry. Toby who? Did I know him?

When he was five, you scorched his tongue with some tea.

Really? Are you making that up?

No. His tongue was stuck to a frozen pole and you tried to help.

I don't remember that.

No, she would've said, *you wouldn't.*

I don't remember, Allison. That was a long time ago, you know.

I know.

Well, I'm sorry to hear about your friend.

Yeah. So am I.

There would have been an awkward pause.

Listen, Allison, I need to know about the wedding.

Then she would've hung up.

Ally let the meatloaf drop back into the puddle of ketchup on her plate. Harry had scalded little Toby's tongue before she'd even known that Toby existed. And on that first night, when she'd called out to Toby from the bleachers, he'd burnt himself with hot chocolate. Did that mean something? she wondered. Was her family somehow destined to hurt Toby, even when all they wanted was to be there, to be around him, to make it better? Did these little things, these small coincidences mean anything at all?

Ally took her fork and pressed the prongs into her chin until it hurt. She had no idea if she wanted the little things to mean something or not.

That night, Adam grabbed onto Vincent's mention of the old place as if it were a dead tree floating along a flooded river. The last few days, he'd begun to wonder for the first time what it would be like to let himself sink beneath numbness. To end it all with a violent *bang, singe, crack* that led to nothing but the same weightless stillness. Then the phone had rung, and just like that, he'd found himself reaching up, grasping for the outrage that still floated somewhere above the surface.

Why hadn't he thought to go back there — that place of memories that had come like a waking dream during his first days in Ruth's apartment, more real than his hand in front of his face? Why hadn't he gone to stand as a witness on the dirt where his people had been robbed?

From the height of Ruth's truck cab, Franklin's shops and houses looked even squatter than that first morning Adam had stepped off the bus. The low sun was already throwing the streets into wide shadow and turning the lake a brilliant, dancing orange. As Adam got to the bridge, it seemed like he was moving over liquid fire, and he slowed down. He might have stopped completely if it weren't for an insistent honk from behind.

The driver was a youngish woman with trendy sunglasses. She threw up her arms in exasperation.

"What's your hurry, bitch?" he asked the rear-view mirror. "Can't somebody enjoy the scenery?"

He reached for the bottle of brandy he'd tossed on the passenger seat. Weeks earlier, he'd made note of the dusty bottle in the cupboard above the fridge but he hadn't been able to imagine drinking the shit until now. With one hand still on the wheel, Adam gripped the cap in his teeth, gave it a few twists, and took a swig. The stuff tasted just as awful as he'd expected.

"You in a rush?" he asked the mirror. "What's the matter? Don't you like fucking sunsets?"

When the horn sounded again, Adam took his foot off the gas and eased as slowly as he could into the new service station. He parked the truck in front of the convenience store and took another swig. *Us poor little city kids,* he silently told the honking bitch, *you think we saw fucking sunsets? We used to get excited over a bit of gas in a mud puddle.*

When he got out of the truck, the smell from the pumps seemed like an old friend. He paused for a moment, just breathing it in. *What else on Earth,* he thought, *could make a fucking rainbow in a pothole and destroy a drycleaners in minutes?*

Adam went inside and lingered behind a group of sport fisherman who were stocking up on junk food for the flight home. *Excuse me,* he imagined saying to the teenager at the cash register, the brandy fresh on his breath, *I have no valid driver's license, but would you tell how I might get to the shit-hole where your people stuck my people?* Instead he lingered by the door, casually spinning the revolving rack of maps until the noisy bastards descended on the cashier.

Back in the truck, he pulled the map from the front of his pants and struggled to spread it flat against the steering wheel. He'd hadn't had a reason to bother with maps since elementary school and was surprised by how spread out everything was. A red square near the bottom right marked Winnipeg, connected to a maze of dots. But as you moved up further, there was really nothing but blank pink land and blue water.

After a few minutes straining to see in the dying light, Adam found what he was looking for — a tiny black speck right in the middle, no bigger than a fleck of ash. So much pink fucking land, he thought, and there was still not enough. Somehow, his people had been stuck with a little speck in a place filled with endless, open nothing.

He took another swig of brandy, tried to remember something that would help him get his bearings. All he could recall was a little yellow sign shaped like an arrow, sitting at the end of the gravel road. He could feel the gravel in his runners as he and his brothers hiked down to the highway, could see them kicking at the sign pole, loosening its grip in the earth and then turning it around to face the opposite direction.

Adam nestled the bottle between his thighs and started up the truck. It looked easy enough. First straight south, then turn left and go east. He pushed the unfolded map onto a floor already littered with Ruth's discarded shopping lists and crushed cigarette packages and eased onto the highway.

It was already nearly dark when Rina heard the familiar sound of a truck pulling over.

Since the funeral, she'd begun retracing the paths where Toby used to train. She wandered further and further along the highway until the bush and rock closed in and she had to steady herself against the passing semis. She did this knowing full well that if Toby had still been there, she wouldn't be walking at all. He would've shaken his head at her in puzzlement and insisted on driving.

On her way out the door that night, Merik had thrown his glasses onto the table and sighed. "Where are you going?" he asked. "You need to eat."

"I need fresh air," she said. But she really meant that she had to get away from those who couldn't understand who Toby was and how it had been when she was with him. She had to get way from those who spewed platitudes that told her that school would help her move on, that in time everything was going to be okay.

As the truck approached from behind, Rina looked over like she always did when drivers pulled up alongside her, ready to give her most reassuring smile — the one that said that said to her concerned neighbours: *I'm not stranded, I'm just a foreigner. Go about your business.*

A few minutes before, it had been the chatty old man who collected shopping carts from the Co-op parking lot slowing up on the shoulder. "I almost thought you were the dead one," he called over as he cruised along like the two of them were taking a stroll. "He used to race up and down on these crazy skis on wheels, funniest thing, all summer you'd see him. But he was killed, eh. Car accident. Lived here my whole life and never so much as a fender bender. But these corners are deadly, especially in winter. This was in summer though, just a few weeks ago. Terrible tragedy."

"Please," Rina had replied, smiling weakly, but wishing he was close enough that she could spit in the face of this harmless man. How dare he speak of things he knew so little about? "Please. I'm okay."

But this time it was different. This time Ally's cousin was leaning far enough over to reach his hand out the open window of Ruth's truck, as if he wanted to scoop her up. His hand looked fat compared to Toby's, and the tattoos across his knuckles looked like sickly green intruders across such smooth, golden skin. His hands were smooth and scarred, she thought, where Toby's had been rough and scrubbed.

"You just walking along the highway for kicks?" he asked.

Rina reached for the door and the truck veered slightly, as if he were afraid she might throw herself under the wheels. Adam braked with a jerk and she climbed in.

He watched her jean skirt rise to mid-thigh as she sat down with no regard for the crumpled map at her feet. He waited for her to say something about the open bottle that rested by his feet, but she only stretched her legs out straight and arched her back, reaching into her back pocket and pulling out some cigarettes. She threw the package on the seat beside him before he could ask for one.

As he eased back onto the highway, the graffitied rocks on either side were muted in the fledgling dusk, their shrill man-made colours lost in a blink of the headlights — here, then gone. Of all of them, it was with the miner's girlfriend that Adam had always felt most confident. He'd seen the way she looked at him, knew what to expect from girls like her. When he'd pulled over, he'd only meant to give himself a little pick-me-up, let her accuse and dismiss him like the bitch she was, give himself the edge he needed to keep driving to who-knows-where for who-knew why. Who could've predicted she would grab the door handle and climb in?

He lit a cigarette and let the match snuff out between his fingers. He could feel her eyes on him, following the delicate line of smoke that rose up like magic from his singed skin.

When she reached down the bottle and took a chug, he eased up on the gas in surprise, and brandy dribbled unchecked down her chin.

As he drove, she lifted the bottle to her lips every few minutes, revealing the long line of her throat. By the time the curving, rocky passes gave way to gravel shoulders surrounded by dense bush which grew more shadowy and less distinct by the minute, Adam still had no idea what was going on. What the hell was she doing here exactly? When she threw her head back for another swig, he remembered how he'd been able to see down her shirt that night on the rock, as if she had been sitting there just for his amusement, so bent over and exposed.

He watched her swallow — once, twice, three times.

"You weren't at the funeral," he said.

Rina busied herself lighting another cigarette, then leaned back against the headrest. She closed her eyes and inhaled. "Please. Let's not talk. Okay?"

"Don't you want to know where we're going?" he asked.

She shook her head, holding the bottle in her lap now, nestled cozily in the dip where her legs met. Although it was almost dark, he could see her left hand playing over her bare thigh, digging little half-moon slits with her nails.

A green EXIT sign flashed by on their right.

"Did that say east?" he asked.

But her eyes remained closed and his map lay trapped beneath her sandals.

Up ahead, a sprawling gas station suddenly appeared from around the curve. A giant, well-lit sign announced: HOME-COOKED MEALS SERVED ALL DAY, ALL NIGHT, LAST STOP FOR THREE HOURS. The intersection itself was marked by nothing but a lonely stop sign. The only way to go was east.

After a few miles, the claustrophobic curves of the last hour became a wide, bumpy straightaway surrounded by the eerie emptiness of burnt-out forest. For as far as the eye could see, there was nothing but a blur of scrubby new growth, no more than one or two seasons along, punctuated by solitary singed trees that stood pale in the dusk like the skeletons they were. Adam found himself speeding carelessly now, like he was joyriding with his friends — except this time he was anxious only to be done, to get the hell out of the haunted remains of the forest all around. Every few miles, fluorescent orange triangles along the shoulder warned of deep potholes left by permafrost, but he paid them no attention. Whenever Rina's head bounced against the headrest, he wondered if she'd actually passed out by now. Then she'd light another cigarette, or take another swig, close her eyes and let her head loll back again.

She was completely oblivious when they reached a giant billboard on the side of the highway, lit up as bright as the gas station, telling them to take a right up ahead for "the best darn fishin' in the North." Adam felt the same sense of bitter triumph as when he'd come upon Ruth's without remembering whether she'd said left or right. In the end, there was no beat-up little arrow, but still, here he was, back at the old homestead with the miner's girlfriend pissed out of her mind. When he veered onto the shoulder, the bottle tipped over in her lap, but there was nothing left to spill.

As he sped over the gravel, the unease Adam had felt in the vanished forest faded away into a pleasing sense of recognition. The rocks pummeling the truck's underbelly made a steady din, and he was once again jostling with his brothers in the back of a pickup, breathing in the sandy dust, yelling above the noisy music of the gravel. He remembered Leonard, still chubby with baby fat but already a daredevil, trying to climb onto the top of the cab while Lucille pounded against the rear window, her mouth ridiculous as it opened and closed to make unheard shouts, until someone, maybe Adam, maybe one of his brothers, pulled at Leonard's T-shirt and brought him down to safety, caught in the bony net of all his brothers' tickling arms. Adam suddenly wanted the road to go on forever, cradled by the tall old spruce closing in on either side, leaving everything in his dust, flying in the middle of nowhere with the miner's beautiful girlfriend blissfully pissed and unquestioning at his side.

But the gravel came to an abrupt end. A narrow street of new asphalt cut across their path while the towering spruce gave way to a strange mixture of buildings.

Adam pulled into a small clearing. The steady *whir* of the engine and thundering racket of the gravel went silent.

Rina opened her eyes and saw what looked like a town, but not a town. They'd stopped in what could've been a graveyard for snowmobiles: four or five of them rusty and scattered in a patch of tall, weedy grass. Through a cluster of poplars to the right, there was a generously lit parking lot, freshly painted with yellow lines and a wide log building that ran along a wall of scraggly pines. An electric sign over the entrance said "Four Winds Lodge" in an attractive collection of yellows and reds. To the left, where the dusk lay blue and undisturbed, she could make out what had to be a school or official building. It was made of bland, dirty brick, with an empty flagpole out front and an old play structure sitting off by itself. A couple of small children were taking turns jumping off a swing and landing in their hands and knees in the dirt, pausing now and then to gawk at the parked truck in the distance. It wasn't long before they sauntered away, as if the very presence of an outsider was cramping their style.

Rina unrolled the window all the way down and watched them disappear into the stretch of colourless, box-like houses that spread beyond the asphalt. Small white satellite dishes protruded from every home like alien eyes. Though she could make out no actual streets, there were cars parked here and there, some obviously sleek and new, some dead and abandoned. All of it was ringed by a perimeter of dense forest, a jagged wall of black against the darkening sky. Somewhere, a chorus of dogs barked frantically back and forth.

When she tried to speak, she realized her cheeks and tongue were pleasantly numb. "What is this?"

Adam grabbed the bottle from her lap, tipped it upside down, and tossed it on the floor. "This is nowhere," he said. "When I was a kid, we got the hell out as fast as we could."

The bottle had bounced against her ankle with a hard *clunk*, but Rina felt no pain or anger. She'd never imagined Ally's cousin anywhere but the wide, busy streets of the city. She'd never imagined such a strange, sad place in this bland, young country.

"None of this used to be here," Adam said.

Although the darkness was nearly complete now, the artificial glare of the parking lot lights filtered through the trees, turning everything around them into sharp edges of brightness and shadow. Rina watched Adam's wide fists grip the steering wheel, his tattooed knuckles almost white, as if the truck was still bouncing over the terrible roads.

Now that the engine had finally stopped, her ears buzzed in the quiet. There was a matching alcohol-fueled buzz in her brain. This place reminded her of something. Something about home, where every image was always askew, where every memory seemed caught between two competing worlds.

There were the endless cafés alive all day and night, the men always winking and arguing, fighting and hugging. But there were also the eerily empty café tables, still set, broken glass sparkling in the sun as she rushed by, hunched low, practically dragged off her feet by Slavenka's insistent pull. There was the opera house where she'd sat front and center, a queen in her red dress, an empty seat for her sister, the princess Olga, watching her mother bow, then bow again. But there were also red velvet seats left exposed to the elements, pigeons roosting in the upper balconies of a tumbled ruin.

Rina knew this place. It was a limbo place, part rusty and forgotten, part shiny and new; half-wild, half-wired. It was as strange and sad and resilient as a polar bear swimming down a warm, winding river.

She turned to face Adam then, carelessly tucking her left leg beneath her and revealing the fleshy part of her thighs. Whatever elation he'd felt flying over the gravel was long gone. Had he really forgotten, he thought, that the old man was dead — deader than Leonard, deader than the miner? Had he really believed this place with the best fucking fishin' in the North would mean anything to him? He thought of the old man walking purposefully with his rifle, a stooped shadow gliding into the tall grass. It was the same grass where they'd chased Ally until she was almost swallowed by the dry, snapping blades. The same grass as the littered clearing they were parked in now.

He remembered the old man had stridden away towards the clouds that burned purple and pink above the trees. Then "look at that sun," Vincent had said, "flat as a pancake on the horizon there," and Adam had wondered, at not quite five years old: *Why must you always talk? Why can you never be quiet?*

The miner's girlfriend was crying silently. Her tears were nothing like Vincent's quick and ready weeping, nothing like Krista's pathetic, begging sobs. They were different, resistant and bitter, without noise or demand.

Adam grabbed her face with both hands, wiping roughly at her cheeks with his fingers, and she didn't push him away. Instead, she grabbed for his hair, pulling him close enough to dart her tongue into his mouth, and in an instant, Adam's entire body tensed with a kind of suspended power, like the moments just before he'd shoved the map into his pants. Only days after the miner had deserted him and his rightful prey, the girlfriend was pressing her perfect little chest into his, letting him taste the disgusting brandy on her tongue at the place where his people had been robbed. What would the wilderness expert think of that?

With her jean skirt already hiked up, all Adam had to do was push a little further until he could feel the silky edge of her underwear, and then just a little further until his fingers were between her legs, and it was even softer and warmer than her mouth, yet still, she did not stop him. She squirmed until she was under him, letting her neck fall awkwardly against the edge of the open window, pulling his head so close that their teeth knocked together as he unbuttoned his jeans and lowered himself over her, oblivious to the gearshift that would leave a nasty bruise on his thigh. Licking her face until he couldn't tell which were her tears and which was his spit, he kept his eyes open for the first time in his life, amazed that she was sweating and straining beneath him, anxiously raising her perfect hips to meet his while her perfect neck rocked mercilessly against the metal doorframe.

When her sobs became almost a scream, he steadied himself against the dashboard with one hand and covered her mouth with the other, then waited for the familiar sensation of suspended release. Eyes shut tight now, he let it come, rolling through him until all he could do was collapse on top of her in disbelief.

The sobbing continued for a moment or two, then stopped altogether. Even with the window open wide, even with an overflowing dumpster wafting from the edge of the parking lot, the smell of brandy was overwhelming. Still kneeling between her limp, perfect legs, Adam reached into the back and found a blanket Ruth kept handy for winter emergencies.

He lifted Rina's head and shoved the blanket beneath her neck, then let his hand linger for a moment against the glistening, spit-covered cheek of the miner's passed-out girlfriend.

When Rina came to, she was alone.

The first thing she did was throw open the door and puke against the wheel of Ruth's truck. Way back in June, when she'd been a silly girl who pouted because her boyfriend went off with his friends, Toby had held back her hair as she got sick all over his shoes, and her humiliation had made her feel even sicker. But she couldn't have cared less if Adam had been there to see her like this, heaving violently even after her stomach was empty, the stench of the dumpster mixing with stench of her vomit. She didn't care what Merik and Slavenka would think of her, wretchedly hanging out the door, sore and raw between her legs, stiff and painful when she tried to turn her head.

What have you done? Slavenka would say. *How could you? A woman's body, it is a gift from God, something to be revered and respected. Is nothing sacred anymore? Your cousin, she was raped at gunpoint like we are nothing but animals. How could you, Rina?*

Merik would shake his head and rub his eyes as if tired, asking questions with answers he didn't want to hear. *Who knows where that boy has been? Do you really think you could go to school while saddled with a child?*

But she didn't care about any of it. As soon as she was able, Rina called out for him. "Adam?"

She waited. Nearby, beneath the growing hum of mosquitoes, there was a rustling sound near the garbage bin. Something was spilling cans onto the ground and Rina couldn't even bring herself to care what kind of animal it might be, or what it might do to her.

"Adam?" she called again.

Then it came, hollow and distant. "Yeah."

Stepping though her foul mess in the grass, Rina stumbled back towards where they'd come from, following the direction of his voice. As she left the lights of the parking lot behind, she grew more and more blind, tripping over small rocks and discarded bottles, barely feeling the grass scratching her legs, until the night was blacker than she'd ever known. She kept going until there was only blackness and a giant, gleaming half-moon, until the sky was crowded with stars that actually twinkled like in storybooks. Never before had she been able to make out every lonely crater and arid, silvery plain of the moon; the dazzling, dangerous, untouchable inferno of the stars.

Rina stood, lost in the dark, and there it all was, so gloriously shining and indifferent.

"I'm here," Adam said, closer now.

She turned towards him and waited to see something, anything, that was here and alive on this earth. It took a few moments before she could make out an outline of a man about ten feet away — large and alone, feet apart, arms probably crossed, still except for the shimmer of one knee. It was as if she could see him and not see him at the same time, and even with the taste of vomit fresh in her mouth, even wretched and sore and unsteady on her feet, Rina knew that all she wanted, all she cared about, was pulling him against her again as hard as she could.

"Is the sky always like this here?" she asked.

Although Adam could barely see her, he could still taste her cheeks, salty and soft. "How should I know?"

He said it with no anger in his voice. There in the shadows, he couldn't bring himself to break the spell.

For the first time that summer, Rina hugged herself in the night air, shivering in her thin T-shirt and bare legs. She wanted to lose herself in the faceless, endless stars, to cling to Adam in the awful darkness. She wanted to, but now that she'd left the brandy a stinking mess against Ruth's truck, she was nearly sober and the past would return unbidden and unwanted, like a pesky child who can't take a hint.

For how could she ever really be free of the one who'd patiently shown her that a dark mystery could be neither dark nor mysterious? Who'd taken her down to the hospital clinic that gave out contraception for free? Who'd gently pulled the pine needles from her palm? Toby came to her now, his brow as furrowed and angry as the day she'd first seen him at the hockey rink, his lips set in a line of hurt and confusion.

"He didn't tell me you were going hunting," she said to Adam. "I didn't know until afterwards."

Adam laughed, short and bitter, as if saying I told you so. No matter how long they both longed for it, it could never really be just the two of them in this moment.

"You went together," she said. "Why weren't you with him when it happened?"

"Because he fucking left without me," Adam said.

But Rina didn't believe him.

"Take me home," she said. "Please, take me home."

Later that night Rina lay in bed, sore and ashamed and afraid to sleep. She couldn't bear the idea of seeing her Toby in her dreams hoisted above the wailing crowd even while she knew she ached for Adam now.

Was it inevitable, she wondered, that sometime, somewhere, she would ache for him? That she could not help aching for Adam just as she ached for herself? Long before, had she seen it in his dancing knee, in the way he pretended not to hear things, in the lies he told?

Such questions plagued her until about four-thirty, just as the first crows began cawing obnoxiously from their high wires. That's when she decided she couldn't go to Winnipeg without Toby. All that was safe and good had been wrenched away in a second and she only had one choice left.

She needed to run away again. Back to that other city, where death had fallen from a clear blue sky, back to the mountains where the night was as dark and as bright as the one she and Adam had stood under.

She had to go back to see it for herself, to make these places real and concrete and alive. To make them anything but the stuff of dreams.

15

～ As DAWN BROKE, Rina lay wide awake, planning her escape, while Slavenka curled possessively against Merik's side as if nothing had changed between them. In the apartment above the store, Adam restlessly wrapped and unwrapped himself in the afghan while Ruth snored, a sound Harry had once likened to a toy lawnmower. In the next room, Ally lay on top of her blankets, socks still on, mouth open, sleeping fitfully.

In the smelter down the street, Lyle smiled blankly at a joke in the lunchroom, thankful for his men's presence, not even hearing the actual punchline, while back at the bungalow, Sharon sat slumped in the armchair, lost in the oblivion of one of Merik's little orange pills.

In the east, the sun rose brilliant and unfettered in a cloudless sky, weakened only by the Earth's relentless orbit tilting the small Northern town further and further away from its heat. Not far south along the highway, the fox sniffed at the morning air, sensing the urgent bite of fall even as the summer smoke still lingered. Though only in its third year, the fox knew it must soon get to work preparing for the long freeze even as the ground still smouldered just a few miles away, ready to ignite again with the slightest encouragement.

Toby neither slept nor stirred. Cradled in creamy-white satin that had reminded Sharon of the tattered trim of his baby blanket, his body was already beginning the long, slow process of returning to the deep, dark earth. But above ground, he loomed larger than ever, haunting all those who had known and loved him with his silence.

It was just before nine when Ally got up to go to the bathroom. Adam watched her as she padded silently across the floor in her sock feet. Her thin blonde hair was matted flat on one side and her flannel pajama top strained at the shoulders, as if she'd just recently outgrown it. She looked like a little kid, like baby Leonard when he'd just woken up from a nap. It made Adam want to jump up and grab his cousin's chubby arm, guide her down beside him on the couch and pin her there so she couldn't leave.

The last thing he wanted was to be alone. Not now, not when he'd begun to remember that sense of wonder he'd known once, so briefly, so long ago, back when he'd still technically been in grade eight but had spent most afternoons trolling the sidewalks, looking for walls to tag after dark.

An older guy who'd hung around the school's back entrances selling cigarettes and pot had showed him the techniques, and from the very first time Adam climbed onto the roof of a restaurant, from the time he'd begun to spray in the sickly light of a flickering street lamp, he hadn't been able to get enough.

Leonard began to brag to whoever would listen. "You need to mark some fucking boundaries, Adam's your man, eh."

Soon, Adam's fingernails were never really clean and his snot was always a rainbow of colours. As the paint sprayed against the brick, or stucco, or plywood, he'd feel it come, every time — that unmistakable sense of being in control, yet not, the rush of an hour that goes by like a minute.

With the miner's girlfriend he'd felt it again — a sense that it was possible to be active in body yet free of its limits, to be in the moment yet free of time, to be trembling yet unafraid. Even after he'd climbed off her and left her there to sleep it off, the sensation had lingered beneath the ridiculously vast night sky. It had been like he was swimming amongst the stars and planets while standing still in a littered ditch, and later, when he'd heard his name, heard Rina of all people call it out, he'd felt as light as a lost balloon climbing to the heavens.

Then the harsh, *take me home,* had cut through the darkness and he'd come crashing down, just like on another warm night. That time, he'd been lost in the middle of a bright blue "w" when he'd felt a jab between his shoulder blades.

A friend of his older brother's had stood over him while Leonard playfully swung a dirty sock stuffed with a billiard ball near Adam's face. "Hey," the friend said, "that's enough with the colouring, eh. We got bigger fucking fish to fry here."

Leonard, not yet too old to still copy Adam sometimes, had kicked one of the paint cans into the street. "You in or are you out?"

Years later, Rina had wept softly in the passenger seat the whole way home, huddled against the door as if trying not to take up too much space. As soon as they'd arrived in town, she asked to be let out.

"Just tell me where to go," Adam said. "I'll take you."

But she'd reached for the door handle as if she might jump out.

"Let me out here," she pleaded. "Please. This is good."

He'd left her at the bridge, where the lake had become motionless and dull and the stars were a million, billion miles away.

Back at Ruth's, he misjudged the length of the narrow driveway and went too far, knocking a row of metal garbage cans against the loading door. He didn't even bother to check the truck for damage. Instead, he blindly made his way up the dark stairs and into the dark apartment. He'd gone to the fridge and squinted into the bright light as if this were a night like any other. The smell of Ally's discarded meatloaf made him step back in revulsion, and this time, there'd been something else, too, something sour, and he remembered how one of Leonard's kindergarten friends had died. One morning, the kid had walked through the backdoor of a boarded-up house and climbed into an unplugged fridge for reasons known only to him.

He'd have been five years old, Adam had remembered, small enough to fit.

Now, as Ally shuffled past, he reached for Ruth's cigarettes and threw them at her feet. "You want a smoke?"

But she didn't even bother to look at him. She was already disappearing into the bathroom.

What do you do when you've spent the night being jealous of a blue-skinned corpse who'd had a sour-smelling appliance for a coffin? When no one seems to look you in the eye anymore? When you come crashing down to earth, and all you have left is the refrain of your own skull bouncing on the pavement?

"Your friend," Adam called after his cousin. "She's pretty horny for someone so shook up."

Ally pivoted around in her sock feet.

"That's where I was last night, if you were wondering," he went on. "I was comforting her in Ruth's truck. I think she forgot her panties in the front seat."

It took Ally a moment to even understand what he could possibly mean. When she'd woken, her eyes opening by degrees, her limbs stretching tentatively, as if no longer sure what they were for, there'd been a few blissful moments when it seemed like nothing had changed.

There were still the same photographs taped to her closet door: an old family picture complete with funny mustache scribbled above Harry's lip; dozens of rectangular, bodiless class portraits, some of friends who'd been gone almost as long as her father; a few shots of her and Rina and Toby, Ally usually in the middle sticking out her tongue, pretending to grab Rina's breast, showing some leg at graduation. There was still the same striped yellow wallpaper that Ruth couldn't get to match at the seams, still the same half-scraped-off stickers on her dresser mirror. She was the old Ally again, already tasting the scrambled eggs that would be cooking in the kitchen, wondering if Ruth had defrosted rye bread or white.

But it had been nothing but an illusion. Everything was topsy-turvy. Adam was saying crazy things about Rina. Her Rina. Toby's Rina.

Don't believe everything that cousin of yours says, Toby had told her. *Just promise me you'll be careful.* It had been just the two of them that afternoon, when she'd imitated that stupid cat on a leash, and he'd laughed.

But she hadn't listened to him. "You're lying," she said to Adam.

Adam grinned. "Why would I lie?"

Ally swayed ever so slightly. It was just one more question she didn't have an answer for. Why would he lie about something like this? Why would you skip your own boyfriend's funeral and then send your friends away like they're nothing but a pain in the ass?

"You're sick," she said. "There's something wrong with you."

Adam shrugged. "You and me, we're not so different. You would've fucked him if you could."

It was not the same, Ally thought. It was not. "Don't talk about him," she whispered.

Adam paused, not sure whether he still wanted to keep her there or tell her to fuck off. He could see the miner standing breezily in the doorway flanked by tall, thin Rina and short, soft Ally, could see him walking sure-footed and easy through the dense bush, could see him watching the thunderstorm as if the sky were putting on a show just for him. And he could see Leonard's little friend, the one they called "Toothbrush" because of the way his hair stuck up, could see the poor dumb fuck nestling into the deserted fridge, running away from God-knows-what. No one had even reported him missing for two days.

Adam watched Ally chew at her thumbnail like she was going for blood. "Your miner," he said. "He was one of the fucking lucky ones, you know."

Ally shook her head, defenseless against the questions. Did he mean he thought Toby was lucky because of who he'd been, or because he'd died?

"Don't you dare talk about him," she said.

Ruth emerged from her bedroom, balancing an overflowing ashtray on an empty plate. Though the store should've been open for two minutes already, she'd obviously just gotten dressed. Her hair was still uncombed and caught up in the back collar of her blouse.

For Ally, it was the last straw. What had happened to the Ruth who didn't take shit from anybody? Who kept her own books and won in bingo? Who the hell was this woman with her makeup undone, who worked for hours doing nothing, who gave out the wrong change, who lent out her leased truck to someone they barely knew? And since when did she smoke that much?

Suddenly, the whole scene disgusted Ally — the stink of days-old ashes, the sight of her mother looking defeated and useless while a line of customers waited outside the door, wondering if they'd been right all along. It's hard to manage such a low mark-up operation, they'd say pitifully, but you have to hand it to her. She gave it a good shot all on her own.

All Ally wanted right now was for things to be the same, and her mother had gone ahead and changed.

"Harry left a message yesterday," Ally said. "He's getting married."

Ruth dumped the ashtray into a bulging garbage bag propped against the cupboard below the sink. Cigarette butts toppled over the side and onto the floor.

It was just like him to chicken out, Ruth thought. Only Harry would leave news like that on the answering machine. Only he would believe Vincent and then give out her number. Only he would be civil to her brother even though he hated him and then sic him on her. Only he would call early in the morning just to mock her.

"I forget her name," Ally said. "But the wedding's soon. Like a couple of weeks."

Ruth steadied the garbage bag with her foot to keep it from dumping over. There were times when Ally reminded her so much of Harry that it frightened her — the way their lower lips jutted out in a half-pout when they were relaxed in front

WHERE THE ROCKS SAY YOUR NAME

of the television. How she chewed her nails, starting with the thumb and moving her way systemically down, exactly the same as he'd done when he thought no one was looking. The way she was standing now, looking slightly stiff even in her pajamas, pretending to make conversation while really passing some kind of judgment.

Only she was not his daughter. He'd given up that right long ago. "Are you going?"

Ally shrugged.

"You're going to go?"

"I have to pee," Ally said.

Ruth followed her to the bathroom. She stood in the doorway, gripping either side as if holding it up.

"Who's going to help me in the store?" she asked. "I can't do this by myself forever."

Ally put the toilet seat down and shrugged again. "I can't just never go anywhere, you know. Have you ever heard of a holiday?"

"You think I like doing this by myself?" Ruth asked. Just yesterday, she'd roused herself to fix a leak in the toilet tank so their water bills wouldn't bankrupt them, and now Ally was talking to her like she couldn't understand the simplest things. "You think I can goddamn find someone in such a short time?"

Ally brushed a black hair from the edge of the sink. Ruth was her mother, yet offered no motherly comfort. Rina was her friend, yet seemed only to get stranger. Adam was her cousin, yet remained as confusing and as dangerous as the first day she'd met him. At least Harry never meant to hurt anyone. He just did.

"He's my dad," she said.

"He's a cheater," Ruth replied.

~ 261 ~

Ally laughed and then said out loud something she'd never really wanted to believe. "He didn't cheat on you. He'd already left. He was gone."

"You don't know what you're talking about," Ruth said.

"Yes, I do," Ally said. "You can't feed me this shit anymore."

Ruth closed her eyes and shook her head.

"Yes, I do!" Ally shouted.

In the bright light of the bathroom, the little lines around Ruth's mouth stood out mean and deep while a tiny crumb of toast dangled from her chin. "And so do you," Ally went on. "You knew he was already gone. He left because he hated it here."

"Stop it," Ruth whispered.

"He hated you," Ally said. "He told me."

Ruth kept shaking her head, like a stubborn child ready to cover her ears and sing a song.

She won't even look at me, Ally thought, *because she's useless.* At least Harry had an excuse. He was away, had always been far away. He wouldn't even remember who Toby was. "I'm going to close the store for the funeral," Ruth had said, not having any idea that it was too late.

Ally stepped in close enough for Ruth to smell her bitter morning breath. "He told me," she repeated.

"Stop it!" Ruth screamed. She shoved Ally away with both hands and the next thing she knew she was watching her daughter stumble back, as if everything that had been happening had turned to slow motion. She was watching Ally falling back and back until she was grabbing at the shower curtain, the little metal rings snapping off one after the other with a soft *ping*, watching Ally's astonished face sink further and further until first her tail bone, and then her spine, landed with a hollow *boom* in the tub.

At first, mother and daughter just stared at one another, both struck dumb with surprise. For about five seconds, things seemed to have slowed to a complete stop, held in a freeze frame like the movies. But then Ruth began to notice a familiar smell. It had been the smell of a party's end when she was growing up. While her mother Mary said her goodbyes, Vincent and the other guys had often stood a few feet away, laughing and drawing yellow pictures in the snow.

Ruth watched the circle of dampness spreading up from the crotch of Ally's underwear, soaking through the soft flannel stretched across her stomach. It was more than she could stand.

She turned away and headed for the door. She ignored Adam, who was sitting up now and hugging his knees beneath the afghan, pretended she didn't notice his eyes following her. She crouched down near a pile of shoes and fumbled through her purse. With a trembling hand, she put on her lipstick without using a mirror and sprayed some cheap perfume under her armpits. Then she went downstairs to let in her morning regulars.

After they'd deserted him, Ruth disappearing down into the store and Ally into her room, Adam felt more sure of himself than he had in weeks. He knew exactly what he must do.

His aunt's violent outburst had reminded him of so many mornings in the inner-city apartment, when he'd woken up to the sound of incoherent threats from across the room. He'd still been on his game and could bring in the goods like nobody else. Their "ace in the hole" they called him, and when things got stupid, he'd just buried his head in a pillow and acted as if still dead to the world. He'd never been the one anybody expected to step into the flash of knives, the pointlessly dangerous game of push and shove, to risk his life to save some fuckers who would throw theirs away over a bottle of whiskey.

But as he hugged his knees, still trying to get the *boom* of Ally hitting the bathtub from his head, Adam knew those days were history. He knew he was worse than those scrappy fuckers. He knew he hated himself as much as he hated the unknown snitch.

It didn't matter that his former life in the apartment had been a dangerous house of cards, a precarious creation of boredom and anger, ready to crush those on the bottom, leaving those on top with nothing but a long, inevitable fall. Even far away from the apartment's tight-knit group, part of Adam would always long for loyalty at all costs: after Leonard was murdered, he'd buggered off on his own; he'd begun to wonder if it was all a fool's game, and so they had turned on him, and so it must be.

Plus there was no denying that on his own, he'd done no better. Twice, he could've easily robbed the old woman, yet had only stood there, uselessly craving her useless death. He'd wandered for days yet no visions had come. He'd held a rifle in his hands yet killed nothing. He'd found his way back to where his people were screwed yet had only managed to screw the miner's girlfriend. What kind of revenge was it when the miner wasn't even around to see?

Adam was clean out of ideas. All that was left was Leonard's *thud* in the doorway. And the miner's mangled truck. And Toothbrush's blue little body. And the smack of his own skull on the pavement. All that was left was to get off his ass and go out and find a way. Release would not come to him. He would have to search it out, but this time, he would find a way. He would not back down.

It was simple, really. He needed to get up, and go out, and find a way.

When Ruth heard his footsteps on the stairs, she was standing on a chair in a back corner of the store, studying an extensive spider web. How in the hell had she missed it, she wondered. How had she allowed a collection of dead bugs to float above her food bins?

She twisted around and saw Adam was wearing nothing but a T-shirt and a pair of ripped boxer shorts. "What are you doing?" she asked him. "Why aren't you dressed?"

He stopped on the last stair. He had no answer. He had no plan. He didn't even have a lie.

"You dented my garbage cans," she said.

He only scowled, his mouth a hard, thin line. *I know something much worse,* his face seemed to say. *There's cobwebs in your store and you hit your own fucking daughter.*

But she didn't want him to go. And not just because of what people would say about her nephew walking around town in his underwear. She didn't want to be alone in the empty store. Not with the smell of Ally's urine still so fresh. Not with the dead bugs so close she could reach out and touch them.

"So did you go?" she asked. "To the old place?"

Nothing was simple, Adam thought. Nothing.

"Everything was different," he said.

Out of the corner of her eye, Ruth could see the spider now. It was making its way high along the wall to her right, swift and purposeful.

She thought of the last time she'd been back on her own, when her mother was dying and Vincent had called her, blubbering incoherently. Harry had offered to go with her but she'd refused. She'd driven down the gravel road all by herself, conscious of every pebble that *pinged* and *popped* beneath his new car.

She went back to that suffocating house and Mary had grabbed her arm, reaching from her sweaty nest on the threadbare couch.

"Get a priest," her mother said. "Get a priest."

Ruth recoiled at the clammy touch, wondering if Mary's mind was failing along with her body. All her life, their mother had scorned the religion that had been forced upon her, had nothing but venom for the solemn-faced women who'd taken her as a young child, who'd shaved her long, lice-ridden hair and strapped her in a desk, told her everything she had known was dirty and wrong, and then sent her back.

"All bullshit," she said to her children later, wiping the spittle from her mouth with the back of her hand.

Yet on her deathbed, she squeezed Ruth's wrist until it hurt. "I've been a sinner," she said.

Ruth tried to remember some of the things Harry always went on about. "Your traditional cultures," he would say, looking up from his book as she warmed Ally's bottle or cleared the table, "we need to embrace their spirituality. They understood the cycle of life. They knew we were one with the Earth."

As Vincent had wept in another room somewhere, Ruth freed her arm and rested her hand awkwardly against her mother's forehead. "You'll be with the ancestors now," she said.

But Mary had insisted, growing more and more agitated, until Ruth finally went and found someone who could perform a mumbled ritual imported from some other time and place.

"She's at peace now," the old priest said gently. But Ruth couldn't tell if her mother's expression — her mouth set in a slight, sly smile — suggested peace or resignation.

Now, she watched the spider magically lower itself by an invisible thread and hang there as if weightless.

"That little Leonard," she said to Adam. "He was something else. I remember one time he tried to light Ally's hair on fire and Harry almost had a heart attack."

Adam couldn't tell if she was smiling, or if her lipstick was just crooked. Either way, this was the most Ruth had ever said to him. For weeks, she'd asked him virtually nothing, hadn't shown the slightest interest except to deliver empty ultimatums. But then this wasn't any other morning — little Ally had gone *boom* in the tub.

Adam hadn't thought Ruth had it in her.

"I watched him die, you know," he said. "They swarmed the house and so he goes out there with a bottle, racing like a fucking warrior, and I stood there with a piece in my hand, right in the front landing. I just stood there, watching through the curtain, through the little fucking window in the door."

Adam waited as Ruth climbed down off the chair and began to busy herself again — walking over to the cash desk, popping open the drawer, banging rolls of change into the tray.

"He shouldn't have run out like that," she finally said.

Adam shook his head. "They would've come in through the windows. There was little kids."

Ruth could feel her hands grow steadier with each *whack*, each explosion of the coins.

"He was always like that," Adam said. "He always went fucking first. He was never afraid."

"Everybody's afraid," Ruth said, slamming the drawer closed.

Adam kept shaking his head. "Not Leonard."

Ruth grabbed the broom and returned to the far corner of the store. With one sweeping arc, she destroyed weeks of delicate spinning. "It's not your fault," she said. "At least you're alive."

Adam laughed, scornful and half-crazed in his underwear. "So what?"

Then with two offhand words, without even knowing what she was doing, Ruth miraculously gave her nephew what he needed.

"That's enough," she said.

Moments later, the door rang in a customer and with just one look, she sent him plodding back up the stairs.

For the rest of the morning, Ally lay on top of her blankets, poking at her bruised tailbone as if needing to know it had really happened, listening to Adam flip through the channels just the way Ruth would sometimes. First it was music videos, then some kind of canned laughter, then the drone of a newscaster. Just before lunch, Adam finally settled on an old horror movie, and the corny music and hushed dialogue made her remember a winter night at Sharon and Lyle's.

It had been a full-blown blizzard, with swirling snow clinging in clumps to the stuccoed bungalow and drifts reaching for the roof. Inside, though, they were cozy — Ally stretched out on the basement couch while Toby sat on the floor, his shoulder blades brushing up against the outside of her right thigh. Rina lay wrapped in a sleeping bag, her head in Toby's lap. "I don't understand this," she said.

Though the movie had already started, she gazed up at one of the high basement windows as if there was something to see in the rectangle of white. "These scary movies, why do you watch them?"

Toby let his head fall back against Ally's knee and sighed in fake exasperation. "Watch and find out."

Ally hummed spooky music and wiggled her fingers in Rina's face. "Because it's fun."

Rina batted Ally's hands away. "It's fun to be frightened?"

"Yeah," Toby and Ally said in unison, and as the wind whistled through the tiny cracks in the foundation, they poked at Rina through the sleeping bag until she was laughing in submission. But as soon as they'd started watching the movie again, Rina had closed her eyes and had a nap.

Adam flipped to the sappy violins of a soap opera and Ally decided that Rina had only been pretending to sleep. How had she not noticed before, she wondered, that Rina was a fake? How had she not known that her friend was the kind of person who would screw someone else while her boyfriend's coveralls still hung in his locker?

Ruth appeared in the bedroom doorway. "I defrosted some spaghetti," she said.

"Good for you," Ally replied.

"I'm going to ask him to help me with the store," Ruth said.

When Ally sat up, her back felt sore and tight. "Who?"

"You know who," Ruth said. "He's down there right now."

Ally ran her fingers down her spine until she found the heart of the bruise. "I don't want him here."

"Who's supposed to help me while you're gone?" Ruth asked.

"Somebody else," Ally said. "There's lots of people."

Ruth shook her head and stood her ground. Earlier, when Adam had stood before her in that ridiculous underwear and told her about his brother, he'd looked eerily like Vincent back when he snuck into her room late at night, trying not to wake her.

"Listen, Ruthie, I'm sorry, eh," he always said, while going through the pockets of her jeans. "I'm a little short. I'm sorry, Ruthie. I'll pay you back. Go back to sleep."

But his son had looked her in the eye and not asked for forgiveness.

"It's my store," she said to Ally. "I'll hire who I want."

Ally stared down into her outstretched knees and poked at her wound.

All Ruth wanted was to step over the pee-soaked panties on the floor and touch the one person who until not long ago, had loved her without question.

"The spaghetti's in the fridge," she said again, then turned away.

That night, Ally dozed off to the strains of a hospital drama's closing scenes and didn't wake again until some time after three. Everything was dark and quiet except for the distant whirring of the fridge. She was trembling.

She'd been having a dream, but not the usual kind. It had been more like her daydreams, but this time she'd been asleep. Toby had been there with her. She could still smell Sharon's fabric softener.

It had been afternoon and he'd stood outside the store with his packed truck. He'd been by himself except for his old dog barking in the driver's seat, coughing and choking like it used to whenever Toby left it behind.

Ally had stood on the curb and he'd come slowly towards her, his hands shoved in his front pockets, his elbows locked straight as they always were when he felt shy or uncomfortable. It was how he'd stood that first night at the pool hall. As he got closer, she'd been able to make out the small blue vein that magically appeared under his left eye when he was tired.

I have something to tell you, she said. *Rina never really loved you. And I don't think Adam ever loved anyone in his life.*

But Toby was already turning away to hush the frantic dog, was already whispering nonsense in its ear like Ally had seen him do so many times before — before she even knew that she loved him.

I wouldn't leave you, she'd said, following after him. *I would stay here, I would go with you. I wouldn't leave you.*

Then the next thing she knew they were driving, just the two of them, but she was in the back seat, watching his damp curls strain against the breeze.

They didn't deserve you, she'd shouted above the wind. And then what?

He'd said something, she was sure it of it. He hadn't taken her in his arms and hugged her for the first time, or brought her cold fingers to his lips, or reached back and squeezed her hand. He'd actually said something this time.

Go to back to sleep, Ally told herself. But the more she willed him back, the wider awake she became. There was the rumble of a delivery truck on its way to the bakery. There was a sliver of light from the street lamp peaking around the edge of the blind.

How could it have seemed so real? she wondered. What do you do when what you want is close enough to touch, yet no matter how hard you try, you can't grab on?

Please, she pleaded silently. *Please.* But it was too late.

All her life, Ally had taken things at face value, had come to rely on Ruth's straightforward, pitiless strength, even when it hurt. She'd put her faith in what she could see and touch and taste, had chosen this from the moment she'd turned away from Harry for good. But then she'd begun to daydream about a boy who wasn't hers; to feel alone even in company; to shelter in the harbour of made-up conversations.

Her faith had been shaken, and there was no going back. Perfect, foreign Rina had made ordinary, homebound Ally feel as if she knew things, when in fact the very opposite was true — she had nothing but questions and more questions, with no mercy for the wounded.

Even Toby, so kind and predictable, had taken his share of secrets to the grave. Who would ever know that he'd dreaded the city more than he wanted Rina? Or that it was Ally he was coming to just before the end? Or that he could never have given his friend what she really wanted?

Wide awake in the wee hours of the morning, surrounded by traitors, all Ally could do was cling to the one thing she was certain about.

"We didn't deserve you," she whispered.

16

∾   WHEN RINA TOLD HER PARENTS that she'd already called her aunt and made arrangements for an extended visit back home, Merik took off his glasses and seemed ready to toss them across the table.

"I know the last while, it's been hard for you," he said. "But once you are at the university, once you have started your courses, it will get easier. You will see."

Rina stared down at the kitchen tiles. Although her hair hid the bruises, she could still feel where the back of her head had knocked against the car doorframe. *If you knew what I did*, she wanted to say, *if you only knew, you wouldn't be so calm and self-satisfied.*

"No," she said, "it won't."

Merik turned to Slavenka, who was standing near the sink, struggling to pull wet rubber gloves from her hands.

"If you aren't ready to start at the university," Slavenka said, "you should stay here for a while. Maybe that's what you need."

"It is still not safe," Merik said to his wife without looking at her. "Your sister should not have encouraged this. I won't allow it."

"Not safe?" Rina asked. She tried to keep her tone even, mimicking the doctor-voice she knew so well. "You wanted to stay when there was still bombs going off everywhere. Now it's over and you tell me it's not safe?"

Merik rolled up his paper and put it under his arm. It looked like he was going to leave the room, but then he turned in the doorway and pointed at Rina like a scolding school-teacher. "There's nothing there for you," he said. "The petty criminals run things, that's what I'm telling you. You should go to university in Winnipeg like we planned. I won't have you do something ridiculous just because you aren't thinking properly. I know you feel terrible now, Rina, but this will pass."

But it would not pass. He and Slavenka couldn't keep their daughter from running back to the distant rubble any more than they could've kept her from the ready safety of Toby's arms. Rina spent the rest of the week on the phone, buying airline tickets on credit cards that were not hers to use, telling relatives back home, who'd watched with a bitter mixture of envy and disappointment when her parents left what they wanted to hear. She stole small bills from Slavenka's wallet a few at a time, and wondered how it had come to this. Ally and Toby had sometimes made her feel like she was a hundred years old, yet they would never have been reduced to such humili-ation. At least they earned their own keep, had their own money. It was she who was the helpless child.

It was she who'd known better, yet let so many people down.

Ruth's storeroom calendar was already flipped to September when there was a faint knocking at Sharon and

Lyle's door. It was just after eight in the morning and Lyle had been asleep for maybe twenty minutes.

"Sharon?" he called out. There was no reply.

By the time Lyle opened the door, Rina was standing on the bottom step, as if she'd almost been ready to give up. Lyle was momentarily confused. Had the girl not been told? Could it be? Why couldn't he remember seeing her amongst the mourners?

"He's not here," he said.

Rina nodded, as if his strange comment was exactly what she'd been thinking. "This was his," she said.

She held out an old sweatshirt of Toby's — navy, and folded into a neat square. Lyle thought of the way Sharon had been handling her son's clothes lately, burrowing her face into his sweatpants and T-shirts. She'd begun squeezing their little grandson so tight that he squirmed away.

"Sharon's asleep," he said. "She's looking after our daughter's little guy every afternoon. He's a handful."

Rina continued to hold out the sweatshirt with a persistence that was almost rude.

"I thought you were my daughter," Lyle said. He was more awake now and suddenly self-conscious in just his ratty bathrobe. "She's got a job washing hair at the salon by the hospital there."

Rina nodded impatiently and lifted up the sweatshirt. "This was his," she said again.

But Lyle refused to take it. He kept his hands busy tightening the tie of his robe. He remembered speaking to Rina the day of the accident, how the sound of her voice had reminded him how beautiful she was. And he remembered her mother's visit later on, how the odd mix of spices in the stew she gave them had left him on the toilet for a good part of the night.

"You keep it," he said. "We've got enough."

Rina hugged the sweatshirt to her chest. She'd come unprepared for Lyle's ridiculous small talk, his oafish self-consciousness, his sleepy kindness. How had she forgotten these people so quickly? How had she forgotten that these people would never ask her to give up her one last piece of him?

"Thank you," she said. "I'm sorry, I should have known you would be sleeping. I'm very sorry."

"It's okay," Lyle assured her. "It doesn't matter. You keep it, sweetie."

But she was already making her way down the driveway, clutching the sweatshirt to herself like a shy student holding her textbooks.

That morning, though the afternoon promised to be no less sweltering than the weeks before, clusters of schoolchildren in new turtleneck sweaters and corduroy pants crowded Rina along the sidewalk. When she passed the community centre at the end of Toby's street, a portable sign proclaimed an extensive slate of activity for the month — hockey practice, bingo, model railroading. Even what little traffic there was seemed be moving with some new urgency. In this place where the weather would soon make dawdling impossible, everyone seemed to hurry now with a practiced, automatic purpose, as if en masse they'd decided: enough was enough, it was time to get back down to business.

This shift in the air only left Rina feeling further behind. As she began the steady climb up towards the centre of town, just as Adam had climbed the day he arrived, not even the precious sweatshirt could keep her from wondering: how long had it been? How long since she'd walked to school feeling as if she were on some other planet, where bombs and snipers were replaced with random thugs who had nothing to do but call out names she didn't understand? Winnipeg's wide streets had been so absurdly flat, making her feel so insignificant, so tiny and exposed in their frozen breadth. They'd offered nowhere to run, nowhere to hide, and yet the strangers who lived there had just kept going about their business, as if there was no danger looming.

"You know what I miss about school?" Toby had asked her once. "The smell of those little pink erasers. Every year, I knew I'd get a new package of them even though I still had a bunch in the bottom of my knapsack, covered in lint and shit."

Rina had smiled at the time, loved him more than ever, but the memory of it made her feel like an alien in this world of fall schedules and new turtleneck sweaters, made her want to find a small, private refuge — maybe a tool shed or child's play house — a place where she might crouch down and shut out the mindless morning routine all around.

What was the point, she wondered, of going to see Ally anyway? What did she hope to accomplish by seeing her friend now? From the very start, they'd had so little in common. Would they have even stayed friends if not for Toby? It was as if the three of them had been a perfect triangle, that symmetrical wonder of geometry Merik had carefully drawn for her when she was still in preschool.

"Look how beautiful it is," he'd said, slowly spinning a scrap of paper torn from her colouring book. "It's always the same no matter how you look at it."

But take away one side, Rina thought, and all you're left with is a couple of lines going nowhere.

Still, she kept climbing, clutching the sweatshirt tight.

Ruth was near the wrapped candy bins, chatting with a customer, when Rina came in. She paused for a few seconds in mid-sentence, then carried on, as if her conversation was too important to interrupt. She pointed up the stairs.

Rina knocked on the apartment door, just as she'd knocked so many times before. She was just about to turn away when Ally opened the door a crack and peaked out. She looked pale-lipped and suspicious and un-Ally-like.

Rina had no idea what to say to this person who wouldn't even let her inside.

"I thought you left already," Ally said.

Rina hugged the sweatshirt. "I'm not going to school. I'm going back to stay with my aunt."

Ally raised her eyebrows as if she didn't believe her. "I thought it was still too shitty there to go back."

Rina felt the fear rising in the back of her throat. She was sweating more now, but not from the climb. Had she ever really expected these people to understand what she couldn't understand herself? Had she ever really believed that any of them could save her?

"My aunt's house used to be right across from my school building," she said. "She says the soccer field is a grave now. No stones, no markers. If you didn't know, you'd think it was just a field."

Ally looked down. There was something about the way Rina was speaking, slightly hesitant, without a hint of a snort, that she found satisfying. Just like the message high and mighty Harry had left that morning, which she'd played five times in a row.

"I know I haven't been the greatest father," he'd said. "But you're grown now, Ally. You're old enough to accept an apology. Let's start again. We'll get you a dress, and you'll meet the girls."

Only once had Ally ever seen Rina falter like this — that night on the rock, with Adam and Toby. Only once had Ally ever really wondered why she'd never asked her friend why. Why Slavenka moped around instead of planning her new, expensive house. Why Merik looked at them like they weren't really there. Why Rina could turn her back on the one she was supposed to love, and fuck the one she was supposed to hate. Why she would want to go back to such a crazy place.

"I miss him," Ally whispered.

Rina nodded, yes.

"I just want him back," Ally said. "I want to go back to the way it was."

She dripped and snorted as she wept, and Rina wrapped the sweatshirt around her friend's shoulders. "I know," she said. "But see I brought this for you." She tied the arms across Ally's chest. "See? There you go."

Ally wiped her nose with the back of her hand. "It's yours."

"Please," Rina said. She dabbed at Ally's cheeks with the sleeves, laughing a little. "You keep it for me."

Ally fingered the soft, worn cotton and let her old self be comforted — the same Ally who had reached for poor Ruthie even as her mother was pushing her away. Who wasn't going to her father's wedding out of spite, but because she wanted the dress, wanted to meet the girls. Wanted to start again.

"I'm going to Harry's wedding," she said. "I need to get the hell out of here."

"That's good, yes?" Rina asked. "That's good."

Ally shrugged, pressing the sweatshirt against her nose. But she was too stuffed up to smell a thing. "Will you be back?"

Rina paused. "Yes, of course," she finally said. "No worries."

She was already about halfway down the stairs when it struck Rina what a liar she really was. She'd told herself she'd come to see Ally, yet all along, she'd known that wasn't all. Her arms suddenly, irretrievably empty, her sweaty skin grown clammy in the relentless air conditioning, she didn't scurry out as quickly as possible. Instead, she dawdled on each step, carefully scanning the store from above, searching for any sign of Adam.

I must go away, she thought, *and never, ever come back.*

Later that morning, Slavenka walked into the crowded waiting room of Merik's office. She told the receptionist that it was an emergency, she must speak to her husband, and the young woman, like so many she saw at the Co-op with their babies — thick-waisted, with a hairstyle that did not flatter — scurried away like a frightened rabbit.

Slavenka could hear her husband's voice before he appeared.

"Please, excuse me," it said, gentle and firm. Then an examining room door swung open and he was there, tall and bright in his white coat, closing the door with a firm, gentle *click.*

"I'm going with her," Slavenka said.

The receptionist stood there dumbly, looking rumpled and concerned. Merik grabbed Slavenka's elbow and led her into the small bathroom at the end of the hall.

"What is this?" he asked. "What are you talking about?"

Slavenka slammed the door hard enough to wake an infant in the waiting room. "You know," she said.

It was the conversation they never had, but that always seemed to be there, underneath everything they said and everything they did, like the elusive trickle of an underground spring. Only this time, she would not let him sidetrack her, would let not him speak so soothingly and factually, as if she were a dying patient. "With Rina. I'm going."

Merik carefully rested his patient's file on the edge of the sink. He was already running forty minutes behind. "Since when? Since when are you going?"

Slavenka threw her head back as if about to laugh, just as her daughter had when speaking with Ally after the funeral. "Since today," Slavenka said, "since yesterday, since always."

Merik sank down onto the toilet seat. He wanted to throw off his lab coat and rip the sink from the wall, leave nothing but a sputtering hole and a thousand pieces of porcelain scattered over the antiseptic tiles. When he spoke again, it was with great care. "You're never satisfied," he said. "You're always looking for something better. But you'll go back and all you'll find is misery. I can tell you right now."

Slavenka got down on her knees then, slid along the bathroom floor until she was clasping his hands in a manner worthy of their language. "Is this life?" she asked. "I want to show her, Merik. The way the dandelions, they grow in the sidewalk cracks in April, Merik, in April, a true spring. And the smells and the colours and the music in the market, so rich I want to eat and sing until I'm one of those old women, fat and hoarse, sitting on a bench, watching the whole wide world go by in an afternoon."

It had been years since he'd heard her speak like that, passionate and articulate and wonderful. There were times in church when he thought he could glimpse it, watching the way she prayed so intensely into her folded hands. Her neck had arched like the hydrangeas that had grown on their terrace, bent beneath the weight of their own beauty.

Merik looked down, his glasses sliding dangerously down his nose.

"It's no more," he said. "Don't you see?"

Slavenka kissed his fingers, opened his hands and held them against her cheeks as if this alone would prove her point. "No," she said. "We should never have left. I was wrong, you must forgive me. The rubble is better than nothing."

He knew there was nothing he could say now, nothing that could make a difference. "From the moment I saw you," she'd said once, not long after their marriage, "I knew I wanted us to make babies. With your hair and my lips, we must do it now and do it often," and so they'd had a child. Then later, she'd said "the world is going mad; I will not do it," and they'd had no more.

Merik let go of her face and gripped beneath her armpits. He tried to pull her to her feet, but if anger had left him ready to tear out a sink, sadness left him weak as a child. Slavenka was left to grab onto the handrail for elderly patients giving a urine sample.

As soon as she'd hoisted herself up, Merik picked up his file. "I'm running behind," he said. "Even more than usual."

Slavenka threw her head back again, laughed for real this time. From the beginning, she'd loved this about Merik, his adorably serious sense of duty, his scientific commitment to order. And yet it had given her no end of grief. There were times when she'd wondered if he were really human at all.

"Aren't you tired?" she asked. "Aren't you tired of speaking a language that isn't your own?"

He nodded, because he was tired and because he knew it was the only way she'd let him open the door.

"Somebody must be there to build," she said. "You of all people know that, Merik."

"We'll talk later," he said, leading her back down the hall, smiling reassuringly at the receptionist. "When I get home, when there's more time."

For the rest of the afternoon, while Slavenka and Rina sat together at the kitchen table going over the list of things they would need, Merik met with his patients one after the other, checking their feet for recurring plantar warts; removing stitches; listening to their heartbeats. He did this until there was no one left to see and his receptionist had said good night with a look of shy concern. Then he went into his waiting room and sank down into one of the chairs that was already beginning to look a little worn. There, in the empty quiet of his highly successful practice, Rina's father was as lost as Ally's cousin had ever been.

The Sarajevo of Merik's student days, with its precarious balance of cultures, where a mountain boy could marry red-lipped Slavenka, had once been a real place. He had seen it with his own eyes. But he knew there was no going back now by plane, or bus, or armoured car. His true home only existed as an illusive ideal, an ever-beckoning destination of human grace and promise. It was why he had no desire to go back. Why he felt no contradiction in hating the idea of his daughter's life with the ignorant miner while also forbidding her return. Why the thought of carrying on without his Slavenka left him afraid to go home to his big, bare-walled house.

Outside, two boys passed by the window wielding hockey sticks and Merik got up to close the blinds. Across the way at the arena, pre-season practice had already begun and a steady business of bleeding noses and broken wrists would soon follow.

Under their heavy bags of equipment, the children seemed to move like happy little beasts of burden. Would they ever know what they were missing? he wondered. Watching them disappear into the giant tin-sided box, he was suddenly relieved that they would probably never know what it was like to see a ski lodge housed in a centuries-old castle, its wondrously slanted roofs built to reflect the gentle slopes all around, admired from near and far, turned into a machine-gun bunker.

But this place too, he thought, would not last forever. Like all one-industry towns, always lurking beneath the cheerful boom of collective opportunity and fortune, was the spectre of change. Someday, most likely before his own daughter was as old as him, the bounty of the rock would come to a grinding halt. The company would close, the brightly painted arms of human initiative left to rust.

What would become of this place of hockey fans and firm handshakes? he wondered. What would become of him without Slavenka?

Merik straightened a pile of magazines on the glass table his wife had chosen from an office-supply catalogue and then wanted to send back because it looked "too sterile." He knew living without her was something he couldn't even allow himself to consider.

He had to believe that she would come back to him the same way he had followed her. That their love was its own country — tiny and insignificant and invincible.

After a while, Merik got up and went to his receptionist's desk. He pulled the commercial telephone directory from where it was neatly stacked beneath the phone. Then in the emptiness of his closed office, he began making some inquiries about the purchase of a piano.

The morning was overcast and calm when Merik stopped for a red light at the foot of the bridge. Slavenka sat up front going through her purse, checking that they had their plane tickets one more time. Rina sat in back, wondering if she was seeing things.

She gazed out the window and willed the world to do as she hoped just this once, even though she no longer believed in such things.

Look over here, she pleaded with Adam silently. *Please, look now.*

He stood leaning against the bridge, looking out over the lake. Moments earlier, he'd pulled over and left the blinkers of Ruth's truck flashing. He was supposed to be delivering a gift basket to the new hotel across the street, but had instead found himself wandering towards the water.

The lake sat motionless, as if already frozen. Up on the rocky outcrop towards town, the backyards crowded with rusting swing sets and old canoes seemed deserted of life. Everything was perfectly still except for a gaggle of geese resting down near the boardwalk.

Adam put a cigarette in his mouth, but didn't light it. The night before, he'd called his father to tell him he would be staying for a while.

"Yeah, you stay put," Vincent had said. "Your mom, she understands, eh. The police gave her a hard time about you. She'll be happy to stick it to them."

Adam had nodded silently, remembering the roundness of his mother's hip, soft and ready to offer comfort even in the middle of the night. He'd thought of her in the hospital bed, her face so small and brown in the white pillow, looking up at doctors who would pat her arm, who would smile uncomfortably before turning away from her.

"I'll tell her you're working for Ruthie," Vincent said. "That'll make her laugh."

It was funny all right, Adam had thought. He'd let her youngest boy die, but at least there was one thing he could do for her — he could stay the hell away. And he could stay the hell away because he'd told Ruth the worst thing he could think of and she'd offered him a job he had no intention of doing.

He looked out over the dull lake, polluted and serene. The geese were waddling into the water, one by one, breaking through the stillness at regular intervals. Along with the dewy aspen, he could make out something else, something crisp and rich, the very opposite of the acrid smoke he'd begun to take for granted.

It smells like grass, he thought, dry and sweet because it's fall.

Adam turned then and saw her, waving madly, like a little kid just learning how. She kept waving until the unlit cigarette in his mouth twitched in recognition.

Rina let her fingers rest against the glass, mid-wave.

Are you fucking crazy? he wanted to shout at her. He knew she was going back to that hellhole. The morning she'd come to see Ally, he'd been hiding out in the bathroom, smoking on the edge of the tub.

He wanted to walk over to the truck and grab the door handle just as she'd done along the highway. But the good doctor would probably think it was a car-jacking and speed right on through the light. So he just stood there as the light changed to green, as the shiny red truck pulled away, as it rounded the curve and was gone.

Though she had everything, she'd cried for his people. She'd pulled so hard that their teeth knocked together. She'd let her perfect head slam against the doorframe so he could get off.

She'd let her fingers fall against the car window, as if trying to suspend the silly wave, reaching for him in a red-light moment that seemed to last forever and for no time at all.

She too was a survivor. She was brave. And she'd wanted him.

Adam pulled the soggy cigarette from his mouth, and found himself grinning. For the first time in his life, he knew what it meant to feel grateful.

Because she'd chosen to turn her back on her father at age five, Ally never really knew what it meant to be ashamed of who you were.

It wasn't until she'd begun to watch Toby watching Rina that she'd started to notice that Ruth's lipstick was too bright, her sweaty arms too flabby, her faith in "they" too simple. It was only then that all the faceless, grasping hands trying to undo her pants in the dark bush had become something terrible, only then that she'd begun wondering if there might be winners and there might be losers—that there might be those who were worthy of love, and those who were not. And when Ruth began to change with Adam's arrival, had suddenly grown unreadable and unpredictable, things had only gotten worse. Ally had found herself hating her mother as much as she'd ever hated Harry.

The night she left, Ally closed her bedroom door and dragged her duffle bag noisily across the apartment floor. It was a bingo night, but Ruth was at home, busy over the adding machine. She spoke without looking up.

"When will you be back?"

Ally kicked around the mess of shoes at the door, looking for one of her runners. When she'd talked to Harry the day before, she'd tried to ignore the hint of disappointment that was always in his voice after he'd got what he wanted.

"We'd almost given up on you," he'd said, "But this will be great. It will. It'll be great."

Ruth stopped and rested her elbows on the mess of receipts. "I asked you a question."

She watched Ally bend over to put on her runners. After closing, she'd automatically made her daughter a snack for the road, then changed her mind. Now, with the pinkish flesh of Ally's back crudely exposed, Ruth was torn between getting the lunch bag that still sat neatly folded in the fridge, and laughing out loud.

"He'll die when he sees you in that shrunken T-shirt," she wanted to spit. "He'll die."

Ally opened the door and kicked her duffel bag through, not bothering to tie her laces. Over her shoulder, she saw her mother was staring down at the stupid little machine as if it held some secret. She looked so alone amidst the mess of papers and overflowing ashtrays, so unnaturally old with her blue-black hair pulled into a high ponytail.

But Ally couldn't cry for Ruth the way she'd cried for Rina. They still needed each other too much to have any room for pity.

"Next Friday," she said, then walked away, laces flapping.

As Ally passed through the store on her way out, Adam was supposed to be moving dated stock onto the lower shelves and stacking the new shipment up top. Instead she found him standing near a bin out front, grabbing handfuls of sunflower seeds and letting them run through his fingers.

She kicked her bag across the shop floor, looking up only long enough to let him see her disgust.

Adam removed his hand and licked some salt from his pinkie. "Are you taking the truck?"

Ally brushed past him and ripped a plastic bag from one of the rolls hanging above the bins. She began filling it with peanuts. "She won't let me."

"The bus is shit," Adam said, licking his fingers one by one.

Raking his hands through the dry goods after the store was closed had become one of his favourite things. He would move from bin to bin, reaching deep down into the bounty, feeling the weight and texture of every kernel, every raisin, every gum drop. There was something satisfying about how the floorboards creaked beneath his step, how the smells all mixed together — nutty and sugary, woody and tart. He would think of the old man, whittling on the step outside, always outside with the aspen sap and the dying grass, and find himself wondering about the old place, even though the old man was long buried, and the yellow arrow on the highway was long gone, and the miner's girlfriend wouldn't be there to call his name beneath the stars.

He watched Ally move onto the pretzel sticks, then the chocolate-covered raisins. "You know, your miner," he said. "He told them I was there."

When she didn't respond, Adam went on confessing. "He was fucking dying and he told them I was still there."

Ally stopped fumbling with a twist tie and looked at her cousin, the one who'd barged into their apartment with his vague family memories and bold challenges. *Why do you sound so amazed?* she wanted to shout. *Don't you know that was just the kind of person he was?* But she was no longer sure if that was all there was to it.

"Just be careful," Toby had told her, but she hadn't listened. If she'd been happy to let Rina keep her unhappy secrets, Ally had at least wanted to know what made Adam paddle so furiously in his dreams.

"Are you going to steal from us?" she asked him now.

Adam jumped up onto the counter. "Do you think I'd steal from my own auntie?

Ally shoved the bags of junk food into her jacket pockets and looked at him hard. The truth was, neither of them was sure of the answer to her question. Still, at that moment, at that awkward point of leave-taking, they would at least pretend they believed in certainties.

"Are you just going to sit there like an asshole?" she asked. "Or are you going to open the door?"

He did, and as she kicked her bag through onto the sidewalk, Adam grinned. "See you, Cuz," he said.

꩜ IMAGINE A COOL EVENING IN EARLY SEPTEMBER.
On this night, just after nine, if you'd been sitting precariously above the highway, legs dangling from the craggy rock which had been blasted away decades earlier to make way for the bulldozers and asphalt, and looked straight up, you would've seen a slice of moon growing brighter and brighter in the navy dusk, as if it weren't a planet that people had walked on but a sympathetic neighbour trying to make up for the sun's impending absence. Down below, you would've seen the lonely headlights of a bus on its way to the city, still seven hours and three stops away from a landscape that would open up into vast, prairie lowlands. Straight ahead, you would have seen very little.

Though you might still be able to make out the vague shape of an outcropping, the warm, Precambrian hues and freshly painted neons would be lost. The outline of spruce would've recently disappeared into the night and the fox's movements, solitary and purposeful, would be long hidden.

But if you were eighteen-year-old Ally, chewing your fingernails, aware that it was still too early in the journey to get out your snack, it wouldn't really have mattered. Even in the dark, just being there would make you think of something about forty minutes in the other direction, something expertly painted in purple and yellow and orange, at your suggestion.

Toby was here, it said.

You would close your eyes. And somewhere beneath the steady hum of the speeding bus, as the fall moon shone coldly and the long ride seemed like it would never end, you would hear a voice.

Do you remember, Al? Do you remember?

BRENDA HASIUK's award-winning short fiction has appeared in numerous literary journals, including *The Malahat Review*, *Prairie Fire*, *Prism International*, and *The New Quarterly*. In addition, her work has been published in the anthologies *Up All Night* and *Kobzar's Children: A Century of Untold Ukrianian Stories*. She lives in Winnipeg, Manitoba.